OUT OF

THE FIRE MIST

A NOVEL

by

Rodger Christopherson

Other books by the author:

A Little Bit of Anarchy
Beverly Hills Women
Monkey in a Tree
After the President Disappeared
Illusions
Three weeks Until Tomorrow
Health and the Real Cause of Illness - non fiction
Beyond Heaven and Hell - The Greater Reality - non fiction
Origins & Meaning - How science and religion have failed humanity - non fiction
Circles in the Sand - Poetry

intercept777@centurylink.net

PROLOGUE

The eagle shrieked in alarm, dropped a wing and turned to get a better look. What were humans doing up on top of those cliffs? It was bad enough that there were so many of them milling around down below, to the south. But he was used to that. This was much different.

He was an old eagle, majestic of wingspan, wise in his way, but in his whole lifetime he had never seen humans on top of those rocks. How did they get up there, anyway, with the walls so steep? Humans can't fly. And then he heard the noise they were making. A most unusual kind of noise, stirring up the air, building in intensity, charging it somehow, leaving a foreboding sense of some impending event about to impose itself on the world. What was it, he wondered, and sank lower in the sky, quite prepared to bank quickly and leave the area.

There had been a dark, rumbling thunder shower earlier in the day but by noon the sky was a clear, cloudless, deep blue that hinted at the infinite mystery of the universe. By one o'clock the visitor's parking lots had begun to overflow out onto the shoulders of the access roads and along the highway. There were automobiles from as far away as Maine, RV's from Florida, a pickup truck and a station wagon from the State of Washington and a swarm of overloaded black Harley motorcycles from southern California. Nearly every state of the union and most of the Provinces of Canada were represented and in the lingering humidity of the day the Visitor's Center had long since passed from a quiet repository of exhibits and artifacts into a teeming clutter of sweaty browed tourists.

Outside, kids squealed and dogs barked and camera shutters clicked. There was the snap and pop of aluminum beverage cans being opened and the rustle of paper and plastic as people reached for Big Macs and fried chicken parts purchased back in Rapid City. There was even a home made, grilled tuna on sourdough being passed back and forth between two friends as they forced their way into the crowd already jammed against the metal railings. Self-appointed experts read statistics about the national monument from government-furnished brochures to their families in authoritative voices as the rest of the thick crowd pressed even closer. Although displeased with all the noise and shoving, most everyone seemed to agree that it was still a sight to behold as they pointed at the disrupted mountain.

A couple of teenagers, however, produced a temporary lull in the din when they tossed a string of firecrackers onto the grass but were promptly collared by Park Rangers and escorted away as things quickly returned to normal. More people arrived and more people wedged their way into the heart of the mob to get a better look at what the combined qualities and characteristics of ambition, self righteousness, dynamite and pneumatic hammers can do to disfigure the granite side of a mountain stolen from the Indians - Mount Rushmore, South Dakota. It was the 4th of July, most raucous of all national holidays. Had it not been for the noisy distraction of the burgeoning crowd, however, a careful observer might have been able to pick out the high, piercing shrieks of the spotted eagle hanging in the sky above the ridge behind the wall of the monument, riding the thin thermal of an air current.

Had such an observer been even more discerning he might have also picked up the rhythmic thump, thump, thump of leather wrapped sticks beating on the rawhide coverings of hand made tribal drums in distant, hypnotic harmony coming from a ceremonial site overlooking the head of Lincoln. And if, in addition to having sharp eyes and good ears, one had the good fortune to be at a higher vantage point than the visitors area, he would have been further privileged to see the circle of seven figures hammering away on the stretched and dried, decorated animal skins they each carried. Two shirtless young Lakota Indians, a young Comanche with a raven feather in his

4

hair, a middle aged Ojibway in a baggy, hand painted T-shirt and, strangely enough, a lean post of a bare footed black man followed by a white man whose face was shaded by a sweaty old Stetson hat and a white woman with more curves under her jumpsuit than a Playboy bunny, all moving slowly around the ancient Oglala in the center. Solemnly the regal old man faced each of the four directions in succession as he smoked his feather decorated, red stone pipe, slowly rotated it in a circle and uttered the words, "As it has been said, so let it be."

It was at this moment, when he had finished enunciating the words in his time worn voice, that the eagle above shrieked again and a sudden, heavy gasp ran through the crowd below. Engaged as they were in viewing the sixty foot high carved faces of the former American Presidents, they were utterly shocked to see the granite face of George Washington begin to swim and fade away. Slowly at first, then faster, the stone features dissolved completely, then restructured and reformed themselves into a beautifully rugged, three dimensional portrait of Sitting Bull, famous Chief of the Teton Dakota who defeated Custer at Little Big Horn in eighteen seventy six.

Even more astounding, the following moments saw Roosevelt become transformed into the great chief and priest of the Oglalas, Crazy Horse, murdered by the white man in eighteen hundred and seventy seven. Then, immediately following that miracle, Lincoln's homely physiognomy disappeared into the chiseled and wizened face of the renowned old man of powerful vision, Black Elk.

Jefferson's face, however, remained that of Jefferson, but in the passing moments the smooth features he had worn for more than fifty years soon became deeply furrowed with the lines of age and the countenance he bore changed from a look of astute wisdom to one of deep and immense sadness. And so it came to pass that in a period of just a few minutes, the entire six years of devoted hard labor of government financed sculptor Gutzon Borglum,

5

way back between the years of nineteen thirty six and nineteen forty two, were completely negated and re configured into something that might be construed to be more in keeping with the true history of the Black Hills of South Dakota.

ONE

Kohl looked at the cheap gold watch he had gleaned off a street vendor in Ecuador and wore on his left wrist. If correct, it was eight seventeen in the morning. Good enough, he thought, and wiped his brow in relief. He had just walked safely across the border at Tijuana back into the United States for the first time in over six months. Something must be working right because no one was waiting with a pair of handcuffs to greet him. And now, thanks to his old friend Mike, he had an untraceable off-shore bank account somewhat in excess of a quarter million dollars and, for the time being at least, was completely relieved of the necessity of having to support himself. Even better, he was invisible and unaccountable to the prying eyes of the computerized modern world and could exist outside the system without benefit of credit cards, credit reports, income tax forms, social security number and other insidious forms of present day life that served chiefly to invade one's privacy and limit one's liberty. Such precious autonomy might turn out to be rather important if he were to remain a free man. Even though the authorities might never be able to prove anything specific, he and Mike had still made a mockery out of investigative expertise and sorely abused more than a few egos along the way, so why flaunt his presence and push his luck.

He looked around. Lights were on inside the immigration building, traffic signals were functioning properly, everything electrical appeared to be working normally. Too bad, what a waste. No mark or imprint left. The rest of the world seemed totally oblivious to what they had tried to accomplish. With that thought nagging away in the back of his mind, Kohl caught the shuttle bus into

San Diego airport only to find that he had just missed the flight to Phoenix. The next would be in three hours. There was time enough to look up an old acquaintance over on Coronado Island.

His friend, unfortunately, was not in when he arrived so he headed down to the beach for a walk on the practically deserted strip of sand. Half a mile of plastic cups, candy wrappers, pop bottles, stinking kelp and thick blobs of washed up tar was enough, however. He was just about to turn back when he happened to look up to see a lone figure standing in the midst of a flock of seagulls not too far away; the birds all gathered about with wings folded in solemn looking assembly.

Keeping his distance so as not to disturb the strange scene, Kohl stopped and watched for a moment. The man appeared to be conducting some sort of Indian ritual. But what was the purpose, Kohl wondered as he looked at the stocky, stern faced Native American with his long, black hair tied back in a pony tail. First the man sucked on an ancient looking, long stemmed, ceremonial pipe, then he mumbled something in an unfamiliar dialect too low in volume to make out as he turned and went through a number of unusual motions with the artifact. Well, what did it matter, Kohl soon decided. The seagulls appeared to understand, even if he didn't. Besides, he had best be getting back to the airport.

Two hours later he landed in Phoenix where he caught a second shuttle northward. By late afternoon he was back in the red rock country of Sedona, the place where the most awesome, moving, grievous and shattering experiences of his entire life had all begun two and a half years earlier.

Strangely enough and innocently enough, like so many things, it had started out as an uncomplicated mental exercise. Based on a purely hypothetical situation, the original intent had been to turn his research into a work of literary fiction. Being more of a scientist and engineer than a writer, however, Kohl and his ingenious friend, Mike, were unable to leave well enough alone. Solving seemingly unsolvable engineering problems they had somehow doggedly extended the field of high energy laser technology far beyond the state of the art of the day. Unfortunately, once such a prodigious piece of equipment had been brought into true physical existence, however, it had a way of lying there staring back at them, begging at first, then demanding to be put to use.

Equally unfortunate, the most challenging of causes to which such an awesome device could be put had already been there, ready made and waiting. It was a cause started by Henry David Thoreau, perhaps, or Teddy Roosevelt, maybe John Muir, the Sierra Club, Greenpeace or Earth First, anyone and everyone who saw the beauty and importance of nature and the need for conservation. It was the same cause brought into clearer focus by the inspired writing of men like Edward Abbey and made more urgent by growing population, over development, outright wastefulness and growing environmental pollution. This was the situation they had found themselves in.

Empowered by a technological achievement which could burn holes through thick concrete and steel with its invisible beam from half a mile away, it had tempted them sorely. Having made it small enough to be carried around in the back of an ordinary Ford van with the resultant high mobility was too much. Seduced by the sophistry of causes, their biggest fantasy had turned all too real and in the end, when it was finally over, what? Courage and conviction be damned, himself included, nothing could be, or would ever be the same again.

While nothing could have been more dramatic than the way they had disabled the power producing abilities of Hoover Dam and Three Mile Island and pulled down all the Mississippi River bridges in St. Louis, what had they really accomplished? Very little, as far as the public was concerned. And as for themselves, well, only one thing was sure, the price was much too high. Willing participants though they were, Jenny and Sue were both still gone. It was time to put away the monkey wrench. All such grandiose adventures and nefarious pursuits had come to an end.

Try as he might, however, it was not that easy to put his feelings aside. Bulldozers were tearing up the Juniper trees in a dozen different places around town, and, obscenity of all obscenities, they were building tract houses in this no longer blissful little community, for God's sake. Equally bad, tourist laden airplanes and helicopters were also roaring through the canyons adjacent to town. The discordant thunder of unmuffered engines was echoing off the rocks, frightening the wildlife and destroying the peace and tranquility of the natives while jeep loads of ground borne sightseers knocked down the brush, trampled over wildflowers and left their trash behind.

Even worse, but on an entirely different level, the Army was using the tiny airport as a refueling stop and kickoff point for Special Forces wherein the skull and crossbones boys could drop into less accessible places in the landscape and play soldier with their explosive toys. And while all that was going on, some obtuse, visionless, uncaring politico and his followers were trying to ramrod a road across Red Rock Crossing, a most renowned and spectacular, international beauty spot in its own right. Was nothing sacred, Kohl wondered? Did everything have to be pulled down to the same motorized, blah, bland, empty headed level of mediocrity that existed almost everywhere else in the world? Why was such extraordinary and irreplaceable beauty as existed here allowed to be sacrificed in the name of progress. Where would it end, he wondered and as he thought about it, he shuddered heavily. Maybe someone should blow up the bridge on the highway south of town. That would slow things down for awhile. It would be hard to condemn such an act, maybe he should do it himself.

He entertained the possibility for a moment, then put it aside. No, he would never touch another stick of dynamite as long as he lived. There had to be a better way. Too many madmen were coming out of the woodwork and innocent people were getting killed. Perhaps if he weren't so lonely, he thought. Then he would have a calmer perspective. If only Jenny were back in his life. Dear Jenny. Beautiful, quintessential Jenny, wondrous woman of his every dream, still the woman of his heart. God forgive him for what he had done. Where are you Jenny, he pleaded. Please come home.

Seeking solace, Kohl began hiking the deep rifted canyons once again but it was a hollow, haunting, hapless venture that left him grasping. Jenny was still the sunlight on the path before him, the shadow in the trees, the bird song in the distance, the hushed breath of the wind moving across the land, the ghost that forever followed on the heels of his trail just out of sight in the fringes of the forest, taunting, teasing, never appearing fully, never letting him forget.

What to do, he asked himself constantly, but there were few answers and in an act of desperation he turned back to the diversions of the town. There were polite poetry readings in the bookstore, brown bottles of beer in the bar, talking circles in people's houses and moonlight drumming sessions around the fire on the hill. There was some minor redemption there, to be sure, but ultimately the poetry became too polite and the beer drinking just plain boring. As for talking circles, somewhere in the process of its growth the town was also turning into a crossroads for the New Age community and the followers of this off beat philosophy had infiltrated nearly everything that didn't require hard cash for admission. These individuals rubbed their crystals together, munched on granola bars and made love donations instead. A peaceful enough group for the most part but for Kohl all the self proclaimed gurus and healers were more than a little confused in their declarations of having ascended powers of light, all embracing spirituality and the keys to universal knowledge. They were just another cluster of poor souls on a foggy trip to nowhere, as far as he could see. Like him, perhaps.

Again, Kohl thought about the solitude of the remote canyons, the place where Jenny's memory always came back most vividly. What better place to stand and fight, he finally decided. He would go back to Nature, the mother of all beginnings. There was nothing dire about the decision, it was just the way he was. He would go back into the wilderness until such time as either answers came or he gave up, as simple as that. There would be no television, no newspapers, no people, no indoor plumbing, no store bought food, no grand drama; just him, his knife, the clothes on his back and the desire to somehow work it through.

Three months later Kohl was back in town. Hard muscled lean and clean of eye and heart, he wandered into the local coffee shop for his first civilized breakfast in all that time. He asked to sit out on the patio in the sun. Moments later he gave the waitress his order, handed her back the menu, took a sip of his coffee and looked around the walled off area to see who else was there. Mostly tourists. Ho hum. But wait, who was that person talking to the blond at the far table under the umbrella in the corner. Was it possible? Hell, it was that damned Indian he had seen on the beach in San Diego when he had come back from Mexico almost six months ago. The one who had been conducting the ceremony on the sand for the seagulls. What an peculiar coincidence!

His breakfast arrived. He gulped it down, keeping an eye on the unusual couple. Then, when he had finished, he wiped the last of his meal off the beard he had let grow during his time alone, rose and went to their table. As he approached, the stern faced man with the long hair, dark skin and steely blue-brown eyes looked up at him. Kohl nodded a greeting. The man nodded back and waved a hand at the empty chair opposite. Wordless, Kohl sat down. It was almost as if he had been expected. Ridiculous, Kohl thought as he studied the pair he had joined. The blond was younger, softer, slimmer and more guarded. She was also somewhat resentful of the intrusion. In sharp contrast, the man's features were bold, scarred and striking. Not a person one would want for an enemy, Kohl thought, wondering if he had made a mistake.

The waitress came, refilled the cups of the other two and gave Kohl a fresh cup. "I saw you on the beach in San Diego," Kohl stated in way of introduction.

"Yes, I remember," he was told as the Indian scrutinized him. "But you didn't have all that hair on your face then."

Surprised that the man recognized him at all, Kohl stared at the Indian. But then, when the stranger finally smiled at him, Kohl relaxed as the suggestion of something supernatural about the whole affair slipped away. "I've been out in the woods for a while," Kohl explained and they began to talk.

The woman asked Kohl what he did, meaning did he work, have a career, or what? Kind of an ill fitting question under the circumstances, Kohl thought, since they had just met. Why did she feel it necessary to categorize and cubbyhole him, he wondered. He gazed at her, then looked back at the Indian. The man's expression was non-committal.

"What I have been doing up to now no longer seems pertinent nor important," Kohl answered quietly, baiting her to see how she would react. "And whatever I appear to be in the process of becoming has yet to be fully decided," he finished.

The Indian smiled slightly, the blond rose and excused herself. "I am called Grey Hawk," he said after she had so abruptly departed. Two hours later they were still talking.

Occasionally after that, they met again for breakfast. Once they went out in the evening, had a few beers together and talked some more. Who the blond was, or had been, Kohl never found out. She was never mentioned. Instead, before he really realized what had happened, Kohl found himself climbing up over the rocks in a lost canyon somewhere in the barren reaches of Apache land far to the southeast, a place which Grey Hawk had told him about. "A mean and difficult part of the world for a man alone

12

and guaranteed to rip a hole in your soul if you survive."

They had talked briefly about "Vision Questing" in some of their discussions, as the Indian had called it, but he had refused to share much of the detail with Kohl, appearing rather skeptical as to what might come of it for one with such pale colored skin. Kohl, however, remained undaunted. It felt like another of those things he had been born to challenge himself with and if Grey Hawk wouldn't give him some guidance in the matter, he would go out and do it alone.

It was on the fifth day. The burning sun was near zenith, beating down, heating the carved and heavily serrated, sedimentary walls of the canyon, bringing them to a point where they were unbearable to touch or to lean on. Everything that was capable of movement had long since sought the deeper cover of the upturned rocks and crevices, or lay silently under the shadow traces of the sparse vegetation. Kohl, totally nude, terribly sunburned and blistered, slid further back under the shade of the sandstone overhang above his head and stared out at the scene below, wondering if perhaps he hadn't overdone it this time. His last canteen was nearly empty.

There was water below, half a mile away, but he didn't have the strength to go after it. So much for questing and fasting and Indians named after birds. What an idiot thing to do! And what kind of a name was Grey Hawk, anyway? What was the significance of it, or did it even have one? What kind of a fool was he for letting himself wander out here into this lonely, desolate no man's land where one could char broil hamburger on the rocks two minutes after sun up. Holy hell! He closed his eyes for a moment and forced himself to shut off the rambling voice of disjointed internal dialog he was always so guilty of. To stop trying to analyze everything all the time, to account for every little thought and feeling. It wasn't easy but after some moments he was able to open his eyes again and still keep his mind at rest. Finally, he arrived at a state of acceptance, a un-focused, non-thinking, disordered awareness.

Slowly it deepened and changed in perspective as somehow his mind, his body and his entire being gradually ceased to exist as a separate entity. He was becoming a part of something much larger and far more extensive. It was as though he were flowing outward from his physical self, out through his surroundings, blending and merging. Then, in turn, it felt as if his surroundings were flowing back through him, rising, ebbing, moving in, moving away, carrying him along in their course. He was the earth, the rocks, the trees, the wisp of cloud in the corner of the sky, the sky itself. Then, almost as quickly, he was himself again but found that he was no longer sitting alone with his back up against the rocks. Something else was beginning to happen. Coalescing out of the heat of the day and the intense stillness of the hour an entirely new scene burst upon him like flowers unfolding rapidly in accelerated motion, anew and anew, swirling, settling, changing once more.

Somewhere a mountain lion snarled. At least it sounded like one. Was it? Tawny and graceful with golden, glowing eyes, the great beast appeared at the edge of his vision, bared its immense white fangs and snarled again. Then, before he could react, the towering, dingy, pollution etched, gray stone buildings of a city sprang up before him with all the dirt and noise of its streets eminently obvious. The big cat moved off into the maze and Kohl followed, flying along behind. People hurried out of their way, running to hide in doorways or down dark alleys. As they went, they bounded over bodies lying in the gutters as other haunted looking faces peeked out from behind closed windows. Everywhere there was the stench of decay and the echoing sound of women weeping and wailing. They passed an ancient stone church with its shamble of broken stain glass windows, home to a hoard of rats that scurried in and out, feeding off the decaying flesh in the streets. The stench was horrific.

Finally, they came to the edge of the city, to a vast landfill where the bounding animal came to a stop and turned to make sure Kohl saw what was happening. An immense, bright yellow bulldozer was working away at a huge, random pile of books of all sizes and colors, thick and thin, new and old, hard back and soft cover, scrolls, hand written manuscripts, letters with official seals embossed on them, the entire history of mankind, or so it could have been, rising almost nearly as high as the tallest building of the city.

Pumping out a trail of thick, black smoke the machine pushed bladefull after bladefull into the mouth of a giant, blazing furnace that belched and bellowed for more. Somehow Kohl felt himself drawn closer, then stood aghast. A skeleton with glowing red coals for eyes worked the controls of the howling mechanical monster and there in its path stood a group of small, ragged children, too frightened to move. Hopelessly, Kohl tried to scream but his voice was lost in the overwhelming roar. He tried to move but his legs seemed to sink into the ground.

"Please," he shouted at the lion in desperation, not knowing why such an appeal should be made to an animal. Incongruous as it was, however, it worked. In the next moment Kohl was running fast as light, rallying the young ones together, hustling them out of the way. But one, however, too weak to move, lay there still. Fear and panic swelled in his chest. He turned back again, scooped the frail and tattered waif up into his arms and with great effort barely managed to move out of reach of the heartless demon of a machine, the heat of the engine burning his back as it narrowly missed him.

Gently he sat the girl child down in the dirt and looked into soft, gray-green eyes big as night and deep as eternity. Unsure at first, the child stared questioningly back at him, then opened her arms and put them around his neck. A tear rolled down his cheek and the entire scene disappeared from view, swallowed up by a giant, swirling dust devil.

Kohl half closed his eyes and raised his hand in protection as a large, sandy colored stone, half as tall as a tree, rose up out of the ground before him. An old Indian with a crooked stick in his hand walked out from behind

15

the rock and began tracing over the lines carved into the smooth surface as if trying to explain their meaning to Kohl. The lips moved and there were intense expressions on the ancient, lined face but the voice was empty and without sound. After he had finished his silent speech the old man sprinkled tobacco on the ground in front of the rock, then looked skyward and began to pray.

A bolt of blue-white flame zig-zagged across the sky and a nearly instantaneous crash of thunder reverberated off the rocks and shook the canyon, wall to wall, as a sudden shower of rain startled Kohl's desiccated body. He shivered in reaction. Who was this old Indian? What strange message was embedded in the petroglyph that he had tried so hard to share? What was it all about? What did it all mean, Kohl began to wonder, only to have his thoughts interrupted by the heavy flutter of wings as a large, princely looking gray colored hawk of tremendous wingspan swooped downward, braked itself with outstretched wings and flared tail, settled on the rocks above and stared down at him.

Transfixed, Kohl stared back for what had to have been half a lifetime. Then, as if some act of judgment had been at last completed, the powerful bird took majestically to the air. Aloft, it made a sweeping circle overhead before climbing higher into the austere sky. Once there it let out a high, piercing cry and dove downward, full speed towards the ground, where needle sharp talons found the muscled back of some creature on the ground too far away for Kohl to see exactly what it was. Lifting the catch easily upward with a flap of wings, the hawk flew directly overhead and let it drop. The stricken creature tumbled once, twice, slowed slightly and changed into something else before continuing the descent. An all white snake flicked its yellow forked tongue, tasting the air around Kohl's painfully sunburned feet where it had landed and spoke to him in a voice he thought he recognized. Was it his own?

"I am the belated messenger from other realms," it said. "It is in things unseen that you must seek both your solace and your salvation. It is on the yon side of self where promise and fulfillment both begin and end, and where true and abiding destiny awaits. The key resides in your own mind. Seek and prepare. It will show itself."

The words hung tenuously in the air for a long, overwhelming moment, then fell back into the silence and heat of the day, along with all the remnants of the strange illusion Kohl had been experiencing. Instinctively he tried to shield his eyes from the intense brightness that flooded him. Somehow the sun had moved significantly higher in its arc across the sky and he was no longer sitting in the shade of the ledge where he had originally located himself. Bleary eyed, agonizingly weak and disoriented, he wiped his brow on his bare arm, licked his lips with a tongue as dry and rough as the skin on his body and groped for the one remaining canteen that he thought had fluid left in it. The container was empty. He swore in a harsh, hoarse voice, threw it over the edge and began to painfully crawl down off the precipitous slab of rock he had been sitting on for all these days and nights without food or shelter.

Far below the breeze murmured gently in the waiting cottonwoods, stirred the leaves into a soft, quavering rustle and created tiny ripples on the rock rimmed, spring fed pond of cool, clear liquid. Still much, much too far away, depleted and totally without reserve, Kohl's wasted body would gladly have given up. But to hell with that, he told himself. He had a vision. He didn't understand what it all meant but it had to be important, dammit. The wild animals were not going to pick his bones. He had to get back and talk to Grey Hawk. He struggled for nearly and hour, clawing his way along on his belly for the last few yards, scrapping the rest of the skin off his oozing blisters. Ultimately, he was at the edge of the pool where, still lying on his stomach, he sank his burned face into the life saving substance and came back to the world.

"I'll be an SOB," Grey Hawk said when Kohl saw him next, showing Kohl another dimension of his personality. He had never heard the man swear before. Grey Hawk examined Kohl's face with microscopic precision. "Damned fool," he said, deciding to let it go at that, after Kohl told him where he had gone and for how many days. The lad had survived, hadn't he. "Not supposed to take water with you on a Vision Quest," was all he ended up with in way of exhortation.

Kohl shrugged in admission of his mistake and asked the Indian if he wanted to hear the rest of it. Satisfied that Kohl was telling the truth about having had such a vision the first time out, Grey Hawk stifled his feelings, nodded yes and listened patiently as Kohl described the depth and agony of his experience in all its vivid detail, leaving out only a very small part as he was instructed to do. Something necessary so as not to invalidate its impact. Part of the Medicine Way, he was told.

"What do you think it means?" he asked, still somewhat weak from all the torment it had presented and not all that sure he really wanted to know anyway.

"Not mine to say," he was told. "That you must determine for yourself."

Kohl groaned. Maybe later, he told himself, when he felt stronger. "What about the seek and prepare part then? Any suggestions on the one?" he asked.

"We'll see," Grey Hawk stated. "But first I must contact my Elders." Again he studied Kohl's face, even more intently this time, still very perplexed. Truthfully, he was as surprised as Kohl about what had happened. The white man was a decent enough individual, he admitted. Clever and quick and with a certain sensitivity. He liked him for the most part but he still had the same misgivings about him as he did about most members of that race. Full of curiosity on the surface but down deep there was little understanding and respect for the old ways and even less desire to give up materialistic strivings in search of something better. The commitment necessary to cross over into the greater world of Spirit was difficult at best, and few succeeded. Why should he waste his time on this one? Still, it was a powerful vision, one that he, himself, had symbolically appeared in. Admittedly, it left him little choice. He was obligated to carry the matter at least a step

18

or two further.

"What Elders?" Kohl asked, having but a small idea of what the man was referring to.

The question was never answered. "Come back in the morning," he was told instead. "Bring your knife, hatchet and a shovel just in case."

In case of what? Kohl wanted to ask, but was held off by a wave of Grey Hawk's hand.

"Follow me," Grey Hawk instructed Kohl shortly after sunrise the following day from the window of his car. He then drove south out of town with Kohl doing his best to keep up to the old Ford which eventually stopped at a remote area in the woods along the creek bed. Here Grey Hawk located and selected a number of tall, slender saplings which he sprinkled tobacco at the base of and said a small prayer over. Then he proceeded to give Kohl an elaborate set of instructions on how to construct a sweat lodge; where it should be located, where to place the entrance, the grandfather pit, the grandmother pit, the alter, the amount of firewood needed, how to select the stones to be heated, a dozen details that must be important. He said it only once and ended the monologue by driving off before Kohl could even begin to ask what it was all about and what it was that Grey Hawk's Elders had said, if anything.

No words were exchanged between Grey Hawk from where he sat on the ground just inside the doorway of the small blanket shrouded, dome shaped enclosure, and the individual moving about outside in the evening air. All Kohl saw when the small flap of a door was thrown open was a delicate looking hand that showed white in the light from the crackling fire in the grandfather pit twenty feet away to the east of the lodge. First a deer antler was passed in, then a small bag of cedar chips. After that a long handled fork appeared with a red hot, glowing rock in it, seven times in a row forcing Kohl to try and shrink back farther away each time. With nothing on but a towel around his waist to protect him, surges of pain coursed through his body as the intense heat attacked the still unhealed blisters from his previous adventure. He was sure he would faint before the ordeal was over.

Grey Hawk said something which sounded like, "Ah-Ho", after he placed each new rock on the pile in the central pit with the aid of the deer antler. Cedar chips were then sprinkled on the additions to the pile and the crisp, fresh aroma filled the steam filled space. The antler and chips were then passed back out and the door resealed from outside, again trapping them in the dark womb of the earth.

Darker even than the darkest of nights inside, Kohl waited and felt a shudder of fear and uncertainty pass through him. Grey Hawk's deep voice filled the tiny space with a husky, chanting prayer as his hand found its way to the wooden bucket and the short handled gourd dipper. Kohl shut his eyes, opened them, shut them, couldn't tell the difference, said his own hurried little prayer and waited.

Cold water splashed on the superheated volcanic stones. Hissing sound and shooting steam filled the already suffocating and, far too small, structure Kohl had erected the previous day, making it even more impossible to breath.

Another chant began. Was it one voice, two voices or three? He couldn't tell. And who were all these strange people who sat with him around the grandmother pit, with their backs against the wall? They had just filed in, in the fire light and sat down after Kohl had already been told to enter nearly an hour earlier. Most of them had long hair. He had made out that much, and the skin of one appeared much darker than that of the others but he didn't have the vaguest idea of who they were or what their purpose was for being there. It was something else to think about as questions came and went.

Kohl felt light headed, dysfunctional and disoriented. At times he was sure he was hallucinating. Must be because it was totally black in there, he told himself. Then something appeared to be rising up from the center of their circle above where the rocks lay piled tightly together. A distinct, glowing and very unusually bright orb, highly visible but yet one which shed no light outward into the surroundings. All else inside the lodge still remained in the void. The orb began to change shape and took on a somewhat human form. What was it, Kohl wondered as he let his towel fall to the ground.

The next thing he knew all four rounds of the ceremony had been completed and he was crawling along the ground past the still hot stones, now twenty eight in number, making his way to the open flap of the door. Outside, he tried to stand, thought better of it, sat on a wooden stump instead and waited, allowing his overheated self to cool, giving himself time to adjust to breathing again. Still sweating profusely, his body cried out and his brain spun as he failed to make any sense of what had happened inside the lodge. Something else to deal with, even more time would be needed to assimilate it all.

Later, when their bodies had cooled and the sweat had nearly dried, Kohl was introduced to his companions. Running Deer, Spotted Owl, One Hand, Rainmaker, James. James? Kohl looked closely at James in the dying fire light. No wonder he was so dark. He was a black man.

Then someone else was standing in front of him. The fire tender. More surprises, it was a woman. A strong but very fleeting expression passed over her face as though he had somehow startled her, yet was too quickly subdued for him to decipher. He held out his grimy hand as he had seen the other men do. She hesitated, then took it briefly, but firmly. Suddenly, he was embarrassed. Barefooted, stringy haired and filthy dirty with nothing on but an old towel wrapped around his midsection, he felt himself at a severe disadvantage to deal with the penetrating look she gave him.

Finally forcing his distress aside, he studied her more closely. There was something awfully familiar about that face and the long dark hair. What was it? Had they met before? Why couldn't he remember? Then, when he was about to give up, an image of a girl in military fatigues carrying a rifle flashed through his mind. Oh, damn, he said to himself and looked at Grey Hawk. Grey Hawk surveyed the two of them with a quick curiosity and shrugged. He had no idea what was going on between them. Kohl turned his attention back to the woman. Now dressed in flannel shirt, blue jeans and cowboy boots that did little to hide her proportions, she proved to be most provocative. At last he spoke.

"Daphne?" he questioned, trying to focus in on an evening almost a year ago. It had been a tense, dark and moonless night with a hurried, skirting hike through the woods under a foreboding set of circumstances. Sirens had been screaming in the distance as helicopters prowled low over the terrain, searching for him and Mike as she had stumbled along beside them down the hill to safety. There hadn't been illumination enough for a close look or time enough for any conversation either, so to this day she had remained an unsolved mystery. There was only one thing he was certain of, however, it was the same girl. What the hell was going on, he wondered, pleased and alarmed, all in the same breath.

He looked again to Grey Hawk for some hint but the Indian had moved closer to the fire where he was talking with the other men. Kohl turned back to Daphne, caught the thoughtful depth in her eyes as he studied her more carefully. It occurred to him that she was beautiful, more strikingly so than anything he could have imagined. But what was she doing here? And what had she been doing out there in the woods that night in her uniform? Why hadn't she called for help on her radio, shot into the air to attract attention or tried in some way to detain them as she must have been honor bound to do? Why? That was the unanswered question he had puzzled over so many times, his rational mind never able to come up with a satisfactory answer. And now, here she was again under an almost equally strange set of circumstances. There was a lot he needed to talk to her about but before he could get over the

22

shock of seeing her, let alone try and approach, she went to Grey Hawk, bade him good night and left. It was then that it occurred to him. The eyes. Her eyes were the same deep and mysterious gray-green, as those of the child in his vision.

Struggling with her own questions, Daphne headed home to the tiny second floor apartment she had rented as a temporary place to stay. Wearily, she climbed the stairs, went inside, slipped out of her stained clothes and stepped into the shower. Being a sweat lodge fire tender was damned hard work, she had just found out. It was also very hot and dirty, too. She felt as though she had sweat even more than the seven men who had been inside the crude structure, something some of them had obviously built for the occasion. She pulled the curtain shut and reached for the faucet when abruptly a strong realization almost caused her to loose her balance. Instead of being privileged to the freedom of the small apartment she was now living in, she was very close to spending half her life looking through the bars of a prison cell. Heaven help her if the truth were known, she had assisted fugitives to escape from the authorities. Not only had she helped them, she was also probably the only person in the whole country who could positively identify them and link them to that awesome weapon carrying van that had created so much havoc across the country. Potentially, that had all the earmarks of a dangerous piece of information.

They had come roaring up the hill in the middle of the night in that big van without lights on and ground to a stop beside her. She had pointed the flashlight in the rolled down window, gotten a look at something in their faces and did that which was in total opposition to both her training and her own good sense. Why, she asked herself again, for the hundredth time or more as she turned on the water and tried to calm herself, why had she compromised herself so badly? And for what? Was there a little bit of anarchy in her own heart that was beginning to surface? Perhaps, and now that she thought of it the side of her that

23

felt that way agreed completely with everything Kohl and Mike had been doing as she had understood it from the media coverage of the events at that time. In the awesome wake they had left behind there had still been some moral code attached. Not one single soul had ever received as much as a scratch from their part in the adventures. Too bad the government couldn't make the same claim about some of its more clandestine operations. Thinking of it in those terms she tried to assure herself that neither Kohl nor Mike would be the ones to harm her. And, except for the little bit she had shared with her own mother, who else would ever know? But then she considered the person her mother was now married to. Maybe sharing hadn't been so wise, after all.

Her thoughts then returned specifically to Kohl. What else had she learned about him from their brief meeting tonight? Friend or foe, there was a solid determination in his face and a steady gaze that left little room to hide. Beyond that, and most unsettling, Kohl was even more handsome than she had remembered. There had been something rather feral and untamed about him too, standing there all disheveled with nothing but a towel around him. Kind of made her feel a little queasy for a moment. That, piled on top of the fact that it was such an astonishing coincidence to have reconnected with him here in such an unlikely place. What a coincidence to have even met him to begin with, and at Ft. Huachuca, no less, where she had been finishing up her enlistment. And how had he and Grey Hawk crossed paths, she wondered further. Had that been another one of those coincidences also, or was it true what they said? There were no such things! If so, should she be concerned or should she feel grateful? There was no conclusion to be reached.

What she really needed at the moment, however, was a tub to soak in. She could always think clearer in the silence of a tub without the spray pounding her. But the shower was all she had, so she lingered there, shampooing twice, soaping herself over again, letting the little water jets work against her skin, soothing her worn and wilted body. Tired as she was, however, the questions keep coming and the thoughts kept flowing. Now that it was over, her enlistment in the service was a happening that she often wished she had gone without. It had served a purpose at the time, however. Well enough, though, and so much for that.

With that conclusion she shut off the water and reached for the towel. A smile crossed her lips. She thought about what might lie ahead for her. Whatever happened to her here in this scenic little northern Arizona town was going to be an interesting experience, that's for sure. She could feel it deep inside and smiled again. Then, to her surprise, she shivered.

"Isn't one Vision Quest in a lifetime enough," Kohl asked.

"No", Grey Hawk told him.

"No! Why not?"

"Just isn't."

"How many then?"

"Depends"

"On what?"

"The path you find yourself on."

"What is that supposed to mean?"

"For some, all of life and living is a quest. You seem to be one of those but we need to find out for sure."

"How?"

"By doing another vision quest in a more official manner."

That is what Grey Hawk had said to Kohl only yesterday. Now they stood there in the frigid, early morning air of a new dawn just beginning, staring at each other. "Are you ready to begin?" Grey Hawk asked brusquely.

"Jesus, Grey Hawk. I haven't fully recovered from the last one, let alone that super heated pressure cooker you put me through again last night. What was that all about, anyway?"

"Purification."

Kohl groaned. "Right," he said. "Not one tiny electrolyte left over anywhere in one remote cell of my body. No food last night, four hours sleep, no breakfast and now you want me to sit inside this little fourteen foot circle without food or water and keep this fire from going out for how many days? How am I supposed to do that? When am I supposed to sleep?"

"A man on a Vision Quest gives his flesh and bones to the Great Spirit. If he is accepted, he goes on living but his spirit is working apart from his body. He has been given a power almost like dying except that he comes back from death. Don't sleep! That's the idea. Only four days this time."

Kohl gave up. Grey Hawk had also taken away all his clothes. With nothing on but a pair of shorts, he bent over the small teepee of little sticks he had assembled in the tiny fire pit in the center of his circle. With wooden match in hand, he grunted. Grey Hawk held up his ceremonial pipe and began to pray. Kohl scratched the fire stick on a stone, cupped the small flame in his hand until it grew stronger, placed it against the tinder and watched it expand. He leaned more sticks against the pile, then stood and faced the east, looking into the sun just beginning to break over the rim of the earth in the distance.

Grey Hawk prayed on. When at last he had exhausted his appeals to the spirit world, Grey Hawk stepped outside the circle. He then instructed Kohl to light the sage bundle and smudge the inner circumference of that circle, one which Kohl had scraped into the dirt the day before up there on that high hill. When the task of fanning the sweet smelling smoke around the jagged line was complete, Grey Hawk began laying down two rows of corn meal, one white and one yellow, defining it even more clearly, locking Kohl inside. With that done, he said, "I'll be back to check on you in the morning," and disappeared into the tree line.

Kohl surveyed the microcosm of his new domain where he was now held captive by the two scattered bands of corn meal and his own imagination. Mostly, the barrier was psychological in nature, he realized, but it felt very real, nevertheless. So did the importance of the four brightly colored sticks he himself had painted with bands of white, red, yellow and black which he had placed to protect the gates at each of the four compass directions and hold back the assault of any supposedly ethereal intruders who might appear. Just in case, Kohl had placed the tallest and strongest at the north, further adorned with an extra fifteen tobacco ties. If there were such things as bad spirits, Piaja would be the one he would fear the most. Piaja was the mad woman with the long, black hair who came in the night and drove men crazy.

Kohl sat down in the dirt. Maybe he had already gone completely mad. What was he doing here, anyway? He wasn't searching for some grand, ritual enshrouded belief system to fill up his life. He had never been able to accept any of the more popular, elaborately contrived conglomerations of sacrosanct mumblings adrift in the world that endlessly revolved about themselves in the name of salvation. Nor any of the lesser ones either. Most definitely he did not want to "step into the light", wherever one went to do that or whatever that meant. Likewise, he had never wanted to set off to Egypt and climb the great pyramid of Cheops in expectation of some bone rattling, earth upending, re birthing transformation and illumination of his soul. Neither did he want to be indoctrinated, saved or be reborn, to turn his spiritual development over to a grand master, grand wizard, guru, shaman or shadrak, nor did he wish to join a movement, society or sect that self proclaimed to have been gifted with the one path to true eternal bliss.

No, he had never in his whole life, blindly aligned himself with the thinking of another. To the contrary. He had always thought his own thoughts, been his own man, quietly listening to what went on around him, questioning, evaluating, working it through. If it made sense and worked for him, he kept it. Otherwise, he threw it away and waited, open to whatever new truth might appear. Yes, he had to admit, life amounted to a "Quest," all right, as Grey Hawk had said. In the very least, the last few years had certainly been that, and more.

So, what the hell, he decided. He would wait this one out also and see what other delusional, eccentric apparitions might come to test the metaphysically constructed boundary Grey Hawk had so expertly crafted round him with his mysterious, hexing, hoodoo chantings. In the meantime, the uncertainty, the enigma and the compelling lure of the one named Daphne would have to keep. Hopefully, she would still be around when he came back down from this adventure, should he be lucky enough not to fall asleep and let this ridiculous little fire go out, that was. A man can live for a month without food, a week without water, but he can die within a few short hours from exposure. It was getting late in the year. Night time temperatures were dropping low here on the high plateau and there were still traces of frost on the ground when they had come up the mountain. With that small thought still in mind Kohl looked up in time to see a red necked vulture make a lazy swing downward and bank into a turn over the tiny circle he was committed to spending the next four days and nights inside of. He yelled and waved the bird away. To him a commitment was something that, once made, you did. It hadn't even occurred to him that there was an easy way out. He could simply leave the circle and walk on down the slope.

TWO

"Don't worry about the houses," Grey Hawk stated six days later as he, Kohl and Daphne happened to be gathered around the breakfast table at the local coffee shop. Grey Hawk was buying Kohl breakfast as some kind of reward for having made it through his second, not nearly so difficult, vision quest. Why Grey Hawk had invited Daphne along was not yet clear, nor was Kohl so glad that he had, ambivalent as he was about her. Still, her presence there, good or bad, had done far more to revive him than two days of sleep and four gallons of apple juice.

But how had he let the conversation drift off along these lines, Kohl suddenly wondered. Why had he started complaining about what was happening to the local environment when all he really wanted to do was talk to Daphne, by herself. To begin with he desperately needed to know what she was doing in Sedona. Since her presence came with an element of sinister implication for him, it made him increasingly nervous. But at the same time Grey Hawk was about to make a point, however, and it did sound somewhat important. Maybe he could get her alone later.

"Why not," Kohl asked Grey Hawk. Returning to the subject at hand, he picked up the decanter of coffee that had been left there by the waitress. Daphne's cup was still full but the Indian nodded. Kohl topped off Grey Hawk's cup and refilled his own, waiting for an answer.

"Grandmother will take care of it," they were informed at last, in a tone that indicated he should have understood.

But he didn't. His mind was still semi-dysfunctional. "Grandmother?" he queried instead, with a puzzled look.

"Grandmother," Grey Hawk repeated, like Kohl had suddenly become very dense. "The Earth. The mother of us all."

Of course, Kohl thought. That Grandmother. He should have known. The Indians considered the earth to be a living entity, as were all things upon it. The creatures, the trees, the plants, the rivers, the very rocks. All were alive, all were a part of spirit. "But how will she do that?" he wondered aloud.

Grey Hawk shrugged, something he had been doing a lot of lately, exposed as he was to so many white people these days. If he truly felt that he had more of a choice in the matter he might have shunned them entirely but he had given his word to his tribal elders and was bound by it. In the verbal history of the forefathers, passed on generation after generation, was the prediction that the white man would come to the redman's land, the land of the Turtle as they called it, and would become the conqueror. The native peoples would undergo wide spread decimation and subjugation and would be forced to withdraw their own knowledge and wisdom from the oppressor.

After five hundred years of domination, however, the keepers of the wisdom would find it necessary to come out of the woods, so to speak, and begin sharing their knowledge once again because by now the planet would be in serious jeopardy, both environmentally and socially. Not only would it affect the white man but the redman as well. With that thought in mind, Grey Hawk made the effort and spoke. "Have you ever noticed that spire of volcanic rock sticking up out of the ground just below the notch near the top of Cathedral Rock?"

Kohl nodded that he had.

"There is no such thing as an extinct volcano, only a dormant one. There is also an earth fault line that runs across the valley floor from Sedona up the hill to Jerome."

Kohl pondered the statement as Grey Hawk continued.

"The entire area surrounding Sedona is especially sacred," the Indian said. "It was never meant to be lived upon in such a dense manner. Those ancient tribes who did reside here maintained balance and harmony with the land. They didn't overrun it or defile it but worshiped it instead, along with the Mother and all the other living things. Those who have invaded the place in recent years, however, have a slightly different attitude, as you so clearly pointed out."

It was more than just the houses too, Kohl knew. They had discussed that part of it also. Missing people, sadistic rites, sacrificial rituals, drugs and other things unmentioned, overlooked and covered up for the sake of the tourist dollar, all happening in the surrounding area. The many symptomatic signs of a failing society were not restricted to the big city alone. Goethe's Shadow of the Giant had spread even further across the land than one could have ever earlier imagined possible, out into the country side and beyond, casting metropolis and crossroad towns alike into increasing darkness through things that too many good people were still not yet ready to start dealing with.

But fault lines, earthquakes and streams of hot lava, that was something else. Would the Mother, assuming that the planet was alive, would she destroy the very beauty she had taken all those eons of time to create? Is that what she might resort to, to restore balance to this area of the world? And what about the rest of her domain? Maybe the increase in number and intensity of natural catastrophes in recent years around the world was just an indication of what might yet be coming. Maybe it was a warning of sorts, stepping up in severity, telling us to pay attention and take heed. But it's not too late, Kohl decided. Nature was trying to tell us that mankind still had a choice. Get things back in perspective and equilibrium or there would be a higher price to pay, perhaps even massive eruption and destruction to set things right once more. There was time left, but not for complacency.

Such thoughts brought to mind, "The Prophecies," for Kohl, as so many people referred to them. The Mayan, the Hopi, the Talmud Jmmanuel, the Bible, Billy Meier, Stalking Wolf, Seth and others. There were ten that Kohl knew of personally, from the Middle East, Europe, South America, southwestern United States and elsewhere, some thousands of years old, some relatively recent. No doubt there were other auguries too, if one were to go in search of them. Broad, horrifying statements about the coming fate of the world, so dismal in fact that the natural inclination would be to try and ignore the entire lot. But how could you when there was so much correlation between them?

So, what about Sedona in particular, as Grey Hawk was alluding to? Was there still another prophecy specifically related to it or was it perhaps part of one of those such as the Hopi, close neighbors to the north, whose own prophecy was actually days long in the telling and never completely shared outside the council of elders? A strange prophecy whose essence was carved on a rock up on the mesa. The same rock he had seen in his vision before he had known that it really existed, depicting two world wars and two-hearted humans walking down the wrong path with a third, yet to come, cataclysmic event if they didn't soon change direction. It most certainly could apply to Sedona where there was a steadily increasing amount of human maleficence towards nature. But if not that, then perhaps it was some private, precognitive insight or vision that Grey Hawk himself had been confronted with.

With the thought of that possibility, the remainder of the bleak and agonizing content of Kohl's first experience in the canyon returned, along with all the other misbegotten illusions of his second quest. How could he dispute such things when every aspect of it supported what the man who sat across the table from him was saying to him now. Was Grey Hawk really able to see into the future? And if the Medicine Man could do that, what ability might he also have to be able to change it, Kohl speculated as a thousand bits and pieces of things read and things heard here and there along the way of his life ran through his mind. It was a complex, challenging subject. But so was the gray-eyed girl sitting there listening to the trend of conversation as she finished her breakfast. Somehow he felt he had better find a way to let her know how much he had appreciated her help without dragging Grey Hawk into the picture. Then he needed figure out what her intentions might be regarding his future safety. If he could stop staring long enough to think clearly, that was.

The sound of the Indian's deep voice grew fainter and fainter. Finally it disappeared altogether as Kohl sighed and mentally began tracing his fingertips gently over Daphne's lips and soft skin, then came back again as Grey Hawk grew silent, lit a cigarette and blew smoke across the table. Awakening slowly, Kohl looked at him, looked at the girl and back again at the stoic Indian who had yielded the floor. "What brought you to Sedona?" Kohl asked of Daphne at last, unable to think of anything else to begin with in Grey Hawk's presence.

"I'm not sure," she said, because that was the truth of it. When they had handed her, her discharge from the military she had decided to take the long way back home, had turned off the freeway to have lunch and had been there every since. Another one of those coincidences? She was afraid to think of it in those terms but what else could it be. When she tried to explain it, however, it didn't sound very convincing. Kohl listened to her words and then, almost before she had finished speaking, suspicion suddenly crowded back into his mind. This young lady had been stationed at Fort Huacucha, home of Army Intelligence, Special Forces and other covert and sinister sounding functions. Maybe she hadn't really been discharged at all, as she had stated, but was really on assignment, instead. An assignment that included Mike and himself, temporarily in limbo because Mike's whereabouts were presently unknown. Why not? Government agents had killed Sue, hadn't they? Deliberately shot her down out there on the highway near Page that fateful night. What would they do next? They had proved they were capable of almost anything. He stared at Daphne, fighting the turmoil, not knowing where to go from there, or even if he wanted to pursue the matter any further, then looked away.

Grey Hawk puffed quietly on his cigarette, giving it his full attention to let them know he was doing his best to mind his own business, should they wish to continue. Not daring to allow himself to be captured by her eyes, Kohl forced himself to look into his coffee cup until he had regained control. "What about the van?" he finally asked and looked up to see if there were any betrayal in her answer. It was a legitimate question. The van was a matter of great concern to him because the van was the one thing he never, ever, wanted dug up. Who knew? There just might be something there they had inadvertently overlooked. A stray fingerprint perhaps, a few human hairs, a tiny, traceable bit of something in the way of hard evidence that might serve to convict them should it be discovered. What a frightening thought. Maybe they should have burned it.

"I think they finally gave up," Daphne said, as if to ease his mind. "The ground was still untouched when I went out there just before my discharge."

"That's good," Kohl replied with some relief, wanting desperately to believe her. However, in his heart he knew that he would never be fully able to do so until he had returned and personally checked for himself - something he wasn't about to do until a little more time had passed.

Then the rest of it came around to him from a different angle. What about Grey Hawk sitting there looking so innocent? He was supposed to have been a part of the American Indian Movement, a veteran of the encounter at Wounded Knee, a man about as anti-establishment as one could be. Up until now Kohl hadn't been at all worried about what the Indian might find out about him, but then, what if he wasn't what he had said he was either? Damn!

For the moment, however, he had to let that one go. Both his instincts and what checking he had done thus far gave the man a clean bill. It was back to the girl. This bright eyed, attentive, beautifully seductive, innocently appearing young women was the perfect candidate to get a lonesome, heartbroken fool like himself to spill his guts. "Dammit", Kohl said to himself again. Why did there have to be so many doubts running through his mind? Why couldn't it just be what it seemed to be? Instinctively, however, he took it a step further. How had these two come to know each other? How did Daphne just happen to be tending the sweat lodge fire that night and why hadn't he run into her around town before then?

"I've been reading about Native American philosophy for years," she said in way of explanation. "I went to a talk Grey Hawk was giving at the gallery when I first moved here, decided I liked what he was saying and asked if I could become an apprentice." At this point the conversation died. Kohl had become too wary to continue and Daphne's rational mind had at last forced her to withdraw and suppress any further interest she might have had in Kohl. Somewhere in the back of her mind her future included a more conventional husband, a house on a quiet street and a couple of kids.

THREE

Like Grey Hawk, Spotted Owl had also been somewhat reluctant to accept Kohl into the scheme of things at first. Considering Spotted Owl's own heritage, this would have only been natural. He was Lakota. Justifiably enough, many of the traditional Lakota held an angry view of the white man. Not only had the white man taken all their land away but now they were stealing from their art, their language, their traditions and their ceremony. Equally bad, both white men and white women were writing glamorized, autobiographical stories represented as true encounters with tribal members where great wisdom was supposedly given over. Others passed themselves off as bona fide shamans, priests and pipe carriers, sang Lakota songs, sold pipes that were claimed to have been awakened and conducted bogus ceremonies. Anything at all to make a buck. Still, while many full bloods would have taken these folks out in the desert, stripped them naked and tied them down to stakes in the ground with rawhide laces, Spotted Owl was himself able to display a somewhat more forgiving attitude.

"If we truly are what we claim to be," he had said on one occasion, "then those kinds of people can't detract from our own relationship with the Great Spirit nor can they hurt us no matter how much they steal. If one truly believes in the spirit eternal, in the end they can only hurt themselves, and in ways that will create far more agony for them than anything that can ever happen here on earth." In that same regard he didn't think the Sun Dance and other ceremonies should be closed to outsiders, only to some of them.

"Don't repeat the mistakes of your former enemies. Judge the person, not the skin color," were his exact words. "Don't say they can't have a relationship with Spirit just because they can't speak the traditional language of

35

the Lakota. But, don't say I have to love Jesus and be saved to get to the great beyond, either, because that offends me terribly."

No, Spotted Owl's reaction to Kohl was not because Kohl was a white man intruding into the ways of the red but because Spotted Owl had fallen passionately in love with Daphne only to find out that the only man she seemed to be at all interested in was Kohl. That was his interpretation of the situation, anyway, skewed as it was and after three long weeks of smoldering frustration he gave up the chase and went back to the busty little red headed Tarot card reader named Star Shower he had known before Daphne had appeared. Now having made such a generous concession, he could only wonder at Kohl's stupidity for keeping such a wondrous creature as Daphne waiting.

At last, unable to bear it, Spotted Owl took Kohl aside. He was a tall man, broad shouldered, wide faced with a hook of a nose; wise enough, but not altogether the kind of person Kohl had thus far become accustomed to being around. Spotted Owl twisted his long, black braid of hair and squinted at Kohl when he spoke. Had Kohl bumped his head recently, was his diet lacking in red meat or had his vision failed? What was the problem? Grey Hawk says work with you, help teach you the way but, I don't know, man. Anyone dumb enough to pass up a woman even half as enticing as that chick, well...

Kohl wasn't about to try and convince Spotted Owl that there was nothing wrong with either his vision or his eating habits nor were there any lumps on his head. But, at the same time, he wasn't about to make any excuses for his own behavior either, peculiar as it might appear to the Indian. Nor was he ready to share the real truth with him, just as he couldn't explain all the implications of it to Grey Hawk at this point in their relationship. He wasn't blind to the fact that Daphne's interest in him had increased somewhat either, but he didn't in any way see it as being romantic. Daphne had a certain way of studying him, all right. That much he was aware of, but, she also had a way of avoiding any situation that might leave her alone with him. Not much he could do about that, or anything else. Spotted Owl would have to think what he liked.

But as for himself, right or wrong, lumps on his head or no lumps, one thing was for sure. Whether she liked him or not, she was beautiful and his own looking at her was beginning to drive him crazy. But what was he going to do about it, that was the eternal question. Since she was really apprenticed to Grey Hawk, maybe that mad Indian would do him a favor and send her off to South Dakota or back to the Cherokee Nation or who knew where one of these days to spend time with the elders of other tribes so he wouldn't have to think about her anymore. Like hell he wouldn't!

Pummeled and drained by the swirl of emotions from within, Kohl dragged through the days, barely able to accomplish even the simplest of homework tasks Grey Hawk had set before him. Such tasks as learning to see the auras of insects and counting and remembering the positions and numbers of trees in a clearing in the hopes of being able to tell if a Sasquatch was about, blocking his presence by telepathically disguising himself as one of the rooted, standing, forest people. What bullshit, he began telling himself at last. There were no auras. None of the trees ever changed position either. How could they? They were anchored to the ground with roots, weren't they? Everybody knew that. Unfortunately, Grey Hawk kept sending him back out to the same old place up near Flagstaff in the tall pines, day after day, and like the good soldier he was trying to be, he kept on going, too weak to protest.

Well, at least it was a lot cooler up here at the higher altitude, Kohl told himself one day as he sat down with his back against a familiar tree. And it had been good for something. He was finally able to identify every one of the individual trees in his field of vision. Who knew when that might come in handy. Damn, he was really beginning to feel Grey Hawk's impatience. Then his thoughts began to drift again as a blurred image of Daphne floated through his mind. He sighed forlornly. All too soon he was fast asleep.

What was that, he wondered, suddenly awake. He scanned the clearing. It still looked the same. He rose and moved around the tree, checking the other side. It too, was the same. Or was it? Hmmm, what was it? There. That small clump of tall bushes off to the west somehow appeared more dense than he remembered. He froze and waited. Something was staring back at him, he could feel it. Holy shit! Now what? What if old bigfoot himself was in there looking at him? What was he supposed to do now? What if that big, hairy thing wanted to hug him or something? Maybe it was time to head back down the hill towards home.

Then he caught himself. Idiot! He had to know the truth. If there was such a creature in existence, well then by God, he certainly wanted to see one. And if it was out there, would it come to him or should he go to it? Should he try calling to it? No, don't talk out loud, use telepathy. Don't try to verbalize, he remembered Grey Hawk telling him. Mind-speak didn't work that way. Visualize the act of coming together in a friendly manner instead. That was the way to do it.

Kohl concentrated as hard as he could, thinking the friendliest thoughts he could put together under the circumstances and tried hard to smile at some imaginary hairy creature who had size sixteen footprints, had to be over seven feet tall and had never seen a bar of soap in it's entire life. "Whew", he said, as he began to move slowly in that direction, thinking of the possibility of getting too close to such a thing.

I mean you no harm, he repeated silently to reinforce the image, I really don't. And I sincerely hope you mean me none either. Then abruptly, he stopped in his tracks and stared. "Goddammit," he said out loud.

An embarrassed little laugh emanated from within the green tangle of dense foliage as Daphne parted the branches and stepped forward, dressed in camouflage apparel left over from her days in the service. Kohl glared at her, waiting for an explanation. She gave none, tried to smile instead, but failed.

"All right," he said at last. "What the hell is this all about?"

"Do you have any water?" she said. "I could use a drink."

He glared at her, sulkily walked back to the tree he had fallen asleep under and picked up his canteen. He unscrewed the cap and handed it to her. She took a large swallow.

"Grey Hawk sent me up here to work on my stalking skills," she said, candidly enough. "Told me to see if I could sneak up on you and steal your hat or something and bring it back but a squirrel distracted me and I stepped on a dead branch."

Kohl was incredulous. "You mean that bastard has just been playing games with me?"

Daphne was surprised at the question. "Why would he do that?" she asked defensively.

"What would you call it? There aren't any Bigfoot here. Only women running around in fatigues playing Girl Scout."

She shook her head, thinking she understood the reason for his anger. "You haven't seen one yet?" she asked.

"Hardly."

She looked at him closely. Should she tell him? She turned to the west and checked the clearing. He followed her gaze. Now that was interesting, he thought. He could have sworn there had been another tree standing there just before he had fallen asleep. Or was there? The question showed heavily on his face as he looked back at her, then faded as she held his eyes with her own.

"Oh damn," something deep within him said as he reached for her. Whether or not there really was another being out there was no longer of consequence. The air was filled with bird songs, the breeze was cool and caressing, the bed of pine needles beneath them, soft and accommodating. What anguish some other creature might suffer from being exposed to the perplexing sounds and motions related to the mating habits of the human species was not theirs to worry about.

FOUR

Grey Hawk was both beside and beyond himself. Goddamn, he kept saying to himself, or to anyone else who happened to be around every time he thought of it, which was at least half a dozen times a day. Goddamn was one of the two and only two, all purpose, swear words he had borrowed from the white man. The other was, son-of-a-bitch, which he reserved for even more portentous circumstances than this one, should they ever arrive. He damned well should have known better, Dammit. His two most promising apprentices had both deserted him, lost to the cause for good. Off somewhere, they were, hiding out, drying up their brains trying to screw each other to death. Well, shit!

He was on the phone one sunny afternoon talking long distance to a Mexican lady named Lupe in southern California, about to commit himself to going out there and doing an exorcism on her sister-in-law, Marie, when his front door swung open. He started to make a move to kick it shut again when Daphne and Kohl walked into the rented, double-wide mobile home where he dwelt along with another sometimes blond named Renee who wandered in and out of his life. The once tandem wheeled dwelling was a unique structure now forever stranded atop a mismatched foundation of used cement blocks and riverbed stones dragged up from the creek nearby.

"I'll call you back," Grey Hawk told Lupe. He put down the phone, reached for an unfiltered Camel and lit up. Two deep inhalations later, he turned to them, determined neither to give his thoughts away, nor to be the first to speak. He waited.

Daphne stood leaning into Kohl, his arm around her waist. The all powerful intimacy that had become theirs

40

since he had seen them last pervaded the air. Kohl grinned at Grey Hawk. Grey Hawk's black eyes stared back at him but he purposely still said nothing, damned if he would speak to them. Kohl continued to grin. "There were three of them," he said proudly.

Grey Hawk scratched his weathered chin. What was this boy talking about, he wondered. But he wasn't about to ask, Dammit. Not after two weeks of not seeing them around. As far as he was concerned, he had already written them off. Undaunted, however, Kohl continued. "Sasquatch," he told him. "Two males and a female. At least we think it was a female."

Hmm, Grey Hawk said to himself and dug some imaginary piece of dirt out of the corner of his eye to hide his sudden spurt of curiosity. He then looked them both over closely. Damned hot blooded apprentices anyway. Still, he was forced to admit that neither their brains nor their bodies were completely depleted. Well, what to do now? Two males and a female, huh. Were they bullshiting him, or what? This was serious stuff. He smashed out the cigarette he had going and reached for his Dunhill pipe, filled it with some of his favorite kinnikinnik and scratched the head of a wooden match across the wall paneling near his chair. He took a puff, then decided they were probably being straight with him. "Hmm," he said again, out loud this time. Maybe he been a little premature in his judgment. He took another puff, pulled the tobacco smoke deep into his lungs. It felt warm and soothing. Spirit was agreeing with him.

FIVE

A man of still pressing and impassioned ambition, Daphne's arrogant step-father was beginning to feel that time was running out. He was getting old. A product of both the Korean and Vietnam wars, he had ramrodded himself up through the ranks to Brigadier General before he had been forced into retirement through one petty indiscretion. He had referred to the President of the United States as an asshole in front of an audience of his peers, many of whose toes he had stepped on at one time or another over the years. What goes around, comes around, they all said and they all thanked him for the opportunity to rat on him and be rid of him. General Bartholomew W. Winsome. Bad Bart, they had called him and dementia praecox was what they had always said about him, behind his back of course and according to the old definition (delusions of grandeur).

For the most part, however, he, himself, went unaware and unperturbed by what had happened. What did anyone else know, anyway? There was still too much to be done before throwing in the sponge to let a bunch of shallow visioned, old fools slow him down. There was a whole world out there that still needed to be conquered - for its own good, of course. Thus it was that he went directly from the payroll of the US. Army to a position of valiant self employment, a much more lucrative, self created venture involving the training and placement of hired mercenary soldiers who were routinely shipped off to out of the way places of the world. Beneficially enough, the sadistical side of his own nature made him a master trainer of the demented and with the global situation such as it was, the demand for his specially indoctrinated, semi-psychotic hoodlums was increasing on an almost daily basis. As a result the effectiveness of his graduates was quickly turning him into a multimillionaire and a person to be reckoned with in his own right. Especially when one considered that all those same graduates were also available for instant recall back to his home base, an elite corps of highly disciplined killers at his personal disposal when the time should come. And now, thanks to Daphne's connection with that man Kohl, he had stumbled onto an even better addition to his arsenal and an even more efficient way to achieve his ultimate goal. Maybe the burden of having married Daphne's mother would come to a good end after all.

Originally he had married the woman because he was thinking of tossing his hat into the political arena when he had first been relieved of his command. She was an attractive widow instead of a tainted divorcee. She was also intelligent, socially acceptable and would have looked good at his side, be he governor or senator. But that had completely changed, hadn't it? For several years now he hadn't needed her at all but had decided that in the long run it would probably be much less expensive to let her have the house and a nice allowance than it would be to get a divorce. Unfortunately, the daughter had come with the package. Now, however, it looked like she might turn out to be a real asset and a bonus after all. He would have to buy her mother a new dress or take her out to dinner or something. It was only fair.

As for Daphne, she loathed him as only a displaced step daughter could. A step daughter who saw this demagogue of a man move into her mother's bed, desecrate her real father's image and proceed to drive Daphne from the house and her mother's life. But, knowing him as she had come to, it should have been no surprise to her as to how desperately he might have wanted to get his hands on that powerful laser of Kohl's and Mike's. With the ability of its invisible energy beam to reach out and silently eat through both concrete and steel from far away, it would have been the perfect weapon for him. But as to how he had found out about the fact that she had met Kohl and Mike, that was still a mystery. She had better watch herself. Obviously her own life might well be at stake.

She thought of her real father. He had been such a complete opposite. Boston University Professor of Art Studies, Poet Emeritus, decent human being, a person of wisdom and gentleness, he was dead at forty eight from an aneurysm deep within a vital portion of his brain on Daphne's fourteenth birthday. Dear Daddy, if only you were still here.

"Have you slept with him yet?" Bad Bart demanded of her from where he sat on his hotel bed. He had come all the way from the east coast and had taken a room at the most expensive resort in town to interrogate her. She glared at him, refusing to answer. "You don't have to answer. I know you have," he said, letting her seethe.

She stood there a while, then made a move for the door. "I wouldn't leave just yet, if I were you," he threatened.

She stopped and turned to him. "You don't know anything," she told him.

"Perhaps not", he said, staring at her. Then he smiled his dark smile. "But if you treasure your mother's future, you had best find out what they did with that little device they created."

"Bastard," she said out loud, with hatred in her voice. Go to hell, she stated silently, not about to tell him anything, only to stall. She needed to get back home to try and persuade her mother to leave this mad man first, if that were even possible. There was no question in her mind that he was just crazy enough to do her harm, but could she really get her mother to believe such a thing? It was highly unlikely. Still, she had to try and she needed time.

Wisely and wordlessly, she waited, hoping he would give her some kind of ultimatum. He did. "Three more weeks," he said, "and that's it. Then I'll send her off to that guerrilla compound in Costa Rica I told you about. Whether or not she comes back will be up to you."

Daphne gave him a cold look to let him know she understood and to show him she wasn't nearly as weak as her mother. Then she shrugged and left the room. Damn. What a situation to be in, she told herself as she left and went to her eleven year old car and drove out of the visitors parking lot. Of course the easy thing to do would be to just tell the General where the van was buried and be done with it. How would Kohl ever know? He wouldn't unless he and Mike ever went back there and dug it up, which seemed extremely unlikely under the circumstances. But, regardless, she would know and Kohl was becoming increasingly important to her. But as important as her own mother? Maybe, but why should she even have to make such a choice? And besides, if she did tell the General where the van was at, then any future relationship she might have with Kohl would be based on a lie, and what good was that? Double damn. Well, the General said three weeks, the bastard so she wasn't going to tell Kohl about it, at least not yet, because it was her problem, not his.

Kohl was waiting for her on her apartment steps when she got home. Maybe it was time to have another key made, she thought as she watched him rise to greet her. They had certainly shared her bed often enough. And his. Willingly, she let him kiss her, gave him the best smile she could manage under the circumstances and unlocked the door. Kohl went into the cubicle that served as a kitchen, put down the grocery sack he had brought with him and began emptying it while she went into the bedroom and looked at herself in the mirror, trying to restore her composure. When she reappeared he was making what he called lunch. "Salami or ham?" he asked. She came over to the counter, let him kiss her again, looked at what he was doing, cringed a little for effect and said, "Ham."

When he had finished his haphazard creations they put them on a tray, walked outside and down to the creek. The running water, forever seeking the downstream mystery, tumbled clear and cool over the rocks, providing a comforting backdrop of sound as it went, obviating any immediate need for talk.

How impossible it seemed to Kohl that just a few short months ago this very spot where they were now sitting had been under some fourteen feet of water due to nineteen days of gray, leaking skies in a row. Benign and picturesque, the little stream had turned rampant and raging, overflowing the old, carving out the new, widening itself from five feet to two hundred. Bridges, walls, trees, cars, mobile homes and more, all had been caught and carried along in the furry. Tons and tons of sand, silt, debris and boulders were rearranged, moved about and piled up along the meandering stream bed. A race of giants with monster machines would have taken years to accomplish the same thing but Mother Nature had done it all in less than three weeks, requiring nothing but that from which clouds are formed. It was a stern reminder, all right, awesome and foreboding. The final word rested not in the hands of man, but elsewhere in things so often maligned and misunderstood.   Kohl pondered it again, then his attention returned to the other wonder in his world - the one he never tired of looking at. How was it possible that he could be so lucky?

Ultimately, it was more than just the physical passion that had driven him to her side. There was a rare depth to her that went beyond anything he had ever seen. Jenny had some of it too, Jenny who would always own a piece of his heart no matter where she was. But one woman did not exceed the other. They were each themselves, so very unique and different, beauty that came from both within and without. Depth of soul was the only way he knew how to describe it. He reached over and put his hand on her shoulder.

"Want to talk about it?" he asked.

She kept looking at the stream bed, feigning an interest in something there. "What? she questioned.

"I don't know," he said gently. "Whatever it is that seems to be bothering you."

She almost cut him off with, "nothing", but thought better of it. Kohl was far too astute to try and play games with. But what say without giving it all away?

"Sometimes I worry about my mother," she said to give Kohl some indication as to what was bothering her. "I don't think she's very happy these days."

"How so?" he asked, never having met the woman and knowing but little about her situation except that Daphne had lost her real father some time back.

"My step father can be such a tyrant sometimes," Daphne said, giving him that piece of it. "She won't admit it but I think he's really probably very hard to live with."

"Ex military man, didn't you say?"

"Yes, twenty four years in the Army."

"And an Full Colonel, wasn't it?"

"Brigadier General."

"Shit," Kohl said, as if that explained it clearly

46

enough.

She tried to smile. "Maybe I'll go back and see her. Spend some time together," she added to learn his reaction.

"Might be a good thing," he agreed sympathetically. "When would you go?"

Not for a while, he hoped. He wanted to run down to Ft. Huachuca to confirm that the van was still buried back there in the trees where they had left it before they got more involved. Damn, it would be good to have that over with, the one lingering doubt that kept him from asking her if they couldn't begin sharing bed, breakfast and shower on a full time basis.

"As soon as I can get a decent flight out," she said, forcing Kohl to have to live with his turbid uncertainty a while longer.

SIX

It was the perfect place, a quaint old house overlooking the creek about ten miles out of town. Fifteen acres of land bordered round by National Forest, hidden out of sight from the highway down a long drive through the mesquite and Palo Verde trees. There were hawks and ravens in the sky and deer, ground squirrels, raccoons, javelina, skunks and coyotes roaming the land. A rattler or two showed up with messages from other realms and an occasional scorpion appeared to teach you not to leave your shoes out on the porch at night.

"You must be crazy to be living out there all alone," Daphne's girlfriend said when she called from Phoenix, the new crime capital of the west.

"Out there" also had fruit trees in the yard, ancient old Cottonwoods next to the wash and Sycamores down along the stream bed. Trout, muskrat, beaver and turtles played in the water, an old swimming hole awaited, hiking trails and Indian ruins were close at hand. It was Daphne's new home, for the most part. She had found it and though Kohl soon had most of his things there and spent most of his time there, he still kept his place and his Post Office box in

47

town. Somehow it was a characteristic thing about him that she wasn't sure she totally understood but accepted nevertheless. Maybe it was something she still needed too, she wasn't sure. Commitment without commitment. What did it matter, it worked.

They built a fire pit in the back yard and a sweat lodge down on the sand, started learning how to do more ceremony from Grey Hawk and started practicing the ways of tracking and survival. For Kohl, it had become a time full of joyful hard work, indulgence and deepening emotion, philosophical wonder, reflection, gratitude, growing awareness and, with good reason, increasing assuredness about his own security.

They had finally made the trip to Ft. Huachuca. The van was still safely hidden away in one of the least likely places one would ever think to look, right there on the base itself, underneath the authorities own noses. He had also been out of the news for nearly a year now, no one appeared to be hounding him and most every night when he went to sleep, Daphne was in his arms, warming his spirit. Snug as he had become, there were days in a row when he no longer even thought of the past.

There was another very noticeable change in his life also. His dream world had begun to come alive. Dim remembrances came slowly at first, then with increasing detail, clarity and occurrence. Ultimately, many places were revisited as a continuing drama unfolded. There was both a conscious daytime wakefulness and a conscious dream world wakefulness which became another complete and even more vast realm of existence with its own set of rules. It was a more fruitful place in some respects also, for to gain access to it the ego was forced to remain behind. And with the overly protective and stubborn ego out of the way, many new things became possible. Problems could be solved, questions of health answered, travels into both the past and the future conducted, the lessons of true creativity learned and perhaps even the essence of eternity itself experienced.

As for Daphne, she had begun to have some of the

same adventures, although not yet of the same depth as Kohl. Other things were, to some extent, still in the way. She had made a second trip back east to see her mother and done her best to imply that the General was not a man to be trusted under any circumstances but it was unnecessary. Her mother wasn't as naive as she had thought so Daphne did her best to set her concerns aside and began to focus her attention on her new life with Kohl. And as for Kohl, as nearly as he could tell she was as equally pleased and contented with her life as he was with his, complimenting his own, reflecting back the feelings he had so freely begun to give away. It was perfect, it should have lasted forever. But then, one bright afternoon after a thundershower had come and gone, they walked up the long path to the mailbox together under the newly washed leaves of the trees, smelling the fresh earth and listening to the birds to see if Daphne's mother had written.

Daphne opened the box, removed both a small letter addressed to herself and another large envelope. She put the letter in her pocket and looked at the envelope in surprise. Noticing the Washington, DC. postmark, she raised her eyes questioningly to Kohl and handed him the packet. Perplexed, he took it from her and examined it cautiously. His name had been boldly printed on the front along with her rural address. They started back down the path towards the house.

"What the hell is this?" he said in a shocked voice as he withdrew a number of 8 by 10 glossy photographs from the envelope. One by one, he looked at the series of expertly taken pictures of the van sitting in what appeared to be an old hanger somewhere, then handed them to Daphne. She gasped heavily and her face grew white. Kohl looked further into the envelope and found a neatly typed but signatureless note on a plain white piece of paper. It said:

As you can see, we have recovered your prodigious invention. For now, it is securely out of the hands of the authorities along with other incriminating evidence you overlooked in concealing it. Unfortunately, the laser appears to have been disabled in some way prior to its entombment and we regret to inform you that we have need of your expertise in order to return it to operational status. If you prize your own freedom and would also like to secure the future safety of your lovely lady friend, it would be wise to render us assistance in this matter. Keep your passport handy. You will be contacted in the near future.

Kohl swore loudly as an angry voice welled up inside. He turned to her, pathos tearing at his heart. He was about to say more but he was caught by the dismayed, painful and guiltless expression on her face and stopped, unable to either speak or to move. He turned again to the path and began to walk. She followed behind. Closer to the house, he stopped and sat down under the shade of the umbrella over the picnic table. Silently, Daphne sat next to him. What could have gone wrong? she wondered. There was a sick, empty feeling of growing terror deep in her stomach as a thousand thoughts raced through her mind. Kohl provided the first bit of insight, however. "We were followed," he stated, watching her eyes, noting every flicker of lash and minute muscle twinge of her face, thinking that by now it would be impossible for her to lie to him.

"But how? We took every precaution," she stated innocently enough, since it was inconceivable to her that such a thing could have happened. She had watched Kohl preparing for the trip down to Ft. Huachuca with intense fascination, checking the car and everything they had loaded into it for anything that might emit a tone, signature or signal that might be used to track them. They had then taken three days and had driven nearly a thousand circuitous miles to reach their final destination which in truth lay but a simple five hour ride away from home. Eyes hung on the rear view mirrors, ears tuned to best multi-channel broadband police and military scanners available, they had doubled back and doubled back again, carefully cataloging the traffic as they went. They had even checked for helicopters and low flying planes. Dammit, she cried inwardly, and began to grieve. It was nearly impossible to have been followed. Kohl knew that and under the circumstances he could come to but one conclusion, as far as she was concerned. She had betrayed him.

First and foremost, however, survival was instinctive to Kohl. He couldn't help himself. Being the successful fugitive that he had become had taught him hard lessons in the process. The statement he had made about being followed had been a reactive ploy on his part, something put there to test her, to give her an easy out if she needed it. One that, had she picked up on it and tried to lend credence to, rather than free her, would have confirmed her guilt. He was sorry the minute he had said it, however. He didn't want subterfuge, Dammit! It wasn't what he wanted at all. Auspiciously enough, however, out of all the possibilities that presented themselves, she did the one and only thing possible that could have saved the situation. Trying to assess all the implications, she said nothing, not even the rapidly growing concern she felt for Kohl.

Deeply relived, Kohl reached for her hand and held it softly, letting his mind proceed, weighing the remaining possibilities. Who had the van and the laser and how had they found it? If it was the feds, you could damned well bet that he would already be behind bars, forever locked away. So that still left two remaining possibilities. A foreign power, or some elite, sinister minded, private organization. Not a very promising prospect in either case. But why had the pictures been mailed from Washington? What was that all about?

It was then that Daphne remembered the letter she had placed in her own pocket. A letter from her mother, she thought, recognizing the stationary. She slid her finger under the flap and tore it open.

Dear Daphne,

Your mother is fine and I'm confident she will continue to do well. Thanks to a recent business success of my own, she can feel free to pursue other avenues of expression. Perhaps she can even come to see you when it is convenient. Let us know.

Fondly,   Your Admiring Stepfather.

Daphne stared at the stark page, then reread it again. Oh my God, she thought. What was she supposed to do now? Ignore it, tear it up, burn it? In all the universe there was but one alternate. She handed it to Kohl.

SEVEN

The loose joints of the kitchen chair creaked as Grey Hawk leaned back and scratched his belly while he finished his ruminations about the story that had just been related to him. This one was far better even than the one they told him about having seen three Sasquatch all at the same place and time. "Goddamn," he said in the muffled way he reserved for such frustrating moments. "How the hell did I wind up with the pair of you as apprentices, anyway?" he asked. "How could I have done that, Dammit? I should have known better," he lamented.

"I'm sorry," Kohl said. "I never thought it would turn out this way."

"Me either," Daphne added.

Then the Indian turned and smiled. After all, there was another side to it, though, wasn't there. "So you're the dude who invented that monster zapper and created all that disruption," he said as if he might still be happy to know the two of them.

"I didn't do it alone," Kohl stated. "And I don't think we invented anything particularly. We simply made a few refinements to some existing technology, that's all."

"Modest, huh? Well, doesn't matter. You sure gave the big boys a run for their money, all right," Grey Hawk laughed. "How come you never got caught, anyway?"

"Thus far, who knows? Besides, as you can see, the game still has a few more rounds left to go, wouldn't you say?"

"So it would seem," Grey Hawk acknowledged, beginning to wonder why they had decided to share their story with him. He looked at the pictures once more. There was certainly nothing extraordinary looking about this vehicle that he could see. Might be good to haul wood in, but that was all. "The laser was inside this?" he asked. It was too incredible.

"Don't let the exterior fool you," Kohl said. "It's a one ton, four wheel drive Supervan with posi-traction, heavy duty suspension and gear train, fully blown, four hundred horsepower engine, all that good stuff. It also had radar detectors, police scanners, military band equipment, etcetera, and a ten kilowatt generator behind the front seat to power the laser. The laser itself, is an invisible, long wavelength infrared, continuous wave, carbon-dioxide device than can melt a hole through eight inches of concrete a mile away. We piped the energy beam up through a stabilized optical periscope so we could point it in almost any direction and could use it while we were sitting still or on the move. A little feature that saved the day on more than one occasion."

"Hmm. I see," Grey Hawk said even though he wasn't sure he appreciated all that technical jargon. But he still knew from all the news reports that this little toy was nothing to fool around with. That was for damned sure. And now, not at all surprisingly, it had been found and carted off somewhere. Just as weak, meek, underprivileged little boys were often prone to dream of themselves as being Superman, so too, every impotent, disordered, malicious nutcase in the adult world must have dreamt about getting his hands on something like this. And if Kohl's and Daphne's suppositions as to whose possession it was in now were true, well, that was not good.

Finally the itch on his belly stopped. He brought his chair back down to ground level and gave a summary nod that let them know he got the full impact of their tale. But that, of course, left him with the final question, the one he was now obliged to ask. "So why did you tell me all this?"

"Because we need your help," Kohl told him.

Grey Hawks eyebrows went up. "My help?" he questioned, quite surprised. "What do you expect me to do?"

"Help us get it back," Kohl said.

The Indian chuckled. A small chuckle at first, then a bigger one that eventually grew into a full blown laugh. "Goddamn," he said again, more poetically this time.

"What's so damned funny?" Daphne bristled and wanted to know, not being above the forthright use of a good strong word to accentuate her speech with on proper occasion, either. Combined with her generous good looks, guileless sensuality and heartfelt sincerity, it made her impossible to ignore.

Grey Hawk looked at Daphne, stifled the rest of it, shut his mouth and shrugged.

"Well, why not?" Kohl asked. "You were in Special Forces. Paratrooper, demolition expert, that kind of thing. They used to drop you behind the lines..."

"How do you know all that?"

"One of the guys told me."

"Who, by God. I'll bust his ass."

"I'd rather not say."

Dammit! Grey Hawk mumbled to himself. This man Kohl was getting to be far more than he had bargained for and perhaps even wanted to have around. Suddenly he felt rather tired. Even though he was still a relatively young man compared to some of the members of his tribe, life was tenuous at best and already growing much too short. He had been to Vietnam, all right, and had been overrun and left for dead on two separate occasions. But that was the easy part, he had survived that. It was the rest of it that he didn't like to think about very often. The cancerous effects of that totally harmless, government approved for dumb soldiers, defoliant, Agent Orange, was eating away at his body, destroying the bone tissue, making it harder and harder to climb the three little stairs up into his trailer home. Obviously they didn't know about this side of the story. It wasn't any of their business either. Not yet, at least. But what was he supposed to say? For the life of him, he couldn't think of anything.

"We just thought you might have some ideas, that's

all," Kohl said, before Grey Hawk had a chance to feel like he had been put on the spot.

Aha, well, that was different, Grey Hawk said to himself with relief. Of course he had some ideas. He always had ideas. He didn't have an advanced degree in psychology for nothing. He hadn't been in the service or taught at the University of Wyoming or written a volume of poetry or smuggled a few automatic rifles or been in the Wounded Knee encounter for nothing either. He knew a few other tricks also, most of which the modern world would never admit the plausibility of under any circumstances. Too bad. It was their loss, not his. And as for this situation, now that he thought about it, it certainly was challenging enough to merit his further interest. "First you have to find out where whoever took it, took it," he told them.

"Costa Rica," Daphne bounced back without hesitation.

"How can you be so positive?"

"It's my step father, remember? That's where he has his training camp. I'm sure of it."

Grey Hawk nodded and looked up at the low ceiling overhead. "Tell me a little more about this man's background, if you would," he said after a moment.

Daphne began to elaborate, filling in what had been left out previously as the Indian's focus never drifted from the spot on the ceiling he had locked on to. When she was done, he shook his head as if in agreement and brought his gaze back down to the horizontal, meeting theirs, studying them. Yes, he had an idea. A good idea, he thought. He wondered if Spirit would agree.

"Go there," he instructed them. "Get the exact location, do some reconnoitering. Find a little hill top if you can. We'll need a spot with good cover but not too far away. Then, when you get back, make yourself each a rawhide drum. Elk skin might be best for this one."

"A drum," Kohl said, perplexed, as Grey Hawk cut him off.

"Talk to Running Deer. He'll show you how. When

you're ready, give me a call," he said and got slowly up out of his chair. End of conversation. He had to use the bathroom.

EIGHT

Kohl handed the big, 8x50, binoculars to Grey Hawk and parted the dense foliage so the Indian had a clear line of sight to the compound. Grey Hawk focused them carefully and studied the scene half a mile away from their vantage point on the small, tree covered, jungle like knoll. "You're sure it's in there?" he asked, carefully examining what he could see of the metal roofed building near the center of the complex.

"Positive," Kohl stated.

Grey Hawk looked some more. "Positive?" he repeated. "What makes you so positive?"

"I was in there," Kohl told him matter-of-factly. "For the second time last night."

Grey Hawk gave him a hard scrutiny and put the binoculars back up to his eyes. There was an eight foot high barbed wire fence all around. Only one way in that he could see and that was through a policed gate. Perimeter guards walked the outer fence line. The locked building was in the center, there were barracks not more than a dozen yards away and at least fifteen men in camouflage fatigues wandering around. Son-of-a-bitch, how did this lad pull that one off, he wondered. "I'm surprised you didn't drive off in it," he said instead, however.

"I considered it but there are a couple of key parts to the laser we removed when we buried it which they didn't find. If it had been working so we could have defended ourselves, I might have. Besides, the other thing to consider down here in this part of the world is, where would just the two of us have gone with it, once we had it?"

"Yes, I see," Grey Hawk said as he handed Kohl back the binoculars. Then he sat down on the thick, high grass and lit a cigarette. "By God, it just might work," he said after three long inhalations of smoke and several moments

56

of contemplation.

"What?" Daphne asked eagerly, for she had been down there the whole time too, searching the country, getting scratched and scrapped and stung and bitten, wading through the forest, biting her nails worrying about Kohl as he made his way in and out of the complex and fighting back some bitter tears all too eager to begin. The fear and anxiety she felt for his safety were bad enough but the growing anger towards her step-father was even worse. And ultimately, of course, what about the consequences, should they indeed recover the van. It was something else to worry about. The old lion would really come roaring out of his den then. That, and the sum total of a hundred other things that tested her and pushed her to the wall since those pictures had come in the mail for Kohl. No wonder she felt like crying, so whatever it was that old Grey Hawk intended to do, it had damned well better be good because she didn't see any weapons in any of the luggage he had brought with him. How would they defend themselves if someone started shooting? And what would the local authorities do if they got caught doing something illegal? No doubt they were also on the General's payroll, in a manner of speaking.

As usual, however, Grey Hawk divulged little of his plan. Talk was cheap. If it worked out, they could discuss it later. He had talked to Spirit and asked for guidance. The signs were good but whether or not it would really work, well truthfully, he didn't have the slightest idea. He had never had the occasion to try such a thing.

"I'll stay here and keep an eye out to make sure they don't move it," he stated. "You get back out, find a phone and make some arrangements for me. I need Spotted Owl, One Hand, Rainmaker, Running Deer and James down here on the double. And make sure Spotted Owl runs by my place and picks up all my ceremonial gear. See if you can find me some decent pipe tobacco too, while you're gone."

Decent pipe tobacco, indeed. Daphne balked and held her ground, refusing to leave. She needed more to keep her going than that. Grey Hawk, however, stood firm. Finally Kohl took her by the hand and pulled her reluctantly away.

"What's he going to do?" she asked Kohl down the trail a bit further. "Why can't he tell us? He could at least do that."

"I don't know," Kohl said, trying to console her. "But under the circumstances we don't have much choice, do we? We need all the help we can get."

"Do you trust him?"

"Yeah, I guess I do."

She was quiet, thinking. "Me too, I guess," she admitted.

It was nearly noon and the humidity reading had climbed rapidly upward right along with the temperature. Both were pushing ninety five. Why hadn't this idiot of a General had enough sense to locate his hideaway somewhere up there in the benign regions of the Costa Rican central plateau instead of down here along the hot bed of a coast, Kohl wondered. It would have made a lot more sense. The men all had their shirts off and Daphne had switched to a tank top. Grey Hawk seriously considered having her put on something far less revealing but somehow that didn't seem fair. He just damned well hoped the boys could all keep their minds on the work at hand, that's all. Himself too, as a matter of fact. Son-of-a-bitch. The trials and tribulations of being human.

Except for Kohl, he had lined them all up in a row facing east, with the girl at the end, out of the way. He struck a wooden match, held it to the bundle of sweet Hopi sage and nursed it carefully with his breath until it was smoking nicely. Then, taking up his eagle feather fan, he motioned to Kohl. Kohl stood facing him with arms away from his sides. Grey Hawk began on the right. "Grandmother, Grandfather," were the divinities he called upon as he fanned the smoke over Kohl's arm, up and across his chest, down the other arm. Then, starting on the left of Kohl's head he said, "Creator", and went down the side of his body, then back to the right and repeat. "Great

Mystery", he said for this one. Then Kohl turned half around in a clockwise direction and Grey Hawk went through the same process over his back. Ah-ho, Mitakuye Oyasin, he stated when he had completed the purifying process.

With that he handed the sage bundle and the eagle feathers to Kohl, assumed a position before him and let Kohl purify him. Then he motioned to Kohl to do the rest of the group while he cleaned and filled his ceremonial pipe with fresh tobacco. Good practice for Kohl. Part of the apprenticeship.

When he had completed his assigned task, Kohl joined the line on the end next to Daphne while Grey Hawk stood alone in the front, also facing the east. He solemnly raised his pipe. "Grandfather," he said, honoring the sun. He lowered it to the ground and honored Mother Earth. "Grandmother," he said. He held it horizontally in front of him. "Creator." He moved the end in a circle upwards towards the sky. "Great Mystery. Ah-ho, Mitakuye Oyasin," he concluded and turned towards the south as the line of people turned with him. The words and motions were repeated, then twice more so that all four directions were honored. Facing back towards the east again, he began his supplication.

It was a long prayer, humble and full of deep sincerity. "Hear me. I am Grey Hawk, last of the sun warriors. He who flies and sees in the distance. The bear-man standing alone in the woods. Hear me, hear our prayers. I ask nothing for myself, only that justice be done..."

Unabashed, Grey Hawk's husky voice pleaded openly and deeply for assistance from Spirit, then began to speak incantations in a loping, gaited dialect unfamiliar to Kohl. Unequivocal, strange words. Hypnotic words that reached out, pervading the thick, humid air surrounding the small clearing in the forest where they stood in an invisible, charged cloak. Grey Hawk began to sweat. Moisture ran down into his eyes, glistened on his cheeks, dripped off his face, saturated his clothes. His expression changed, his voice grew stronger, the body more erect. Then, for a moment, his being turned vaporous and translucent to Kohl in a most mysterious manner, fading in and out of focus more and more. At long last he was silent. Appearing solid enough once again, he struck a match, lit the pipe and sucked on it to make sure it was going.

Another puff. "Grandfather." Another. "Grandmother." And so it went, through the final honoring at each of the four directions with the pipe live and burning this time, smoke carrying his final words upward towards the Creation and the Great Mystery. When he was again silent they all took up their rawhide drums and rattles and formed a circle around him.

Grey Hawk produced four home made candles, placed them at the inside periphery of the circle at the four directions and lit them in sequence, starting at the east. Spotted Owl led the drum beat as they all began to move around Grey Hawk, sunwise as if he were the pivot point of some large, spoke-less wheel. The sounds they generated lifted the veil that had covered them and pushed outward through the dense green of the forest, driving across the terrain, building in tempo and volume. They permeated the dense muggy air, pierced the fence line of the guarded compound, penetrated the very sides and roof of the locked, corrugated metal building, and finally, unbeknownst to those bad tempered souls on duty within the compound, it came at last to some intense point of convergence somewhere inside.

The great elemental secrets of life are so simple that few see them, few know they even exist. To Western man especially, they are cut off from sight. Never having been a part of his thinking, non conjectural, they remain implausible. Not a part of his definition of reality, they therefore do not exist, and remain impossible to reach or to witness. Thus such secrets become the well guarded estate of a chosen few who would unselfishly honor them without the abusiveness so characteristic of civilized man.

"As it has been said, so let it be," Grey Hawk said at

last, in confirmation of such ideas. "Ah-ho!"

What more was there to say? The drum beat came to an end, the group stopped circling, came together in the center and put down their drums and rattles.

"I hope someone brought some beer," Spotted Owl said as he lit up a cigarette.

"There's some in the cooler in the back seat of the car," Daphne pointed out but sat down on the ground instead, not about to run errands for the boys. Let them get it themselves.

James and One Hand left the group and went to retrieve the ice chest. "Bring the food, too." Grey Hawk instructed them. "I hope you bought some salami," he said to Kohl and Daphne.

Half an hour later the ice chest had been completely devastated. Kohl dumped out the rest of the ice water, picked up the dozen expended aluminum beer cans, the baloney wrappers, cookie wrappers, potato chip sacks, pieces of bread crust and cigarette butts and tossed them inside. Then he sat down beside Daphne next to Grey Hawk in a last ditch attempt to try and protect her from some of the ogling eyes which were getting progressively braver. Grey Hawk burped a loud, ungracious burp, patted his belly and said, "Well, I think that ought to have done it. Should we go see?"

"See what?" Daphne asked, not sure what he was talking about.

"Come on," the Indian said and got up heavily. Forcing his legs to work again, he led the way to the edge of the clearing. "Got your binoculars?" he asked Kohl.

Kohl started to hand them to him. "No, you look. Tell me what happens," Grey Hawk said as he shut his eyes and concentrated deeply while Kohl brought the binoculars up to his eyes and focused in. After a moment he saw one of the guards leave the barracks and head towards the metal building. As if on command the man unlocked the side door and looked in, then quickly turned around and ran shouting back towards the barracks. Within seconds they had opened the big sliding doors on the front of the building and the entire detail was standing there talking and waving their arms. Daphne gasped suddenly as another figure appeared in their midst. It was her stepfather.

"Well," Grey Hawk demanded, as he opened his eyes.

"It's gone," Kohl stated in disbelief. "The van is gone."

"Gone?" Daphne questioned. "Gone? How could that be? Where did it go?"

Grey Hawk took the binoculars and looked himself. Then he smiled slyly. Son-of-a-bitch. It was gone. How about that? Spotted Owl didn't smile, however. He merely nodded in confirmation. There had never been any doubt in his mind, he had infinite faith in Grey Hawk's power. One Hand, Running Deer and Rainmaker nodded too and began to talk about going home, away from all this oppressive humidity and all these damned bugs. They had enough. James, however pulled the binoculars away from Kohl and made his own observation. "You're sure it was in there," he asked Kohl.

"It was there," Kohl assured him.

"Hmm," James said and kept looking, afraid he might have missed something. By now the armed men below were examining the ground around the building searching for tire tracks or other evidence, of which they found none. Finally James lowered the glasses. "Hmm," he said again. He was deeply impressed. He gave Grey Hawk a reverent glance and backed up a couple of steps, out of the masters way.

"So what happened to it?" Daphne demanded, not about to be put off any more. "And what did the ceremony have to do with it?" she wanted to know. She had thought all that liturgy was just the prelude to the main event. A ritual that would give them strength in their final endeavor to somehow recapture the van, like dancing the war dance before going into battle. But now Kohl had confirmed that the van really wasn't inside the building anymore. My

God! What exactly had happened to it? Where had it gone? She needed an answer now more than ever, one that made some sense. She might be just a lowly apprentice but that didn't mean she didn't deserve to know the truth. She had the right to demand as much of her teacher as he demanded of her. Fair was fair.

Seeing that she wasn't going to give up, Grey Hawk answered. Unfortunately, the explanation wasn't one she felt very comfortable with. "I sent it off into another realm," Grey Hawk told her without elaboration, as though that simple statement was good and sufficient enough to handle it.

Like Daphne, Kohl also had his problems with the explanation. On some remote, intuitive level it was almost acceptable but on a higher, logical level in the cold light of the day, it explained nothing. Undeniably however, regardless of all else, the van had been securely locked inside the storage building. He had seen it there himself, late last night. But, when the doors were opened?? Could it have been a case of mass hypnosis? It was doubtful. Once the big doors were opened he had seen the General walk in and stand in the very spot where the van had been parked. All the hypnotic suggestion in the world wouldn't have allowed him and half his men to walk through it. It had truly disappeared.

NINE

Within half an hour the General had personally examined and re-examined the padlocks of the building in great detail, checked all the metal panels of the structure to see if they had in any way been tampered with, walked every last inch of the fence line bordering the compound, interrogated all the guards, scratched his butt, scratched his head, cussed, swore and tore his hair. Impossible as it should have been, the van had disappeared. What in the hell? How, Goddammit?

Only yesterday he had brought in a gas laser specialist right out of the Research Division of Rockwell International, sworn him to secrecy with the promise of great financial recompense and worked well into the night right by his side in an attempt to overcome whatever it was that had been disabled and bring the big laser mounted in the rear of the van back to operational status. Later on, when the hour had turned late, he had stood there and watched the guards lock the building with his own eyes and had then spent the rest of the night sleeping not more than fifty yards away. Goddammit to hell!

Mentally, he went back over the chain of events for the twentieth time, then he swore again. Some time back someone had told him that he should have had trained attack dogs on the premises but he had shunned their advice. Rightfully so, it had appeared at the time. Dogs were untrustworthy critters in his opinion. Most every one he had ever met had developed an instant dislike for him, especially the larger jawed ones. No, he had believed in his men instead. He was the one who had personally trained them. They were the real mad dogs.

Thinking about it, he swore once again. Somehow, in spite of their most exquisite indoctrination, they had failed him. The dumb shits, damn them all. Somehow, some one or some thing had somehow absconded with his most recently acquired and most highly prized possession. Could it be that someone had tossed somebody a chunk of money so large they couldn't refuse?

Hours later, since there was no longer anything worthwhile left in the compound to guard, he ordered everyone inside the administration building. Securely barricaded in the conference room, he made them all reiterate every last detail of their life from late last night until the moment this morning when he had gotten that mysterious sounding phone call. The call from an unknown source that had urged him to send one of his office staff out to check the contents of the building.

He really put it to them hard. Had they coughed, sneezed, smoked a cigarette, looked at the stars, sneaked off to take a piss, what, what, what? Was anyone ever out of anyone else's sight? Had anyone heard anything at all?

The big sliding doors squeaked when they were being opened, what about that? And why weren't there any tire tracks or anything at all? Jesus, shit, men, what the hell happened?

It had all came to naught. He dismissed them one by one, brought the research genius into his private office, sat him down in a chair, police station interrogation style, and began to harangue him in a most heavy handed manner. At last he gave up. This guy might be a gee whiz, wonder boy when it came to technical whatevers but other than that he was barely competent enough to find his way across the hall to the restroom. Such were the extraordinary consequences of over-specialization in the contemporary world of widgitry. What to do next? He bruised his fist pounding on his desk, wore a path through the varnish on his hardwood floor and pulled out another pound of hair. There was but one last option, John Paul Rapier, the sneaky, squeaky, stealthy, clandestine little bastard, publicly known to be without present employment, black balled in the realms of governmental undercover activities, adrift and angry in the harsh, compassionateless world. What better, heartless, nasty, weasily, S.O.B. to help him get to the bottom of this. But where to find him, and quickly, that was the question.

John Paul Rapier stared into the depths of his bourbon glass. So this is what his life had come to. Not even Scotch, just bourbon, and a cheap imitation for Seven Up, for Christ's sake. And no matter how tall or how full the glass, always at the bottom staring back at him was the same old scene. There he was, standing up there in his second floor office looking down at that man Mike smiling craftily back at him after the whole wall of his building had been sliced open with the big laser and had fallen away, laying him bare to the entire world. How totally and devastatingly embarrassing. Not even the White House staff had known where he had been sequestered away to conduct his top secret duties. But yet, those two destructive bastards, Mike and Kohl, they had found him somehow, unveiled him and so cruelly exposed him. Dammit, he should have shot them all, back then when he had the chance to have done it in an official capacity. Now, however, it could no longer righteously be swept under the rug. It would be an act of murder instead. There would be no Presidential pardon either, not for the likes of him anyway.

Regardless, someday, somewhere, somehow, by God, unlawful act or not, they would pay. This time he would get them, damn them, and worry about the consequences later. But how? Not only had they stopped their baleful blitz on the overindulgent American way of life, but they had gone completely underground. Where to start and what to do? It wasn't all that easy anymore without access to Military Intelligence, FBI files and his own staff of super sleuth investigators. He downed the rest of the cheap mixture and found a stable place to set the empty glass on top of the pile of dirty dishes in the stained sink of the old cabin high in the Ozarks. Then he went out on the termite weakened, wooden deck of a front porch and sat down on the sun frayed straps of the old folding chair. Worst of all, he wondered, what in the hell was he doing here?

The nights were the worst. Darker than the inside of a bloated cow, they were absolutely terrifying. Perhaps they reminded him of his childhood when his tyrant father insisted on shutting the door of his dark, windowless bedroom. Or, perhaps they just reminded him of the dark side of his own nature, hidden away in the shadows of phobia and non comprehension. Or maybe it had something to with dying.

John Paul knew about death, all right. He had seen it in his victims eyes when their lives were seeping away. On the one hand there was a good side to it. When he had stood over them with gun in hand, it had always filled him with a god-like power that had given a warped importance to his own life. On the other hand, however, after the high had faded away, it again became a demonic reminder of his own puny mortality that always came back to haunt him. And now, what worse place could he be in, completely alone with himself and all those fearsome, frightening and foreboding shadows, real and imaginary. Not only was it dark out here in the woods but the silence was so thick you could hardly walk through it, another reminder of the emptiness he visualized at the end of life's misbegotten road. However, no matter how many demons invaded his privacy, as long as the bourbon held out he could still blur the edges of that world sufficiently enough to make the days go by. But then, only as long as he could catch his breath from time to time. Drunk or sober, the air out here in this end-of-the-world, nowhere place was so pollen laden that he was hardly able to breath the whole time he had been there.

This broken down old hovel might be the one remaining real asset he had left to his name, inherited as it was from his second cousin Willie on his mother's side of the family; and the taxes might be dirt cheap, but, somehow he had to get back to the city. He would take concrete, asphalt, exhaust fumes, sirens and the sounds of shots fired in the night any day. Perhaps if he approached her nicely for a change, he could borrow a few dollars from his aunt Mable up in Minnesota. Just a temporary thing until he found employment, mind you. Maybe he could take a new name, too. Surely some private investigator somewhere would hire him. He could build up a little nest egg, then one day, hopefully not too far away, he could pick up the trail again. It ought to work, he told himself in as positive a sounding way as was possible. Unfortunately, he did a poor job of it and remained unconvinced. Dismally, he got up, about to go back inside and retrieve the one unchipped glass in the house from the sink when he heard a noise in the distance. It sounded like a car. Yes, it was a car, coming up the long dirt road that led up the hill to the isolated old cabin. The first and only car other than his own to ever make the trip since he had been staying there. He watched it bump its way over the last fifty yards of ruts and pull up into the weed covered front yard. A tall man with a crew cut dressed in surplus Army fatigues got out. "Mr. Rapier?" he questioned.

TEN

"It has to be them bastards over in the CIA," the General insisted. "No one else would have the resources to pull this one off so smoothly, unless it was the Israelis. But they would have come in with automatic weapons blazing away, instead, not somehow sneaking the thing out in the middle of the night. So you watch yourself, Rapier, these guys are mean. I've seen them in action."

"Yes sir," Rapier replied to his new employer. "Me too."

Working out of a briefcase was hardly equivalent to sitting behind a polished mahogany desk in Washington but it was a start and he would have been willing to lick the General's boots for that, if he had been asked to, that was. But General Bart wasn't at all interested in his boots at this point in his life. He wanted that van with the laser in it back, by God, and if Rapier was somehow able to do that for him, then by God, if that's what it took, he would be willing to lick Rapier's boots instead, right down to the bare leather.

So there it was, a marriage made in heaven. Rapier was particularly thankful because Bart had given him back his life. And whether or not those two hoodlums, Kohl and Mike, had somehow managed to steal their clever toy back or not, he would still take advantage of his new position to catch up with them again. Beyond that, if he handled things properly, who knows? Anything was possible. He might even be able to leverage his way back into the good graces of the President himself, and get his old job back. With that thought in mind he commanded the flunky corporal Bart had assigned to him to bring round the jeep. It was time to be heading off to the San Jose airport to do some fact finding of his own. Suddenly he felt as if he were hovering three feet off the ground. What a joy to be faced with something more challenging than a sink full of dirty dishes, cobwebs, holes in the roof and a bottle of bourbon that was almost always empty. He floated out to the waiting vehicle and lofted himself aboard. With a roar they were off through the open gate, heading down the narrow road carved through the oppressive greenery of the steaming coastal jungle cauldron. The General's copious words still hummed happily away in his mind. "Find the van and I'll give you a bonus equal to twice anything you would have accumulated from the Government," he had promised.

Strange, how fate plays out its hand. Almost a whole year of shameful nothingness, sheer desperation and soulless confusion and now, within just the last forty eight hours, two very major happenings had occurred in Rapier's life. First, the General had given him back his self respect and, second, he was on the way in search of his old enemies. Sure enough, his inquiries at the airport in Costa Rica had turned up a notable lead. A half dozen American Indians had arrived in the Republic the day before the van had disappeared and left again the following day. A fact that he, Rapier, had uncovered, even though it had taken the General to see the full significance of it.

But, so what. After all, it was the General and not he who had been to that part of the world most recently and was thus aware that both his step daughter and the man Kohl had a close association with some rebellious Indian called Grey Hawk and some of his friends, all of whom fit the descriptions he had gleaned from his inquiries. And, guess what? They had arrived from and departed for Phoenix, no less. Unfortunately, no one had seen anyone who completely fit the description of either Kohl, Mike or Daphne and the airlines had no record of any passengers listed under those names. But that didn't eliminate them one bit as far as he was concerned. That fellow Kohl and his partner were much too clever to implicate themselves that way. And whether or not the General could bring himself to believe that they were capable of craftily stealing the van back, somehow they were involved. Rapier knew it. With all his puny being he knew it, he could feel it in his bones. Leave the General back there with that chubby young, brown skinned girl he had seen sneaking into his private quarters, he, Mr. Rapier, had better things to do. The chase was on.

Back home once again, Grey Hawk would share little with Kohl and Daphne as to how he had actually conjured up the disappearance of the van. They had not completed their apprenticeships as yet for one thing. Even then, should they find the dedication to accomplish that, it would still bring no guarantees of their being fully qualified to share in the deeper knowledge involved. Patience, he stressed. Wait and see, but don't count on it. It would depend.

"On what?" some ex apprentice had once asked.

"On what do you think?" Grey Hawk had been considerate enough to reply at the time. But, when the candidate confessed that he didn't know, Grey Hawk had little choice in the matter. Some things you do, some things you don't, because it was extremely rare when that kind of knowledge had ever been shared with a white man. Not all that many Indians either, Grey Hawk knew as a matter of fact. The white man, as well as so many of today's red men, lived in the hard and solid world of materialism where things existed in external separateness. A tree was a tree, a rock a rock, an animal an animal. People could not see around corners or walk through walls or blend with the eagle in the sky. They could not because, for one thing, they did not believe such things were possible. Unlike some of those in other less civilized cultures, they did not understand that each thing is brought into being in the physical world by Spirit, is composed of Spirit and sustained by Spirit. How could they? Having overlaid the distorted views of modern science on top of monotheistic nonsense, they had betrayed both their minds and spirit and severed their intuitive connection with nature in the process.

Once this connection was lost, or never had to begin with, it was almost impossible to find the way back. Caught between the cold and heartless abstractions of economics and technology, the haranguing, muddied waters of modern religion and the mindless maze of pseudo-psychic blatherings on the shelves of New Age bookstores, there was little place to go. If a person kept insisting that life had its origins in pure chance and pond scum, roadside clay and Adam's rib or that Spacecraft Commander Ashtar had Archangel St. Micheal's younger sister artificially inseminated with expresso beans, what chance was there of every learning the truth. On the other hand, if a person could at least grasp that his body was the embodiment of his spirit and that there was no such thing as inert matter, then there was hope. And if one could understand the further implications embedded in that, well...

Regardless of his feelings on the matter of Kohl's and Daphne's deservedness of such higher wisdom at this point, however, Grey Hawk obviously still viewed them with considerable deference for he honored them both with the gift of a ceremonial pipe which he had personally carved out of red pipestone. Not only were the gifts given, they were presented in full celebration wherein the pipes were properly awakened to the spirit world. Medicine pipes that they were free to use in a good way in accordance with the promises they themselves had made to Spirit, knowing that each pipe has a power of its own and that it will gain in power with each wise and unselfish use. Once awakened, however, not only does each pipe have the power to help and to heal but it can in like manner bring equally bad medicine to the bearer if over stated promises are made and the pipe is misused. These were the things to be remembered, Grey Hawk explained as he handed them over.

There was another honor attached to being a pipe carrier, also. Grey Hawk reserved all the critical ceremonies for himself but each pipe holder among the apprentices was given his or her turn to lead the sunrise ceremony on those days when they came together. Of all the ceremonies that Kohl had witnessed it appeared as though this one in particular was to be done in a very specific manner. The words, positions, gestures and everything else leading up to the main prayer and concluding the ceremony afterward appeared rigidly established. It was one of the things he had a problem with but he was determined to do his best and had pretty well convinced himself that some things are just to be accepted. He should have given Grey Hawk more credit.

Worried that he might do something incorrectly the first time out, Kohl mentioned his concern to Spotted Owl. Grey Hawk somehow overheard what he was saying and took him aside. "You really don't think the Creator expects us to be perfect, do you?" he asked Kohl.

"I don't know but it's seems highly unlikely to me."

"Right on. What is perfection? And who says so?"

"I see what you mean."

"Okay, just remember that good intent is the key element here, and what is in your heart, not the ritual. The ritual is secondary. It is symbolism, not edict, and as such, it too is alive. It is meant to help, to lead somewhere, to open doorways, not to close them. Being alive, it must therefore be allowed to evolve and change also, otherwise it becomes dogma. Dogma is the sign of death, one of mankind's greatest enemies. It keeps him frozen in the past and prevents his spiritual development, and, without spiritual development, as we know, the race has a bleak future.

ELEVEN

The other gratifying thing about Grey Hawk was that no matter how contradictory to his own views, nothing in the realm of philosophy was closed. Not only did he tolerate other outlooks, he encouraged their discussion and, in that regard alone, an apprenticeship under him was most unusual. Chopping wood, carrying water and hoeing weeds had a certain value, perhaps, but the idea was not to try and glean spirituality out of subservient labor but to teach people to think. To that end Grey Hawk had developed a required reading list. It contained everything from Stoicism to Behaviorism to Taoism. The day after Daphne conducted her first sunrise ceremony Grey Hawk told her and Kohl that he didn't want to see them again until they had read everything they could find on Plato. "And after you explain it to me, we'll discuss it with the rest of the group."

"Listen to this," Daphne said after a couple of days. "Emerson said that; 'Out of Plato come all things that are still written and debated among men of thought.' Is that possible?"

"I don't know but I think Plato said something quite pertinent to what happened in Costa Rica," Kohl replied.

"Really. What?"

"Life is a dream, rather than a reality. We perceive only the shadows of objects and think them the actual realities."

"And somewhere in that is the explanation of how he made the van disappear? Is that what you're saying?" she asked.

"Not the whole answer," Kohl said, "but some clues. However, there are probably clues everywhere. There have to be. We just need to become more aware, that's all. And reading Plato with a little different perspective in mind this time is probably as good a place to start as any other"

"And how come you know so much about Plato, anyway?"

"Philosophy was one of my favorite subjects in college."

"But I thought you majored in Physics?"

"I did, but ultimate answers have to come from

somewhere. Physics wasn't very satisfying in that respect. Not back then."

"Which means what? I was a college dropout, remember?"

"You can't find out where the life force in a frog comes from by killing it and dissecting it under a microscope. And, you'll never be able to understand the workings of the universe by insisting that the ultimate particle is a solid piece of material hiding somewhere which ten billion dollars worth of slamming sub atomic pieces of matter together is going to find."

"I don't know about slamming sub atomic particles together but I do happen to like frogs and I wouldn't cut one up to save my life. What else did Plato say?"

Kohl referred to his notes. "The soul cannot come into a man if he has never seen the truth. By making the right use of things remembered from former lives and by constantly perfecting himself, a man becomes an initiate into diviner wisdom."

"How can you make the right use of things from former lives if you can't remember any of them? And who believes in reincarnation anyway, except Hindus?"

"Early Christians did, before the Romans took control of their ideas, modified and submerged most of the key tenets and turned it into a religion. Prior to that it had nothing to do with idolization, worship and dogma but was a body of philosophical teachings. The concept of reincarnation was a part of it, just as it is a part of many other native cultures. But even in the western world there have been many famous people who believed in reincarnation," Kohl said and dug through his notes. "For example, Henry Ford, Carl Jung, Goethe, Kant, Voltaire, Emerson, Ben Franklin, General Patton and Walt Whitman. And there are a lot more here on the list."

"But if reincarnation is true, what purpose does it serve? Is that part of our spiritual development... Of course it is, why did I ask?" Daphne said. "But what about Karmic debt? Where does that fit in?"

"Do you believe in original sin?"

"It always been a little ridiculous to me."

"Indeed. There's Karma and then there's Karmic debt. I think Karmic debt is the westerner's misunderstanding of what someone thought Karma really meant. Karmic debt and original sin are not cosmically imposed burdens put upon us for punishment. There is no such thing. If they exist at all, it's because we burden ourselves. We come into the world to learn and to grow. Problems not faced this time around might be chosen to be faced in another life. Karma might be said to present an opportunity for development, not punishment, should we choose to take that road. But it is never mandatory. Free will still reigns and we are always presented with choice."

The discussion continued. In addition to Plato and the rest of the standard fare of college curriculum, they had also read and deliberated over Castanada and Mubimbar. They had also read Steiner, Blavatsky, Brunton, Roberts, Cayce, Sugrue, Rand, Davis and a few others that even Grey Hawk had missed by the time they went to see him. The Indian was impressed and had to smile once or twice in admission that even he had learned a few things from the discussion himself.

"Oh, by the way," Kohl said as they got ready to leave. "I brought you this."

"What is it?" Grey Hawk asked as he flipped through the one hundred or so page document Kohl had handed him.

"The Talmud Jmmanuel."

"What's that?"

"Supposed to be the original Bible before the scribes and priests got a hold of it."

"You're supposed to be reading this stuff, not me."

"I have."

"But what would I do with it? I'm a Red man," Grey Hawk stated as a way of putting it off. He couldn't be allowing his apprentices to gain the upper hand. Not yet, anyway.

"I know. But it's a very unique document. Thought you might have an opinion about it. Especially the prophecy part."

"Suit yourself," Grey Hawk said, and tossed it on the kitchen table.

The next morning Daphne and Kohl were up early and still at it. They talked about dim recollections of things in their own lives that might be indications of past memories resurfacing. They talked about dreams, the illusions of time and space, cause and effect and the definition of reality. None of it led to a clear idea of how Grey Hawk might have accomplished what he had in Costa Rica, however. But there were some clues and they were as real as any of the rest of it.

"Enough," Daphne said at last. "Let's go for a swim."

They took the hillside path down to the creek, made their way upstream over the rocks to the swimming hole, shed their clothes and waded in. "What about us?" Daphne asked after a bit as she paddled up to Kohl in the cool water.

"What about us, what?"

"You know," she said and splashed water in his face.

He reached to grab her but she ducked and swam away. With a few powerful strokes, however, he soon caught her in shallower water. Able to touch bottom he held her from behind, hands cupped over firm breasts and erect nipples. He kissed her neck and gently bit her ear. "Mmmm," she said, as he ran one hand downward over the smooth skin of her belly.

"Don't get fresh. You haven't answered my question."

"What? Do I think we have a past soul connection?"

"Do we?"

"I hope so," he said as he pulled her towards shore.

On the sand, however, Daphne became the aggressor. She forced him down onto his back, and laid on top of him. "Were we lovers, too?" she teased.

"Nothing could be this good without previous practice," he said, fondling her. "But I'm glad I don't have any clear memories."

"Really? Why not?"

"Because each time I look at you and touch you it's a fresh experience, always exciting, sensuous, beautiful and new. I'd like to keep it that way," he said very seriously and rolled her off onto her side where they lay still looking at each other.

She gave him a sweet peck on the nose, a bite on the ear and then attacked his mouth with hers, attempting to swallow him. He raised on his elbow, prepared to turn her on her back when instead, he froze.

"What's wrong?" she asked almost immediately.

"I saw a glint from something up on the hill."

"What was it?"

"A pair of binoculars, probably."

TWELVE

"Rapier may have been pretty slick when he was ensconced in the underhandedness of Washington but he certainly is a washout when it comes to playing lone man out trying to make it as a private investigator," Kohl said to Daphne as he sat at the table soldering wires and components together on a small device he was in the process of assembling. They had the television on loud and the ceiling fan was going over head. Together they did a good job of drowning out their conversation for the bug Kohl had found hidden behind their bookcase after he had discovered they were being watched.

"Do you think he's back working for the government?"

"Rather unlikely, I suspect. Maybe your step-father. Who knows what he's been up to since the van disappeared."

"My step father hasn't even called my mother, the bastard. It's been over three weeks."

"Just as well, don't you think?"

"Probably, but what can we do about Rapier?"

"This thing might help, if I can make it work. I wish Mike were here. He was always better at this kind of stuff than I."

"What is it?"

"Since Rapier tapped our phone I thought I'd tap his. We should know what he's up to in a couple of days."

"Listen to that," Kohl said as he played back the recording he had made of Rapier's latest phone conversation. "He sounds a little frustrated, doesn't he?" Daphne said.

"Do you blame him? Listen to the General bellow," Kohl said as he turned down the volume on Bart's heavy words.

"I can't do it all alone," Rapier stated and the conversation ended with the General agreeing to send two of his best men to keep tabs on Kohl's house while Rapier searched out other places where they might have hidden the van, should Kohl and Daphne indeed be the ones responsible for its disappearance.

Whom else, Rapier had tried to convince the General, once and for all. Since he had finally completed his background check on Grey Hawk, Spotted Owl and One Hand and learned of their combat experience, their involvement with some of the more radical American Indian groups and the fact that Grey Hawk had a rap sheet for gun running, among other things, whom else could it be? What else would such a wild bunch have been doing in Costa Rica, for God's sake? As far as Rapier had been able to learn, none of them knew another soul down there nor had they every set foot on that soil before in their lives. It was too much of a coincidence, he had told the General very bluntly. The General, however, was still reserving his final judgment. Kohl might be pretty slick but there was no way that he and a bunch of savages could have gotten the van out of there right under the noses of himself and his elite troops. It had to have been a much more sophisticated endeavor than that, by God. He hadn't made it clear up to the rank of general for nothing, now had he?

It wasn't all that easy from Kohl's point of view, either. The van might be tucked safely away in some other reality, whatever that meant exactly, beyond the reach of any and all of the likes of the General and Rapier, but what now? He would have been content to have just settled in with Daphne, relaxing and taking the days as they came but he knew that these antagonistic, mad men would never give up. Rapier, for sure, would be an enemy for life. So too, the General, once it became clear to him that Rapier was right. Who knew what they might resort to then? For the moment, the General had underestimated them but eventually he would get it straight enough in his head. And, at that point, beware. Even Daphne's life might be in jeopardy. What could he do then? Kohl wondered. He couldn't be with her twenty four hours a day, every day, for the next twenty years. Grey Hawk had helped him once but it wasn't right to involve him or the other apprentices just yet, and hopefully not at all. Not their problem. Besides, making the van disappear was one thing, this was something else. Try as he might, however, no clear solution came to mind.

"You can't be serious," Rainmaker said.

"Do raven's squawk?" One Hand stated.

"Couldn't be," Spotted Owl laughed. "You don't even have a social security number."

"I know. But my uncle sent me the letter. They want to audit me," One Hand said, waving his hand at the teepee he was living in out there in the woods. Everybody laughed. One Hand laughed too, went inside and came back out with the official looking letter in his hand. He handed it to Spotted Owl who read it and passed it on. All the rest of the apprentices read it and laughed some more.

"I didn't know your name was Clarence," Rainmaker said and smiled.

"Yeah, well, shit. My mother did that to me when she sent me off to school. Wanted me to fit in, if you can believe that."

They kidded him about the name, decided that someone a little more established than he must be sharing it with him.

This, of course, led into a discussion of all the abusive IRS horror stories and someone told One Hand the government would probably put a lien on his teepee. "And your moccasins," someone else jived. But then, something else happened.

They didn't remember who, but it was probably James, dwelling so much on what had taken place in Costa Rica as he was, who had come up with the idea. Bizarre, off the wall, but intriguing.

"This is the feds you're screwing around with," One Hand cautioned.

"So! Let's do it."

"I'm in."

"Me too."

"Same here."

"Do you think it will work?"

"Of course. All we have to do is convince Grey Hawk."

"And who is going to do that?"

"Who else. Daphne and Kohl."

"What? Why us?" Kohl wanted to know.

"Daphne has a great smile," they were told.

"I like it," Daphne confided later.

"I do too," Kohl said because it was a much more subtle way of continuing the skullduggery he had been doing with Mike before he had met Daphne. It also gave him something to think about other than what Rapier and the General were up to. To his surprise, however, Grey Hawk balked and grew silent when Kohl was able to toss it out to him. At first the Indian thought it would be a gross misuse of his power. And secondly, he had always successfully avoided becoming a taxpayer, so what did he care. It was the rest of societies problem. Still, the longer Kohl and Daphne talked about it the more the idea began to intrigue him. Finally he chuckled that mischievous, knowing chuckle of his and said he would give it his highest consideration. Two days later he called and said, "Come on over."

They took along a six pack of beer and sat out in Grey Hawk's front yard where the weeds were high enough to tickle one's chin through the lawn chairs and began again. It was a most ambitious and unique plan. Even Grey Hawk could not deny that it had merit. The bottom line was that, although some segments of the government would become a bit annoyed (madder than hell, actually), it would be a way of helping the people of the country, especially the lower and middle classes.

"Makes it sound communistic," Daphne pointed out.

"But it's a great rationalization, don't you think? You have to give me something," Grey Hawk said.

"How about, you don't solve problems by treating the symptoms."

"Which means what?"

"Police don't attack the cause of crime. Laws don't prevent corruption, collecting aluminum cans won't save the environment and saying that God is on your side doesn't justify war," Kohl said, and went on. Maybe a little too long.

"You orate well," Grey Hawk stated. "Just like Marlon Brando in that Mark Anthony movie."

"Sorry," Kohl said.

"Don't apologize," replied Grey Hawk and smiled at Daphne. "We all have our moments." Then he looked up at the vapor trail of a distant airliner as it fanned out over the sky and shook his head. What a sad and contradictory state of affairs the world was in, he thought to himself. "Unfortunately," he said. "Those who have done the most to create the world's problems and are in a position to provide the most help are also the ones most likely to want to keep things as they are."

"Human nature at its best," Daphne said. " I'd certainly like to see the looks on some of their faces when it happens."

"It hasn't happened yet," Grey Hawk pointed out. "And it might not. But, if we do it, we'd better find a deep hole to hide in."

"Well, I was hoping you would teach us how to become invisible in the meantime," Kohl chided him.

"One thing at a time," Grey Hawk said half seriously and they scheduled another meeting two days hence to discuss it further. Grey Hawk wanted all the apprentices there this time.

Kohl was outside working in the yard when the phone rang. As expected, it was Grey Hawk, but he didn't invite Kohl over. Instead, his voice had lost its usual calmness and he wanted directions to Kohl and Daphne's house, a place he had never bothered to visit as yet. He was coming right over.

Fifteen minutes later he was there. Brow covered with cold sweat, he exited his old Ford with ceremonial pipe in hand.

"We need to do ceremony," he said with great urgency, laying his pipe case on the rusted hood of his car. "And then we need to talk."

He untied the thongs of the flap, took out the pipe and all his accessories. He assembled the pipe, lit a sage bundle, smudged it, smudged Kohl, then proceeded to run through his sacrament in a most compelling manner. When he was done he handed the pipe to Kohl and told him to smoke it also.

Kohl was a little shocked at first. He had never seen Grey Hawk ask anyone to share his pipe with him. The look on the Indian's face, however, let him know that he had better not hesitate before doing it either, if they were to continue their relationship.

"What the hell's going on?" Kohl asked when he had finished and returned the pipe to Grey Hawk's hands.

"Where did you get that damned document?" Grey Hawk demanded.

"What document?"

"The one you gave me."

"The Talmud?"

Grey Hawk glared at him and nodded.

"From a friend in L.A..

"Where did they get it?"

"Supposedly it came from Billy Meier in Switzerland."

"The guy who has all those UFO pictures?"

"Yeah."

"The good ones, I mean. All nice and clear and up close. Even one parked in his driveway?"

It was Kohl's turn to nod. "So what happened, anyway?" he asked. Now he was becoming concerned.

Slowly the tale unfolded. Grey Hawk had been having breakfast at the coffee shop with Renee when a one armed man came up to him, called him by name and asked him if he would mind running out to the edge of town to talk to some friends of his. Why not, Grey Hawk had said. That was what he had come to town for, to talk to people and share a part of his Redman's ways. Breakfast over, he left Renee and went out to Fay Canyon with the man who then led him up the trail a ways to where three people were waiting. A man and two women, one of whom he at first was surprised to think was Renee from a distance, even though it didn't make any sense.

They asked him if he had read the Talmud. He said, part of it, why and so what. He wasn't sure exactly what they said next but it had something to do with Joseph and one of the Celestial Sons. Whichever one had secretly impregnated Mary and brought about the immaculate conception.

Must have done it in a well scrubbed hospital room, Grey Hawk said to himself and then demanded to know what the hell this was all about.

"Come," they had said and led him off through the trees to a small clearing. There, sitting on the desert floor with the sun glinting off its shiny surface, was a small spacecraft which the four visitors boarded and flew off in. With that admission Grey Hawk looked carefully at Kohl to catch his reaction.

"What the hell did you get me into?" he wanted to know.

"I have no idea. All I did was give you a book to read," Kohl said, looking carefully at Grey Hawk to see if he was playing games with him.

But there was no trace of a smile on Grey Hawk's drained face, not even a tiny crinkle. Only a cold, disturbing glare. "You gave me that damned document," he said as if Kohl had done some terrible thing to him.

"Sure, but so what," Kohl stated. "I've read it at least three times and nobody ever came to see me in a UFO."

It was a stalemate, both men wondering if the other was being truthful. Grey Hawk was first to concede. He had an impeccable faith in his pipe and Kohl had done pipe with him, therefore Kohl must be speaking the truth. Kohl, however, had no such stratagem to rely upon. All he could do was resort to what logic he could bring to bear on the situation.

Here was a man who had not only taken lives in the war but one who had also been forced to look his own death in the face on more than one occasion and had kept his wits about him the whole time. There were also his confrontations with the FBI at Wounded Knee as well as the now more imminent fact of the disease gnawing away at his bones. What point was there in making up such a strange story? What was there to be gained from it, especially from telling it to Kohl and in swearing him to secrecy over it? Only the truth could be this bizarre. Or could it? If not that, what was it then that had caused him to become so outwardly disturbed here in the bright light of the day? It would have to have been one hell of a hallucination to make anyone sweat this badly. All Kohl could do for the time being, however, was to take Grey Hawk's story at face value and wait and see what developed. Who was he to decide, anyway?

Other than for one rather startling and peculiar close hand experience he had personally never seen strange lights dashing about high in the sky, let alone a genuine, full size space craft or even anything that might be construed to be one. He had never been a contactee or an abductee or had even met anyone who ever had made that claim or even claimed to have known someone else who had. Not until now. And that was saying a lot for all the time he had spent living in and around such a far out place as Sedona. My God, he wondered. Was it possible? If so, what next? If Grey Hawk was telling the truth, would they be back? And what about their plan to sabatoge the IRS? Whoever these people were, they had sure put the old kibosh on that. Grey Hawk was hardly in the proper state of mind to bring that one off, not for a while, anyway. And what else was wrong with the Indian? He was angry about something.

"They're the enemy," the Indian told him after he put his pipe away.

"I see," Kohl said, except he didn't see at all. He asked for an explanation.

"Down through thousands of years in all the old legends that have been passed on by my ancestors, the star people have always been considered to be the enemy. They were here before and every time they came they created problems. Wars, destruction, slavery. I don't trust the bastards and I don't want anything to do with them," Grey Hawk said emphatically and with that concluding statement he left for home.

Kohl called a couple of days later, thinking he would offer to buy Grey Hawk breakfast but no one answered the phone. It was nearly a week before he connected and Grey Hawk offered no explanation for his absence when they met at their usual place. Kohl held his questions as long as possible. "Did they come back?" he finally asked, after the food was on the table.

Grey Hawk made a wry face and nodded.

"Well, tell me," Kohl said when the Indian sat in silence.

Grey Hawk studied the texture of his fried eggs for awhile, sprinkled more salt and pepper on them, looked glumly around the room and spoke in a rather dismayed tone of voice.

"Renee went to California and had an abortion."

Confused, Kohl shook his head. What was he talking about? Grey Hawk tried to clarify things. "Of course you've heard those stories about the second coming of Christ that the Christians are always yapping about?"

"Of course?"

"It's in some of the other prophecies, too. Only we're not talking about the son of God here who will lead the pure into the white light and ignite the fires of hell for the rest."

"What are we talking about, then?"

"Somehow 'they' knew she was pregnant. How, I don't know. I didn't even know myself, until I confronted her. They told me the child she was bearing was destined to become the new Jmmanuel, or Jmmanuela. Not Christ, get on your knees, kiss my feet and ass and start praying you sinning, fornicating sheep before you can be lofted into heaven, but a prophet and real live human leader to help us out of the mess we have created here on earth. This time it might be a woman."

Kohl's eyebrows went up. Good grief. What could he say to that one? Although it was a much more palatable scenario than the other versions of the second coming that were out there being circulated, it was still god awful bizarre. Maybe the real explanation was simply that the man's mind had snapped. If not, well.. Maybe someone had slipped some celestial seed into someone's orange juice. He shrugged. What next?

"Anyway," Grey Hawk said. "I told her what they told me and the next thing I knew she up and left. Now there is no child." With that he clammed up and assaulted his breakfast. It wasn't until he had completely wiped his plate clean with his toast that he spoke again. "Spotted Owl and the rest of the boys are coming over this afternoon to talk about your idea."

"Okay," Kohl acknowledged, surprised at the sudden shift in Grey Hawk's attention. "Good." Since Grey Hawk seemed rather bitter about the fatherhood that had been denied to him perhaps it would help get his mind off his problems.

THIRTEEN

Now more than seventy pounds overweight, Erma Servill's husband consumed at least a twelve pack of beer every Saturday and another on Sunday, along with a large package of pretzels, two sacks of chips and two packs of smokes in front of the big screen which ran all day long set at full volume, commercials and all. Like a lot of fans, watching sports tested his limits. Physically, intellectually and emotionally. During the week he was even more severely challenged in his job as watchman for a local manufacturing company where his main function was to operate the electric gate into the employee parking lot. The rest of the time he was asleep, either in his TV recliner or in the queen sized bed, snoring out of control, rattling the window panes, loosening the plaster on the ceiling, keeping the multiple, acid caused lesions on Erma's stomach lining from healing. That was the better part of their relationship. Which was why Erma was almost out of control too and why, consequently, she was in the habit of going to work early and coming home late.

Monday, the first day of April, thirteen days before the tax deadline, was no exception. She arrived at her desk in the Ogden, Utah office of the Internal Revenue Service at six forty five, sat down and got ready to bring her list of accounts up on the computer screen. It was something she always did, even before she went to make her first cup of coffee. Conscientious, dedicated and determined, no middle class Yuppie American was going to sneak one by her, by god. Never.

Besides, she needed a raise, and soon. Clarence, poor man, had gotten too fat to push the lawnmower, fix dripping faucets and do all the other minor things that she was now forced to pay someone else to do. Not only that but he had also switched from drinking cheap old Olympia Gold to Heineken and sometimes he did in an extra six pack or three during the week as well, along with a couple of handful's of imported cigars. Such is life. Still, his

87

presence was a comfort. Anything was better than coming home to an empty house.

Erma's favorite case number was N 1072654. Willy O'Hannahan, the tricky devil. She had been after him for years and one of these days she was going to get him, by Hannah, or her name wasn't Erma. Surprisingly his return had shown up on her desk late Friday afternoon and if she had just had another hour with it, well...

But she had to leave for home or Clarence would be complaining about his dinner and if she didn't get home he wouldn't get his favorite meal of wieners and beans which he always liked. Sort of set him up and got him in shape for all the yelling and cursing he was forced to do at the TV screen over the weekend. Anyway, thank god for Monday which finally arrived. Now she could pick up right where she left off, on the last page of O'Hannahan's charitable deductions. How dare he deduct a contribution to Molly Malone's, the cad. What did he take her for, anyway? Everyone west of the Mississippi knew it was a pub in West Los Angeles.

She reached down to the side of her terminal, rocked the switch to the power ON position and waited as the screen came to full brightness. Somehow it was a little slow this morning, she thought and reached into her desk drawer for her note pad and a pack of Doublemint gum. Something was wrong, she decided at last. She was in the process of stuffing the third stick of gum into her mouth and the screen was still blank, lit and blinking, but completely blank, not a single word or icon on it. She punched away on the keyboard, entering commands. Nothing. More commands. Still nothing. A half hour later she was still fussing with the machine when Mrs. Barley came in, another early rising, dedicated wife and public servant.

"What? What did you say?" the Treasurer of the United States shouted into the phone, on the other end of which was the Commissioner of the Internal Revenue

Service. "That's not possible!... What happened to it?... I don't believe it!... Goddammit... It couldn't have... Well, hell. What are you going to do about it?... You don't know what to do? Don't you have back up files somewhere?... Goddammit. How could they be? That's impossible... What about print outs? Don't you have hard copies of everything?... What do you mean, not exactly?...Am I going to tell the President?... Not me, not today. And neither is anyone else, do you hear me?... Why not? It's the First Lady's birthday today and if anything interferes with her party she will probably throw his buns right out on the White House lawn and I'll be out of a job, that's why not. Do you understand?... Good! But tomorrow, tomorrow will be a new day and YOU will be calling him first thing in the morning. Is that clear?... Don't give me that. You're Civil Service, I'm an Appointee, got it?... Good! And absolutely no press releases. Pass the word downward. All employees. I want a total and complete news black out. Anyone violating that order will lose his pension, his social security and his ass in that order, is that clear?... All right, their ass, her ass, whomever's ass. Ass is genderless, you idiot," he shouted for the last time and slammed down the phone.

He cursed once more, buzzed his secretary and told her to come in.

"Yes sir," she answered and appeared at his door in something less than two seconds. He motioned towards the wet bar in the corner. Automatically, she moved to it and prepared him a tall scotch and soda. Then, checking the look of agony and near hysteria on his face, she poured in two more ounces of scotch, brought it over and sat it down. "Perhaps you'd better have one too," he said to her.

She returned to the bar, fixed herself the same and returned to the heavy chair he nodded to in front of his desk. Something must really be wrong, she told herself, something totally dreadful must have happened. The sky must have caved in. In all the long years she had known the man he had never, ever asked a lowly secretary to sit down across from his own desk, let alone share a drink with him. Except for that one cute young thing a while back. But that request had been to sit on his lap, not in a chair. Much different.

As instructed, she sat down and took a heavy swallow. When she looked up again she saw that he was crying. It took two more drinks and half a box of Kleenex to get the full story out of him. Somehow... Somehow, something, some weird quirk of fate, some flukey fluke of fickle finger, some grizzly gremlin had somehow infiltrated the internal revenue computer network. Yes, the entire taxpayer network, as best as could be determined. All the files were gone. The long forms, medium forms, short forms, amended forms, delinquent forms, all of it. All the back up files, everything on computer tape, cassette tape, hard disks, floppy disks, CD disks, microfiche, everything. Every last magnetic, metallic and ink based symbol, right down to the very last byte, was gone, disappeared, wiped away. Vanished as if it had never existed.

Yes, sniffle. There were the taxpayers returns themselves. Some of them. The ones that had been mailed in so far this year. But all they had on them were the taxpayer's names. All the numbers were gone on them, too. Employer identification numbers, social security numbers, even the numbers from the addresses, income amounts, interest payments, withholdings, deductions, every last, lonely digit. Bad as that might be, however, it was only part of the problem. Inspection and testing of local, regional and national computer equipment had been conducted from California to Maine, from Wisconsin to Mississippi. In every case the answer was the same. Functionally, everything tested out correctly, meeting and exceeding every single one of the manufacturer's specification parameters as well as those of the customer, the IRS.

There was just one small problem. Data could be entered in a normal manner. The machinery appeared to accept it without defaulting but it was as though numbers were somehow no longer a part of the language. They did not seem to exist. They would neither appear on the monitor screens nor would they print out when commanded to do so.

The government's top computer analysts then had all the master programs erased, dug the originals out of the archives, reformatted and reprogrammed and recompiled all the mainframes, ran everything through the diagnostic routine, all to no avail. Hard drives and tapes had been replaced, programs revised and rewritten, the wonderboys of the major software companies called in but no matter what, the answer was always the same.

"Our technical experts are unable to offer an explanation at this time," the CEO of IBM stated, speaking both for himself and the head of Microsoft who was in a strategy meeting trying to decide how to best sidestep some of his competitors copyrights. "However, given half a chance, we feel confident that we will soon be able to offer a viable plan of action to solve the problem."

"How can you offer us a viable plan of action for solving the problem when you don't even know what the problem is?" asked Senator Highpiler, acting committee leader. "In the meantime our equipment is still malfunctioning country wide and you have already billed us over three and a half million dollars for services rendered. Is that the best you can do?"

The CEO brushed back his silver gray hair, straightened his tie, straightened up in his chair, coughed to clear his throat and said, "I believe that the only clear recommendation we can make is to install all new equipment."

"That would seem to be indicated," seconded the entire conglomeration of Data General, Control Data Systems, DEC, Apple, and all the other big boys in the business as well as the local manager of Radio Shack from Oildrip, California who had somehow wormed his way into the hearing.

A gasp of disbelief passed round the government's half of the oversized conference table as the entire

91

membership of the Senate Investigating Committee turned pale. It was a very long time before anyone summoned the bravery to ask the next question. How much more would that cost?

"Conservatively?" the CEO asked.

"We don't care," answered Highpiler. "Conservatively or otherwise. Just give us an idea. Guess if you have to."

"With installation?"

"Do you think we can use it sitting on the loading dock?"

"What about operator and programmer retraining. This is fifth generation equipment?"

"Jesus," Highpiler exclaimed.

"Hmm...Let me see," the CEO puzzled. "Yes, I'd say five or six billion, plus or minus a billion or so. That's in the ballpark, anyway."

"And how long would such replacement take?" the Junior Senator from Oklahoma wanted to know. A question that probably shouldn't have been asked under the circumstances.

Half a dozen hmms later another highly specific answer was rendered.

"If we diverted all our commercial orders into this channel, reopened our old facilities in Willming, East Bingling and West Elmhurst and held up all our overseas orders for a time, we might be able to complete the task in two or three years. That presupposes, of course, that this would be a joint effort between my company and my fellow competitors here in the room. Regrettably, however, to be perfectly honest with you, I still don't think it's possible because I don't think the stockholders would ever let me do that."

"What?" shouted someone from the ranks. "Why not?"

"We would lose the world market. Forever! It's exactly what the Chinese and East Indians have been waiting for," the CEO said as the balance of other company executives all nodded their heads in agreement.

"Same here," they said.

Highpiler pounded his forehead to show that he was dumb struck. "What then?" he asked at last, for he too was getting a little tired of hearing how the foreigners had again beat his fellow countrymen at their own game. Maybe they had been responsible by sneaking an especially viral virus into the network. Wouldn't put it past them at all, he wouldn't. But instead of mouthing that suspicion he was forced to ask if there were any other alternatives instead. The problem was there and somehow they had to fix it before the entire country collapsed.

The computer boys huddled their heads together for a few minutes before risking an answer. "Spread deliveries out over five or six years and we may stand a chance," they said.

It was Highpiler's turn to say, Hmm. He said it three more times before he asked, "Will you take vouchers for payment? Temporarily, of course. Until we start collecting some revenue again."

Once more the heads went together down at the end of the table, all accentuated by deep groans, harsh hand waving and hoarse mumbling. Then, there it was.

"Not on your life," they said. "Nothing personal you understand, your Honor, Mr. Highpiler, but, business is business."

Although the Senator was surprised at the reply, he wasn't all that surprised. After all, he was seriously thinking of resigning his own post and going back into private practice if they didn't soon get the mess resolved. The credit card companies had already made it quite clear they wouldn't accept IOU's for his accumulated debt. His young wife would leave him, for sure. He excused himself to make a phone call. When he returned he stood at the end of the streaked and poorly waxed conference table next to the dusty American flag and said, "The President has dispatched a team of accountants to Fort Knox. Although there has been some pilfering going on during previous administrations, he thinks there is enough gold bullion left to foot the bill. Or, at least to get the IRS up and running in the more affluent, high income sections of the country where we stand some chance of collecting revenue."

FOURTEEN

Difficult as it is to believe sometimes, everyone has his place, purpose and function in life. Joe Fray was no exception to this rule. The total obstructionist, his claim to fame was that he was always in the way. His, and everyone else's. Such was the extent of his inborn, singular aptitude that his own mother had left him on the front steps of the County Courthouse at the age of six and left town. His estranged father put up with him for two more long years, then turned him over to his grandparents, and so it went.It was the story of his life, which is exactly why he had ultimately been placed on the White House staff. He was hired solely to run interference between the President and the public. And now that the difficulties that the IRS had engendered had somehow began to leak out, the President was being besieged. Even though the line of individuals knocking on the door extended more than four blocks down Pennsylvania Avenue, the President still felt quite safe, however, for Fray was in the way.

Along with everyone else, he was also in the way of one John Paul Rapier and had been for nearly a week now. But unlike most of the waiting crowd, Rapier really had something important to say, both for his sake and for the sake of the country. A bell had gone off in his head when he had learned of the time and date of the IRS phenomenon. It was exactly the same time he had been hiding in a manzanita bush spying on Kohl and Daphne, watching the strange ceremony taking place out behind that junk pile of a trailer that crazy Indian lived in and it was the same Indian who had been seen coming and going in Costa Rica when the van had disappeared. That confirmed it. There was a connection. He didn't quite know the how or the why of it but he could certainly understand the what for, thus there had to be a connection and he knew it.

Now, if he could just get in to see the President...

94

He had called all his old cronies but the word was still out. Shun Rapier or loose your job. So there was no alternative, he must go straight to the top. Except that Fray was in the way, damn him and physically terminating the man might well be worth considering if he didn't soon find a way around the clown. But then it occurred to him. Surprising as it might be, he and Fray had something in common. They were both outcasts. He professionally and Fray socially. He had to be. Who in the world would want a person like that for a friend? It was a place to start. What do you suppose he liked to drink?

"I think you are completely mad. Such a preposterous story," the President said to Rapier some days later. "How dare you wheedle your way in here with such nonsense," he glared at him and began to reach for the buzzer to summon a Security Guard.

"Wait! Please wait," Rapier pleaded. "Hear me out."

The President scowled, put his chin in his hand, rolled his eyes as if he were in the company of a total whacko and waited while Rapier seized the moment to extend the cast of characters involved in the two episodes. When he finally mentioned Kohl's name, not only did he gain the President's full attention but he also found himself being offered a chance to be back on the federal payroll. Provided he could come up with enough hard evidence to convict the man, of course. It was exactly what Rapier had hoped for, his dream come true, it didn't matter that nothing was coming into the federal treasury to pay his salary.

Still, sitting there, having suddenly regained his credibility, being treated with respect again... what was it? He'd didn't know. Then, before he realized it, he heard himself declining the job offer and at the same time questioning the sensibility of that choice and desperately attempting to shut himself up.

Fool, he told himself later. Just because they threw you out before doesn't mean you have to reject them now.

Is your ego getting in the way, John Paul? That could be dangerous, you know. But thinking about it further he knew that it wasn't his ego. It was much more fundamental than that. It had to do with character, his and General Bart's. Bart was far more resourceful, inventive and ruthless than anyone he had ever met in the ranks of any of even the most clandestine of back alley governmental agencies, with or without Pentagon or Presidential integument.

Bart, therefore, was a man to respect and to learn from, even for him with his thirty four years of cold hearted sleuthing. Besides, working for the General might more quickly bring him face to face with the two people he hated most in the world, Kohl and Mike. That was why he had turned the President down. Kohl and Mike had stolen his credibility from him, and his dignity. Next time he was allowed back in he would have to try and explain his situation to the man in the White House, if that were possible. Dealing with Presidents was not an easy task.

Talk about ego. He had worked for five different Presidents over the years, each one successively worse, the balloon heads. However, he still hadn't done too badly. The man was a bit perturbed by his refusal but he had still walked away with a consulting arrangement of sorts, agreeing to keep the White House informed in exchange for access to certain classified data bases. Then he swore. Damn Kohl and that Indian. What if they decided to wipe out all the computers in the intelligence network? Were they capable of that, too? Quite possibly. Would they do such a thing? What then?

"Why the hell didn't you tell me sooner?" Bart growled.

"You weren't here, remember? And no one knew how to reach you," Rapier defended himself, stretching the truth a little. He knew very well where the General had been. Knowing where people were was the business he was in and knowing your own employer's whereabouts was especially important, even though he didn't quite dare to say so. Sure, he could have gotten back a few days earlier but so what. He had met with the President on two different occasions, by God, and that might turn out to be good for both himself and Bart before this was all over.

Besides, what was Bart complaining about? Obviously his own little trip had been successful. Two dozen of his boys were on their way to the airport right now, headed for Africa to provide some lucrative assistance to some fanatical warlord while another dozen were being readied for southeast Asia. Additionally, the man had been to several of the old Soviet Republics along the way and, although he wasn't talking about it, something good had came of that, too. Particularly in the Ukraine because he had ventured down into Panama before seeing Rapier. Hidden in the jungle, another facility was under construction, one that would be capable of handling and storing nuclear materials. Conceivably, the man was negotiating for surplus warheads from the Russians.

At any rate, Bart nodded when Rapier reminded him of his being away and asked to be brought up to date. Yes, he had heard about the computer difficulties the IRS was having. "Just the excuse that asshole needs to declare martial law." (He still referred to the President as, "that asshole," even though it had been more than three years since he was expelled from duty.)

"It wouldn't surprise me," Rapier confirmed. "Things are beginning to get out of hand back there."

Officially acknowledged or not, the word was leaking out and things were beginning to snowball. By the thousands, people had stopped paying taxes for the first time in generations. The incident had given the average working person a real shot in the arm and a whole new attitude about life. Government request or no government request, they were not about to make voluntary payments as long as the computer system was out of order and there was no way to track them. The prevailing attitude of the day was now, to hell with that. Having had a taste of keeping that sizable percentage of their own money which

97

had formerly gone to support corruption and bureaucratic bumbling, several strong coalitions had been formed in major cities across the country to bring about the legal abolishment of the income tax, once and for all. Carrying it a step further, another group of liberated extremists had even begun tossing firebombs into IRS facilities in the middle of the night to further the cause. In that respect, things were almost out of control.

On the other side of it, the general populace was in a state of rising euphoria. Based on the rumors that it would be at least two years before the IRS was back in business, the economy had suddenly blossomed. New housing starts shot up twenty five percent, productivity in hard goods manufacturing had increased eighteen percent, the GNP rose nine percent and the stock market had soared to the greatest heights in history. Potentially, it was a very dangerous time. What would happen when the government had the ability to collect taxes again and tried to re-impose itself. It might take more than martial law to do that.

But getting control of the tax situation was a different issue, one that the General wasn't particularly concerned about. Mostly, he was just plain envious and didn't want the President to wind up with the dictatorial kind of power that martial law would give him. Thinking himself to be one of the few people in the world truly deserving of such a position, the General had mentally reserved that role for himself. Not so far away, he kept telling himself, he would find a way to cash in on the government's dilemma yet.

Then he sat back in his oversized leather chair and listened to Rapier's report. It left him nearly speechless. Holy Christ! It was unbelievable. If Rapier's suppositions were true, what the hell was he wasting his time trying to deal with the nuclear weapons black market when all he needed was Kohl and a few of his Indian buddies to conquer the world. He almost tipped over backward with excitement.

FIFTEEN

Wisely enough Kohl understood that, sooner or later,

Rapier and the General would somehow connect the disappearance of the van with the malfunctioning IRS computer network. It was merely a question of time. And when that happened it was time to disappear and go underground. Regardless, it was time to move away from Sedona anyway. Something about the very town itself, and the surrounding area, had changed also, just within the last few months. Yes, there were still some very good people there, like everywhere else, working hard to make the world a better place to live in but something deep and fundamental was wrong. It was as if its very soul had withdrawn. Now just another place over run with people, Sedona was no longer sacred.

Although she still dearly loved the region, Daphne thought she felt it too. Whatever Kohl decided was best, however, that is what they would do. She left it up to him. Then, within just a couple of days since they had last talked about it, Grey Hawk called again and spoke with Kohl. There was a new woman in his life. One who had a recent divorce settlement sitting in the bank waiting to be put to good use. Her name was Claudia.

Fortunately enough, Grey Hawk had just the place for her money. They had purchased sixty acres of remotely located land in the Colorado mountains with two old houses and some out buildings on it. The ultimate plan was to turn the place into a retreat and learning center. Ceremony, herbs and medicine, survival skills, community living and everything else necessary for staying alive was to be there by the time the earth changes Grey Hawk believed were eminent had begun to come to pass.

Unfortunately, after having made a sizable down payment on the property there was little left to bring the place up to a livable condition for the coming winter. At eight thousand feet the snow would get deep. While there were deer, antelope, elk and rumorings of bear in the thick forest that Grey Hawk might bring down with his white man's recurved bow for the larder, there was also firewood to be cut, roofs to repair, water pipes to mend, automobiles that needed attention and six dozen other things waiting for Kohl's talents. There was more to talk about, too, when he got there, Grey Hawk assured him, in regard to the visitation he had back in Sedona.

While the rest of the story about the aliens might just make it all worthwhile, Kohl had balked because Daphne didn't want to come along. Since Grey Hawk's new lady had gone back to Kansas to stay with her old girlfriend until the place was more inhabitable, Daphne felt that it would be an opportunity for Kohl to spend time alone with his friend and spirit guide. Finally, with many assurances from her that she would be all right, he threw his tools into the back of the old truck and before she knew it he was waving good-by. Dammit, she would miss him. Maybe she should have gone along.

Slowly she turned and went back into the house. She picked up the book she had been reading, found her mind wandering without comprehension and put it back down. It was time for a walk. The creek bed was alive with the gold and rust colors of fall, the sparkle of sunlight and upside down reflections of landscapes on the water, the chirp of swallows and the laborious flap of Raven's wings. She sat on a smooth, large gray boulder, brushed her long, dark hair that now almost reached the middle of her back and looked for fish in the water. Swimming upstream, a muskrat broke the mirrored surface with his nose and came ashore on the opposite side. Then Daphne rose and moved further up the bank to an ancient cottonwood, leaned back against the course bark and shut her eyes, letting her mind drift. Except for her mother, life before Kohl was but a smattering of pale shadows no longer important. This was her new reality and Kohl had very nearly become the center of that universe. An uncertain universe, to be sure, especially with the things they had become involved in. But that aspect of it did not frighten her. There was little that did anymore. It was something she had learned from Kohl. Ah, Kohl. Life didn't need a blueprint all laid out in five year increments with promises, projections, milestones, commitment and guarantee all wrapped around the safe, preconceived ideas of acceptability and success dictated by others at all, as she used to think. No, that wasn't her definition of living. Not anymore. It was giving up on life. Little house on a quiet street be damned.

A long ten days later he was back, sweeping her up in his arms, then laughing after her as they climbed the ladder to the loft where she had her bed. Later they sat by the old wood burning stove and talked. Her days had been full of self imposed solitude, his, well...

She lit some candles so she could see him better. She loved to watch him when he talked, blue eyes sparkling, face so full of feeling and intensity. Hard work and little sleep was most of the story. Spotted Owl and One Hand had been there also. They had towed the rusted hulks of abandoned automobiles out of the yard, dragged downed trees in from the woods and sawed them up, installed a water heater, fixed the chimney, the kitchen stove and, and... and talked late into the night and then tried to sleep to the broken background of Grey Hawk's prodigious, snoring rumble. And then one evening the rest of the apprentices all showed and after the evening meal they all agreed that what had been done to the IRS was a bit severe. So, with that in mind, they did another ceremony and recreated a number of income tax files. The lower income groups were still in limbo but for anyone making over two hundred thousand a year, their taxes were all doubled. They would have another meeting around Christmas time and re evaluate the rest of it then. And. as for the rest of it, the Grey Hawk had claimed to have had two more visitations from the people in their shiny, wingless craft. People who, except for their long earlobes, looked every bit the same as humans.

"Oh, wow. Do you think he's flipped out?" Daphne asked.

"I don't know. But something doesn't quite make it. Either Grey Hawk is lying, Billy Meier is lying or there are some imposters on the scene."

"How so?"

"Because I had a friend call Switzerland while I was there. Billy Meier claims he's never been to Sedona in his life yet Grey Hawk tells me that was the name of the man who sought him out in the restaurant the first time and took him out to meet these people who, incidentally, just happened to have the same names as Billy's visitors. Ptaah and Semjase. Unfortunately, according to Billy, Semjase had a serious accident a few years back and is supposed to be off recovering somewhere and won't be back for at least another sixty years."

"How could that be? She'll be dead by then."

"Well, supposedly, just like Moses, Noah and all those other Biblical characters who lived to be seven and eight hundred years old, so do these people."

Daphne had to think about that one, choosing not to take issue with it just yet. "What did they tell him this time?" she asked instead, as if it were all true.

"That instead of continuing to be their enemy he would soon have a change of heart and begin supporting them."

"Really?"

"Who knows. Anyway, he said he told them to leave him alone, that he didn't want anything to do with them."

"Some story!"

"Yeah. Distressing. Our friend, mentor and spirit guide seems to be cracking up. Where do we go from here?"

But what could they do about it, they wondered. Nothing at the moment, they decided. They left it at that and turned back to the more urgent, everyday concerns of living, like doing the wash and pressing their bodies together. The days drifted by. A week, two, three, and in all that time they were together constantly, Kohl reluctant to leave her out of his sight. The house was still under sporadic surveillance.

Utah, Kohl suggested one day. Enough was enough. Sounds good to me, Daphne confirmed. The scenery there was every bit as spectacular as that where they lived now, maybe even more so. "We'll run into town in the morning", Kohl told her. "And leave as soon as we get back".

"Why don't you go," she said the next day, however. "I'll stay here and finish packing."

"I think you should come. We won't be gone long."

"You worry too much, Kohl. I'll be all right. I have a lot of things to go through. It will save time in the end."

He was still reluctant, but then perhaps she was right. He was overly prone to worrying about her, he admitted.

As soon as he had left, Daphne set to work. For some reason she had accumulated more clothes and things than she had realized. She emptied out the closet and all the dresser drawers, sorting as she went, laying everything on the bed. She had been at it no more than thirty minutes when she thought she heard a car pull up in the drive. It was much too soon for Kohl to be returning. She was on the way to the window to see who it was when the front door burst open. A short, middle aged, dour looking man in a gray suit stood there with an automatic weapon in hand, staring at her. Although she had never seen him before, Kohl had described him accurately enough. It was Rapier.

"Well, well, well," he said, evaluating her. Although he was not much of an expert on the finer qualities of womanhood, she was much too good looking to be related to the General by blood, no doubt about that. Unfortunately for him, as he sometimes felt when he saw one as bold and beautiful as this one, there had been little time in his life for such indulgence. It was just as well. He had never been much of a performer in that area, even as a youth. Work, a much more trustworthy endeavor, had become his mistress instead. Therefore, except when forced to deal with them in business, he had shunted women aside with derogatory rationalizations and left them alone. It was less embarrassing that way. Still, she was quite startling, even to him. So much so that it almost caused him to sigh. Someday, perhaps, a tiny thought crept

103

in and said, indicating that he was still partially human, for a small, unclear dream still lived on in the hidden recesses of his mind. But then, before it could fully emerge, he spoke.

"If you would please accompany me," he said in his flat sounding voice. "My driver is waiting."

Daphne evaluated the situation carefully. The gun was a forty five, the safety was probably off and the kitchen door more than twenty feet away. Not very good odds, especially with this man. She was face to face with the cold hearted killer who had gunned down the woman Mike had been in love with. Would he shoot her too, she wondered. Only if she forced him to, she decided. Instinctively she knew she was being taken hostage and that her value would depend on her being alive. Reluctant to give in so easily, however, she asked, "Why should I?"

"Don't toy with me, young lady," he warned her.

She turned slightly, took a step backwards, her eyes on the door. A deadly roar filled the house as a heavy slug thumped home into the thick ceiling beam over her head. She froze and nodded slowly. No sense in pushing her luck, she decided as Rapier motioned with the pistol. She passed slowly in front of him and went outside to the waiting automobile. They got in the rear seat. Daphne looked at the back of the closely cropped driver's head as he put the car in gear and drove up the dirt drive to the end where he made a hard right turn. What an ugly gorilla, she thought, surprised that they were heading back into Sedona. Rapier reached for the cellular phone and dialed a number. "We're on our way," he said.

"If that's the General," Daphne said angrily. "Tell the bastard he'll be sorry for this one."

The second Kohl turned down the drive he noticed the fresh tire tracks in the dirt and the hair on the back of his neck bristled. He pulled the truck off to the side and got out. Big car, new tires. They had come from the south, left to the north, throwing a trail of gravel behind as they had pulled onto the asphalt. Someone was in a hurry. He didn't have to go to the house, it simply confirmed his suspicions, especially when he dug the misshapen piece of lead out of the beam. Angry and upset at himself for having left her alone, he went back outside and walked around the yard trying to regain control, fighting back the pain and agony of her absence. It was then that he heard the jet. Although the hilltop airport in Sedona was nearly five miles away you could sometimes still hear an occasional aircraft taking off when the wind was right. This one was exceptionally loud. It should have been. It was a private, twin engine Leer and it came screaming low across the terrain, then pulled up steeply when it reached the house and banked towards the east. Kohl ran back inside and began sorting through Daphne's personal items. Finding her address book he stuffed it into his pocket, went back to the truck and hurried up the drive. When he came to the end he went left, the shortest way to the Interstate and to Phoenix, the nearest major airport.

SIXTEEN

Former inspector Digand Pry's wife had bought him a new leather briefcase with burnished brass hinges and a three digit, combination lock. A Gucci, no less, and with his own personal monogram engraved in gold. Under the circumstances it was the proper thing to do. He had been promoted to FBI Branch Head and transferred to the Phoenix office. It was the rightful place for him because he dovetailed quite nicely with the redneck politics in vogue in the area at the time. It also fit well with his personal life because he liked to go to bed quite early and Arizona was the only state in the union backward enough not to have gone on daylight saving time as yet.

But as for Phoenix itself, his wife absolutely refused to live there. Why should she? This smog choked, grossly over grown old cow town was full of look-alike, barf-bag tract houses whose have-less and have-not portions of the city were doing their very best to make the place the top contender for the new murder capitol of the country. Even with such fierce competition as that coming from

Washington DC., New York, Chicago and Los Angeles, it was gaining steadily in the ratings. She had also heard that all the city restaurants soaked their hors d'oeuvres in green salsa. No way was she going to live in such a place.

No way was she, nor Pry himself, about to let the boys grow up and go to school in such a place, either. Absolutely not. She believed in family values and because she did their home, like those of so many of the newly affluent, psuedo affluent and suddenly snobby, would be located far out in the environs away from the disgusting debasement of the city. Not some previously lived in, second hand home, either, but a brand new one. It was only right, especially when there were still hundreds and hundreds of square miles of vacant land out there waiting to be built upon, much of it still within easy distance of an air-conditioned shopping mall or two. There was only one problem. The land itself was over run with nature's two hundred year old cactus creations, creepy, crawling critters and carnivorous, canine creatures. How could anyone be expected to live in harmony with such things as poisonous insects and reptiles, prickly plant life and howling coyotes.

"You can't," she said. "Cut them down," she told the building contractor. "Stamp them out, poison them or shoot them. And when the house is done we'll plant grass seed and petunias and spend our leisure time playing bridge and croquet. Let the rest of the world take care of itself," she said vehemently. Mostly, however, she was eager to join the burgeoning crowd of all too average pioneers whose only known spiritual skills were in finding their way back to the dress racks in the upscale department stores which sold the same clothes as K-Mart but with a different label for more than three times the price. These creative ventures were best done while their dishwashers, automated sprinkler systems, swimming pools, foolish, frothing decorative fountains and golf course ponds worked overtime sucking the desert water table dry as a bone, creating even more life threatening problems for the plant and animal life indigenous to the area. Again, so what, who cared? Nobody, of course. Humans came first. If they didn't there wouldn't have been any city or suburbs there to begin with. So with that attitude in mind she set out to make a new life for her family, lecturing poor husband Digand almost daily about the fact that, except for what his new job might demand of him, he was to disassociate himself as much as possible from the rest of the depressing non-life of the city and its distasteful turmoil.

"But dear. I have to think of such things," Pry tried to explain to her. "It's part of my job."

"No you don't, Digand," she had responded. "You're not just an ordinary cop anymore, you're part of the haute monde. Once you're in your office you only have to deal with elite criminals who keep their fingernails clean and commit things like fraud and other white collar offenses, not all those petty hoodlums, drug dealers, wife beaters and murderers like common policeman do."

"But dear, I can't spend all my time in the office. I still have to drive to work."

"Yes, but you only have to drive through the east side to get there. Play those bongo tapes I bought you on the way and think of something else. If it still bothers you we'll have the serviceman put another layer of window tint on your car."

Pry sighed and did his best to follow his wife's instructions, but, it wasn't always that easy. Like all big cities, the place was a sewer. And, like it or not, everyday the local crime statistics crossed his desk and he was forced to look at them. Here, as was the case almost everywhere else in the American social order, moral turpitude was like a runaway, airborne green mold that had gotten out of control.

Regardless of the blinders his wife would have him wear, Digand was still aware of the broader view, however. He could still see quite well that presidents still committed dubious, treasonous acts and pardoned each other in the process. Federal and state senators and congressmen committed larceny and fraud, governors had their hands in the public's pockets, city councils flagrantly abused their fringe benefits, executives of the banking and savings and loan industry regularly stole from their clients, the aerospace industry stole from the federal government, private industry stole from private industry, employers on every level sucked out the souls of their employees, hospitals and doctors carved up and killed their patients for profit, cops pounded the weak and the voiceless into the ground and attorneys turned man against man in petty meanness purely for the purpose of acquiring a heavily weighted percentage of the proceeds.

No wonder the American dream had gone sour, Digand had acknowledged one day more than twenty years ago when he was younger and fresher, the edifices of common decency were sinking into the muck. On and on it went, too, with the middle class, of which he was now part of, taking the lumps because the tax assessor kept on handing them the bill for all the profanation. But, instead of taking stock and standing up straight, the middle class made an additional contribution to the disorder by padding their own expense reports, stealing the pencils from the boss's desk, his steaks from the freezer, his merchandise off the loading dock, called in sick, made substandard contributions in return for the paychecks they collected, lied, cheated and stole in turn.

And, even worse, far worse, they helped to perpetuate the indignity by looking upward at the administrative officialdom of pirating executives over them and turned away in silence. A silence which granted an unspoken approval of sorts, thinking that if somehow they, themselves, were cleverly devious enough, then they too might someday rise upward through the murk. Then, when they had achieved one of those privileged, pardonable positions, they, too, would be able to steal really big and have an offshore bank account of their own.

And when Digand had taken the trouble to allow the back one eighth of his right brain to kick in way back then, he realized that it was no wonder that there was violent behavior on the part of the disadvantaged. It was poverty

108

and disenchantment speaking out. Deprived of decent food, adequate shelter, sufficient education, proper medical attention, self respect and the legal right to steal like degreed professionals, they were conveniently and contemptuously designated non-people and left without human dignity. Ignored, trampled over, beat upon, faltering without hope and ordinary promise, what else could they do? The social system they lived in was tailored to force them into becoming exactly what they had become. Nothing more, maybe even less. Tragically, few saw it, or wanted to recognize or acknowledge it. Not the government, the church, the institutions, scientists or psychologists for they, too, were too busily engaged in their own surreptitious finagling for personal gain. And on the individual basis, forget it. It was far too big and far too self incriminating because to some extent, one way or the other, everyone had a hand in it and no one was about to give up anything to help solve the problem. Why should they? The tone was clear, role models were in place and strong examples had been set, everyone might as well join in on the fun.

Rather than help contribute to Digand's moral growth and conscientiousness over the years, however, his wife had always taken the opposite tack. "That's just the way it is," she had told almost every day of his working life. "You need to learn to accept things and not stew about them all the time."

Thus it was that after having being married to this same woman for an uncountable number of years, to a large extent even Digand Pry himself was somewhat predisposed to callousness when it came to the disenchanted underchurnings of the city and the territory he had been sent to protect. As the more mature human being his wife had helped him become, the bottom line was, what did it matter anyway? He had a better than decent office, a sudden, new level of prestige, a steady and inflated paycheck and, now by god, thanks to his promotion and his increasingly snobbish wife, he had a very expensive new briefcase and two extra pairs of top of the line dress shoes which she had put on her latest credit card.

"That's just the way it is," Digand reiterated to himself that Tuesday morning as he parked his car and walked into the building, that already hot, dry morning in May. He was not a savior in a world beyond saving. Assignments came and went. He was simply there to narrow his focus and do his best to solve the problems that funneled themselves through his office. Beaming proudly in spite of his shortcomings, Digand stepped spryly off the elevator on the fifth floor of the headquarters building on Jefferson Avenue and turned left, proceeded past his secretary in his new shoes carrying his new Gucci high enough so that everyone would be able to see his initials on the fine leather. He said good morning in a bright voice and proceeded into his office.

Placing the briefcase on his cluttered desk, he dialed the combination lock numbers he had personally selected, opened it and withdrew a manila folder which he placed face up on the desk. Then he sat down in his big chair, pulled the bottom drawer of his desk half way out, oriented himself so that he could put his feet on it and picked up the slimmest file he had ever come across in his twenty one years, two months, three days and fifteen minutes of dedicated service. Code name, "Havoc." Case number G-297211R. It contained two type written pages. The first page, which had been previously circulated to all branch offices across the country, summarized the illegal act. Violation of federal statute-XYZ-91234, the wanton destruction of governmental records. Devices or specific method employed--unknown. Suspects--none.

The second page was dated several months later and he had only received it on the way out the door last evening. It was a very brief summary of a conversation between the President of the country and a now private citizen, one John Paul Rapier, formerly with NI-5. Unfortunately, not one of Digand's acquaintances knew specifically what NI-5 was. To make up for that they had termed it, Nearly Invisible, for lack of something better. It had been appropriate enough since no one seemed to know who these people worked for and no one was ever able to contact such persons directly. If there was contact, they contacted you, mostly in the same manner that they had contacted the then lowly "Inspector" Pry some two years ago. That had been by tersely informing him that all his case files were to be shared with some, as yet unstated, individual and should that individual (who later turned out to be Rapier) choose to make any decisions regarding the case, he was obliged to support him. With his life, if necessary.

Fortunately, it had never come to that. The suspects, Mike, Kohl, a bum named Buck Hudson and their three women friends were alleged to be in the business of destroying power generating plants, bridges and other edifices of the modern world, acts which served to severely disrupt the everyday workings of society. Extensive and destructive as their efforts were, however, as far as anyone could determine they had never directly harmed another human being, a dog, a cat, a mouse or a chickadee. Nor had any serious shred of evidence ever been turned up to link them to these allegations. No, it was all still pure, unsupported speculation.

As for harming other human beings, that was Rapier's area of expertise. The overzealous, conniving, cabalistic little bastard had willfully shot and killed Sue Loring that ignoble night out on the highway without due cause or provocation. None whatsoever and Digand knew it. Unfortunately, he had been there without prior knowledge of Rapier's intentions. Regardless of the fact that he probably could not have prevented it even if he had been more informed, it was the one thing in his life that still kept him awake at night. And it probably would to his dying day, too, because it was his own cowardice that had kept him from reporting the truth of it at the time. By now, however, too much time had gone by. No one would believe him. It was too late.

In the end Rapier had paid a most painful price for it, however, the worm. Discredit and mandatory retirement had served him right, the glory grabber, for stealing Digand's case in the first place. But, what the hell was this new report all about, Digand wondered as he read it for the fifth time. The President had let the darned little devil back into his office and in doing so Rapier had somehow also implicated Mike and Kohl in the scandalous erasure of the IRS data banks through the use of Native American ritual.

Native American ritual!! What kind of silly drivel was that? It was preposterous, absolutely preposterous. What in heavens name had happened to the chief executive, endorsing such ludicrous nonsense? He was acting almost as batty as Rapier. Jeees! Digand said aloud. He put the file down with renewed disgust as something suddenly occurred to him. He began arduously searching through his desk. At last he found it, the presidential campaign button he had worn before the last election, and threw it in the wastebasket. Maybe it was time to start voting Democrat again. Then he buzzed his secretary. "Ask Spinnet to come to my office," he told her.

"Yes sir," Spinnet said when he appeared at his boss's door. Pry waved him to the chair in front of the desk and he came in and sat down.

"This is yours," Digand said to Spinnet as he handed over the two page document to his main man, thanking himself for having had the wisdom to speak to Spinnet's wife about all the garlic she had been putting in the meatballs she cooked all the time. Now that he could afford to get a little closer to him, Spinnet wasn't such a bad guy after all, Digand had decided. Kind of clever, too. Even knew how to change the sparkplugs in his own car, he had found out.

Spinnet opened the folder and scanned the report. His eyebrows went up, narrowing his forehead down to a puzzled furrow. "What's this?" he asked.

Pry simply shrugged. "Good luck," he said, dismissing him without answering the question.

Spinnet would have liked more clarification on the matter but he had heard through the in-house grapevine that his superior had just flunked the exam for his sixteenth degree in the Masons that he had been working on for the last eleven months. Best to leave him alone, he reluctantly decided. Probably wanted to hit the books some more. He got up. "Nice briefcase," he stated, nodding in the affirmative.

"Thank you," Pry said.

SEVENTEEN

The large, two story, old stone house sat on an estate sized lot on the outskirts of Chevy Chase. The hedges had been freshly trimmed and the smell of new mown grass was still in the air as Kohl came through the gate, up the walk and ran the bell, late that afternoon. Eyes more blue than gray, still very attractive, it was obvious where Daphne had inherited all her beauty from.

"Hello," Daphne's mother said somewhat cautiously, looking him over quickly, obviously not missing much. Then she looked at him again. What was it, she wondered. Should she know this man?

"Hi. I'm Kohl," he replied, doing his best to downplay his reasons for being there.

"Of course. I should have known from Daphne's description. Please come in."

Why was he here, she wondered after they had chatted a bit. And without Daphne? He seemed very concerned about something. She made tea and served it with some pastries she had picked up at the bakery that morning.

Although he had missed lunch, Kohl ate slowly. The conversation was far more important than his stomach. But where to go with it? What did this woman know about her own husband? Would she even be open to discussing it? And what did he have to go on, anyway? Other than the spent bullet he still carried in his pocket, there was nothing factual. Only the gut wrenching conviction that Bart was involved. But how do you tell someone that their daughter

113

might have been kidnapped by her own stepfather? Would it be fair to burden this kindly woman with such presumptions? Only if it was absolutely necessary, he decided. And was it? Is that what he had to do? He didn't know. All he really knew was that he needed to find the son-of-a-bitch, and quickly. Was he in Washington or down in Costa Rica? If neither, where then?

Still, he managed to subdue his concern and worked hard at being sociable. Fortuitously enough, the General's name soon came up.

"It's my one regret," she was saying, suddenly very open with him about it, perhaps because, in one sense, she now saw Kohl as a part of the family. Or was it because he was being receptive? Maybe it was just because it was long overdue and here was an outside ear. Whatever the reason, it was prompted by a comment he had made about her daughter.

"I suppose I should have waited a few more years before marrying again but I felt so desperately alone after my husband died. I know it was hard on Daphne but the truth is I never realized how much so until she came home on leave that first time after basic training. Why she never told me earlier, I'll never understand. I would have left him, I know I would have. But now that she's grown and off on her own it doesn't seem all that important. I have a nice home, my own circle of friends and the General is always off, somewhere. We rarely cross paths. I hope she understands." It was almost like an apology.

"She's a bright girl. I'm sure she does." Kohl assured her, wondering if Daphne had shared the rest of the story with her when she came back to visit last summer. The part about the General trying to intimidate her by alluding to potential harm that might come to her mother. Apparently not. Daphne's mother was being much too kind to the man who had threatened to do away with her. And if this woman really didn't know, what then? Was it his place to tell her just how badly Daphne hated the man and for what reasons? He would if he ran out of options. If the General wanted something badly enough to take her by force, Daphne's life could be in danger. But first there would be a moment for stating his demands and a period of negotiation. She would be safe until then.

Kohl wanted to conduct that negotiation face to face. He needed to see that face, to look into the bastard's eyes, to make his own first hand measure of the man and a personal assessment of what he and Daphne might be up against. It was the only way he knew how to do it so he made up a story.

"I have a friend who served under the General in Vietnam. He was badly wounded and is having a problem collecting his disability. I thought perhaps the General might be able to help somehow. Maybe a phone call or something."

"He must be a very good friend if you came all this way to just do that," she said with a trace of a question in her voice.

"Actually I was on the way to New York to take care of other business," he added. "So I took the opportunity to stop and thought I might help an old friend in the process."

Almost imperceptibly her eyes narrowed. She studied him carefully. "Is Daphne all right?" she questioned.

Well, that was it. What else could he do now? He told the truth, trying to do it casually. "She was all right when I saw her last," he told her.

"When was that?"

"This morning."

It seemed to satisfy her. Best to leave it at that for now. She got up and went to the study. When she returned she handed him a sheet of personalized stationary. It had addresses and phone numbers on it.

"He was supposed to be back in town yesterday but I haven't heard from him. As I said, that's not unusual, however. He has an apartment in Georgetown which I'm not supposed to know about, either. Unfortunately I don't know the address or phone number for that one."

"Well, I have a little time. I'll see if I can find him. Otherwise it will have to wait. No need to tell him I'm coming, though," Kohl said. "Since he doesn't know me personally it might be more effective if I just dropped in."

She nodded her understanding and they said good-bye.

If there was nothing else that sitting out on a hillside alone without food or drink for days on end had taught Kohl, it was patience and perseverance. Along with a few dollars into the right palms, they had ultimately brought him to a high-rise security building of luxury apartments. He was now inside the subterranean garage waiting for the car which would ultimately pull into its assigned parking space. Hopefully it would be soon. The apartment was empty at the moment but he had learned that the General was in town. Kohl wanted to catch him off guard. Way off guard, damn him.

And, if he judged him correctly the smug bastard would be basking in his success right now, playing the game of fear, making Kohl wait before contacting him with his demands, working the psychological lever of anxiety and worry. Well, we'll see, he told himself, his anger growing. He looked at his watch. "Jesus", he said out loud. Why hadn't he thought of it earlier. He ran to the elevator and found his way back up to the tenth floor, picked the lock and let himself in. No ordinary apartment, this. It was large, lavish and self indulgent, occupying the full end of the floor with views of the city on three sides. From the living room, the study and the bedroom.

Kohl pulled several drawers out of the dresser and chest and dumped the contents out, letting them fall. He went into the king sized, walk in closet, removed some of the General's dress uniforms from their hangers, dropped them on the floor and wiped his feet on them. Back in the study he rifled the oversized glass topped desk with all the souvenirs on it, threw papers on the floor and made a grand mess. Then in the back of another drawer he found an address book, thumbed through it, tore out some key pages and put them in his pocket.

On the wall behind was a gallery of framed photographs. Old cronies, politicians, the Secretary of

116

State, the Israeli Premier, Nixon and Eisenhower, some younger women prominent in the New York social scene, but, not a one of either his wife or his step daughter. Kohl removed a number of them and dumped them in the wastebasket. Then he found a clean sheet of paper and wrote and wrote: "Your envoy left this behind. Thought you might like to have it back." Kohl put the unsigned note in full view on the desk, reached into his pocket, removed the slug he had dug out of the beam at home and placed it on top. Then he headed for the door. There, you son-of-a-bitch, he said. That should give you a little taste of what its like to be violated.

Passing the front closet, he stopped. Curiously he opened the door and turned on the light. An automatic rifle leaned into the corner. There were more weapons on the shelves. His eyes swept over the accumulation of other things, then came back to a two way radio and lingered. Was there another one? Yes there was, but a different model. He looked some more. Nothing. He went back to them, picked them up, turned them both on and checked them against each other. They shared the same frequencies and the batteries were fresh.

Leaving the closet, Kohl went back to the desk and searched through it some more, finding what he wanted. He clipped one radio to his belt, turned the other back on but with its volume down to the lowest setting and the squelch control on high. It would broadcast effectively but with little danger of giving itself away. Tearing off several pieces of heavy tape from the roll he had found, he attached the unit to the underside of the desk, out of sight but as near to the phone as possible. Now he had best be getting out of there. Again, however, he stopped at the closet. Wonder if there might just happen to be a small recorder in here somewhere, he asked himself. Luck was with him once again.

Kohl had his hand on the front doorknob when he heard the key in the lock. Quickly he retreated back into the closet. Fortunately it did not also serve as a coat closet. There was little chance someone would open it when first

117

coming in. He clicked off the light just as the front door opened. Footsteps went past. Whatever happened next didn't matter. The sounds coming from the coarse voice he believed to be the General's were worth every bit of the trouble he had gone to.

"What the hell?" the man bellowed as he discovered the disorder. Kohl opened the closet door a crack and waited. Sure enough, whoever was there went exploring further. When he heard the loud, "Dirty-rotten-low-life-son-of-a-bitch", from the bedroom he slipped out of the apartment, walked down around the corner out of sight from the door, removed the second radio from his belt, turned it on and listened.

He didn't have long to wait. He soon heard noises. He turned the miniature cassette recorder on and placed it near the ear piece of the radio and listened to the sound of desk drawers being opened and slammed back shut. Next there was a long, munificent string of additional, course and crude profanity that could only have come from an ex military officer. The General must have found the breached address book and the note Kohl had left him. There were other sounds. He was making a phone call. Too bad the concealed radio under the desk wasn't a bit more sensitive. He might have been able to pick up the tones from the phone as the man had dialed the number. They could have been decoded later. However, it hadn't, so he would never be completely sure whom he had called. More than likely, though, it was Rapier, as deduced from the sound of the one side of the conversation he was privileged to hear.

Another call was made, the General still mad as hell. He beat on the phone heavily as he dialed. Kohl could hear the sound of more buttons being pushed than before. It must be long distance, perhaps his and Daphne's own phone in Arizona. There was a long wait with no answer. The man hung up and dialed another seven digit number.

The voice was politer and much more subdued than it had been to the first recipient. It must be his wife. He said

118

a few placating words to her about his still being out of town on business, asked her how she was and cautiously steered the call around to her daughter and her daughter's boyfriend, patronizing her. How were they, had she heard from them? There was a short period of silence while he listened. "Nothing?" he said at last, in a rather disappointed and confused tone. Perhaps he had inquired too sweetly, somehow too out of character, or perhaps the very fact that he had inquired at all was out of character. Whatever. It didn't matter. She must have picked up on it and lied to him.

Good, Kohl thought with relief. She had not divulged his presence in Washington. Thank you, he told her silently as a wave of compassion swept over him. Now the poor woman would really be worried about her daughter. But what could he do? Nothing, he decided. He had enough to worry about right now. She would have to live with her anxiety a little longer. But in his anger, Kohl's mind began to blur. Should he go back and knock on the door of that apartment, confront the General now, before he had recovered from the intrusion, or should he force him to sit and wonder, make him wait as no doubt he had set out to make Kohl wait? What to do? Suddenly he felt very tired. It had been an extremely long day. He needed a decent meal and some sleep. Let the slime ball wait, he decided. Let him fume and fuss for a change. Let his frustration build, as it surely would, for here was a man who was used to making the rules, a man who governed by edict. Other people jumped, not him.

EIGHTEEN

At last the cold, cumbersome handcuffs were removed from her wrists and Daphne was pushed through a heavy door that slammed and locked behind her. Hands now free, she reached up and pulled the blindfold from her eyes, something she had been forced to wear since they boarded the private aircraft back in Arizona. Interesting. They didn't care that I had seen their faces, so, obviously they just don't want me to have any idea of where I'm at.

She looked at her watch. There was no way to tell where she might be either, other than it was approximately five hours away by jet. East coast, she speculated, making a quick assessment of her surroundings, but how could she be sure. She was in an older building that was probably a house which now had all the windows boarded up. Recently too, by the look of it, tightly and effectively without regard for cosmetics.

She explored the rest of her prison. In all, she had access to something akin to a sparsely furnished sitting room, an adjoining bedroom of sorts and a bathroom. The hastily and poorly made, twin sized bed was obviously newly purchased, the linens and blankets also fresh from the package. Uncoordinated colors, sheets not tucked in, pillows poorly stuffed; no woman would have done such a thing. The same was true in the bathroom. A pile of new towels were on the counter, a toothbrush still in the package, toothpaste still in the box, soap still in the wrapper, toilet paper still in plastic. There was no deodorant, however, nor cosmetics. Well, she thought, at least the sink and the ancient old cast iron tub standing on its four metal legs along the wall under another boarded up window appeared to be relatively clean.

But to hell with all that, she declared. How do I get out of here, she asked herself, and set about examining the premises with that singular thought in mind. It wasn't going to be easy, she finally concluded. The only entry and exit was the heavy door she had been pushed through earlier. And from what she could tell, it had at least two locks on it. It also had a small, reversely installed, optical viewer in it that could only be used from the outside. She wanted to scream her lungs out. But why bother, she decided. She was tired. Better to save her energy for something important.

She went into the sitting room and collapsed onto the cold naugahyde of the couch and put her feet up on the scared wooden coffee table. It then occurred to her that there were no paintings on the wall, either, no television, no books, not even a magazine. Her stomach growled.

"Dammit," she said. The bastards hadn't even feed her. And then, as if right on cue, there was a knock on the door. She got up and went towards it. When she was still four steps away a man's voice commanded her to stop.

"Stand there where I can see you," he said gruffly. It was the same man who had driven the car she been abducted in and the same voice she remembered from the plane. She stopped and waited. The door opened. Still wearing the same uniform as before, he stepped inside carrying a tray and kicked the door shut behind him. "Move back in there," he ordered, nodding with his head towards the room she had just come from. She went. "Sit down," he told her.

She sat and faced him glaringly but he ignored the look, put the tray down with a bang and left abruptly. When she heard the sounds of the door locks again, she inspected what had been placed before her.

"Yuk," she said. It was a TV dinner warmed in a microwave. Dry chicken, soggy green beans, runny mashed potatoes, weak colored gravy, some unbuttoned, day old bread, a plastic glass half full of water, plastic knife, plastic fork and paper napkin. She pushed it away. Five minutes later she picked up the fork and cautiously probed the beans and potatoes. Then she touched the chicken with her fingers, squeezed the bread to test it and reluctantly began to eat. When she was done she wiped up some of the remaining gravy on the napkin, went to the door, smeared the tasteless substance over the viewing lens and went to bed.

NINETEEN

Kohl was up shortly after dawn the next morning, leaning against the wall in the hallway outside Bart's apartment. He had expected such a disciplined man as the General to be an early riser. Unfortunately, he was only half right. It was nearly eight o'clock before he heard the door and ducked out of sight. He waited until the door was locked, counted to ten, stepped back out into the hallway behind the General and slowly followed him towards the elevators.

The General stopped at the call panel. Impatiently, he hit the down button three or four times in a row, then stood there staring at the floor numbers above the door as he shifted back and forth. Tall, trim, graying at the temples, dressed in pants pressed razor sharp, a starched white shirt and a gold buttoned, dark blazer, he scowled heavily, playing the role of one much too important and preoccupied to turn around and see who else had stopped to board the lift. Not that it mattered particularly for he wouldn't have recognized Kohl anyway, never having seen as much as a picture of him before. Kohl, however, very definitely wanted to make sure he was noticed.

The General got on the elevator. Kohl followed him in and stepped to the side. The elevator made two more stops on the way down and picked up two more passengers, both of whom got out at the lobby level. Kohl also moved towards the door but purposely bumped into the General. The General growled as Kohl apologized and started brushing off the General's sleeve with his hand. The General jerked his arm away and glared at Kohl. Good, Kohl thought. He'll remember my face now. With that he smiled into the General's face and got off, leaving the General to continue on alone down to the parking level. Enough time for Kohl to get outside and start up the rental car he had waiting in the street.

The General's Washington office was housed in an old brownstone building next to a pawn shop down a narrow side street boldly located not more than half a mile from the White House. From the front it went unannounced. There was no sign above the door or any other indication of its use or purpose, only the street number on the column near the entry. Inside, however, it was much more remarkable. The front door entered into a well appointed lobby complete with waiting area, restroom and a receptionist strategically located behind a paneled partition. Behind the receptionist, in turn, was a solid wall with an electrically controlled door that could only be opened by the button under her desk. It was a black button, located next to another red one that activated a buzzer somewhere in the far reaches to the back.

Although not all that wide up front, once inside and further back the premises bent around behind the pawn shop and took up the entire rear portion of the building, clear to the alleyway behind, with the General's own office consuming a goodly portion of the southeast corner. The computer and communications room comprised a good one third of the rest while the remainder was devoted to offices and work areas for his staff, which at times numbered as many as ten or twelve. Unseen from below, there were also four microwave antennas of various sizes on the roof, six floors up, along with a number of radio and television antennas. The largest microwave dish was pointed slightly south and west of zenith towards a classified satellite whose transmission code had been broken by one of the staff experts. Two of the other dishes pointed towards other buildings in the downtown area and collected spuriously reflected signals that emanated from across the Potomac over in Virginia while the last was tied directly into the phone company giving the General quick and easy access to global communication.

In addition to being the location of a sophisticated, round the clock, intelligence gathering center, it also served a much humbler function. It was the General's recruiting office. Offbeat ads were routinely placed in a number of large, east coast cities soliciting persons looking for high paying, adventuresome, overseas jobs willing to take risks and live under adverse conditions. Resumes were reviewed first, followed by phone interrogations. Those remaining after several steps of screening were administered a battery of psychological tests and their profiles prepared. If their profiles fell within the bounds of what might formally be classified as borderline psychotic, they were then invited to come to Washington, all expenses paid. Ultimately, if they passed a face to face interview with one last intermediary, they became privileged to personally shake hands with the General.

Kohl waited ten minutes before stepping through the front door into the lobby. Just long enough for the General to get comfortable with his first cup of coffee, he hoped. "May I help you?" the sharp eyed, middle aged woman asked.

Kohl stepped up to the counter. "I'd like to see Bartholomew," he stated with authority.

"Bartholomew?" She looked at him strangely. "There's no one here by that name."

"The General," Kohl clarified. She caught the hard look in his eyes and hesitated, wondering if she might have to find the red button under her desk. She put one hand down in her lap and asked Kohl if he had an appointment. "No," he said, "but the old boy might just be expecting me."

The derogatory use of her employer's full first name had caught her off guard but she quickly regained her composure and her authority.

"I'm sorry but HE doesn't see anyone without an appointment. Besides, I'm not sure he's in as yet. If you would like to leave your name and a number where you might be reached I can call you if he should decide to meet with you," she said superciliously.

"Give him this," Kohl said and handed her a photo copy of one of the pages he had tore from the General's address book.

"What's this supposed to be?" she wanted to know.

"He will understand."

She looked at it and shrugged, reached for an envelope, put the page inside, picked up her pen and asked, "May I have your name, sir."

"My dear woman," Kohl said. "Those are my credentials. I don't want you to put that in his incoming mail basket. I want you to personally take it back and hand it to him. I assure you that he will then invite me in. Quite promptly, no doubt."

Contrary to Kohl's expectations, the General never drank coffee first thing in the morning. His first priority was to stop in the computer room, should there be some communication which had come in during the night that required his attention. If there were no urgencies he then walked a short block down the street to where he had his usual breakfast of corned beef hash, eggs, rye toast and tea. For this he allotted himself exactly thirty minutes. Then the real work of the day began. Strategy update, logistics appraisal and timetable evaluation. Money, manpower, weaponry, all were equally important.

He had given himself five years. Two had already gone by. He was behind schedule. Interruptions, always interruptions, unpredictable interruptions caused by unpredictable people, the consequences of having to deal with so damned many undisciplined civilians. And now the most unpredictable of all things had happened. Somehow that man Kohl had found a transgressor brave enough to dare break into the General's private quarters and violate his personal world. Who would be dumb enough to do such a risky thing for him? Who else could it be unless it was that mad Indian friend of his.

Yes, that was the most plausible possibility, what with the man's service record. The intrusion had all the earmarks of an Army trained, Special Forces, Southeast Asia veteran, no doubt about that. Then the General paused in his condemnation. Why hadn't he seen it earlier? This was exactly the kind of talent he was looking for. What the hell, forgive and forget. There was always room for a good man somewhere in his growing organization. Instead of being put out about it, why not present the man with some nice incentive to join the team. Indians liked to have cash in hand just like everyone else. Maybe a few deposits in a Swiss bank account to sweeten it up. Then wouldn't he be able to laugh like hell. And, if the price was right, maybe the Indian could even help him get that big laser back.

The General smiled generously to himself at first. Then something more important occurred to him. Even if he had the laser back he would probably still need Kohl to help make it operational and that would require some very

125

strong leverage to get him to cooperate. Indian or no Indian to try and win him over, it was best to keep the girl hidden away. Thinking thusly, the General decided to forgo calling Kohl until later. Since the Indian was obviously in town, he would no doubt be soon showing his face. He had best think about what other enticements he might use to further his recruitment should some misguided loyalty or other objection enter the picture.

Having proceeded this far with his thinking, and not having made it down the street to breakfast yet, he was not overly surprised when his receptionist found him in the computer room. She handed him the piece of paper and waited, fully expecting to be told to call the police. Instead the General merely smiled at her, or was it to himself? She wasn't sure. "Bring him to my office," he instructed. "I'll talk to him there."

She led Kohl back through the long hallway past the now closed doors of the other rooms and offices, stopped in front of the carved oak door in the rear and knocked twice before entering. The General sat behind the expanse of his nearly barren desk, hidden from view by the Wall Street Journal, as if he had nothing more on his mind than to be casually reading the morning paper. "General, this is..." the receptionist said. "What did you say your name was Sir?"

"I didn't. But for the record, it's Kohl," he said, noticing the almost imperceptible movement of the paper when he spoke, wondering what it meant. Why should the man be surprised at the mention of his name?

The paper slowly descended as the General folded it carefully, taking the time he was doing it to examine the person standing in front of him. He scowled briefly when he realized that Kohl was the same man that had so brazenly bumped into him in the elevator earlier. The rash bastard, he thought, but then quickly swept it aside as he waved the receptionist from the room and smiled.

Have a seat," he said politely, as he pointed to the low chair directly in front of the desk. It was another of his little devices. There were two visitors chairs in the office. One, the normal companion chair to the room which had been placed against the wall for now, and this one, purposely slightly shorter than most. Just enough to place the occupant in a slightly uncomfortable, slightly disadvantaged line of sight whereupon he had to look upward from this subordinate position to see the General's face when he spoke.

Kohl, however, ignored the offer and said, "I won't be staying long."

The General frowned and shrugged, his mind working as he waited. Other than basic formalities, he wasn't about to speak first. What could he say, anyway? Open confrontation would solve nothing at this point. Silence predominated. A full minute went by. Say something, dammit, the General said to himself. And for Christ's sake, sit down. How the hell are we ever going to begin negotiating? But Kohl, the nonconformist, neither spoke nor sat. For someone as easily aggravated as the General, it was too much.

"Well," he finally said with forced humility. "How can I help you?"

Instead of answering, however, Kohl looked around the room, saw the wet bar in the corner, went to it, opened the small refrigerator, found a soft drink and helped himself. Then he came back, leaned on the desk and stared hard into the General's eyes.

"I came to take Daphne home. Would you like me to wait out in the lobby while you make the arrangements?"

"Daphne? My step daughter? Is she here?" he feigned. "Her mother didn't tell me. What are you talking about?"

"If I was back in Arizona you would be calling me about now, making some demand or other," Kohl responded curtly. "So let's just cut the crap and get down to business. What specifically do you want?"

The General hesitated and his stomach growled. Show some respect, Goddammit, he said under his breath. Someday I'll be your master. Then you won't be standing there like some smart ass, drinking my last cream soda. You'll be on your knees, instead, by god. Rather than speaking his mind, however, he leaned back in his chair in a show of confidence and said, "I assure you she is well and comfortable. Now if you would just sit down, we can discuss the matter."

Kohl sat down but he didn't like the feel of the chair one bit. He got up again, saw the other chair by the wall and dragged it over, placing it more directly in front of the desk before sitting again. "Please continue," he said.

The General let out a sigh, sat up as straight as he could in his own chair, cleared his throat and began a very difficult conversation.

"I must apologize. Please understand that we didn't bring her here to place you in a compromised position. Rather, it was done to gain your attention so that we might sit down as gentlemen and discuss a venture which might prove to be mutually advantageous on many levels."

Kohl laughed derisively. "Kidnapping precludes calling yourself a gentleman, don't you think?"

"Perhaps, but I thought it necessary."

"You're pathetic. You are really pathetic."

"Maybe, maybe not. We shall see. I have something you want, you have something I want. Don't try so hard to insult me and maybe we can come to terms?"

"And what is it that you think I have?"

"Good. I'm glad you asked. First, the van with the laser."

"I'm sorry. You had it last, as you proved by the pictures you sent me."

"But not anymore, as I'm sure you are also quite aware. Let's put it this way. I read all the newspaper accounts and most of the classified reports regarding its capability and I also had my own expert look at it. Although I don't feel I want to share the reasons with you just yet, I could certainly put something with that capability to good use. I admit that we might have been a little shortsighted in trying to deal with you the first time. Now, unquestionably, if you returned it to me, you would deserve to be compensated for it. Let's say half a million for starters. Provided it is brought back to its original working condition, of course," the General stated, looking at Kohl to see what impact his offer had made.

There was none. Kohl's gaze never wavered.

"And the girl goes free," the General added quickly. "I will trust you to perform. All I need is your verbal acceptance."

"Sorry. I refuse to bargain under duress."

"What does that mean?"

"Release Daphne or the discussion ends, here and now."

"If you value her life," the General said, the tone of his voice suddenly changing, telling Kohl that he meant every word of the threat he now expressed. "The discussion will continue until I decide it has reached a satisfactory conclusion. So please be patient and hear what else I have to say."

The only answer Kohl would give was in the cold blue of his eyes as they burned into the General. Bart fumbled with some papers on his desk and continued. "Perhaps half a million is a little low. I might go more. A lot more, if you would train some of my people in its use," the General said, bringing his eyes back up while tapping his fingers on the desk top, doing his best to sound tempting. "Beyond that, you and your friends also have some other unique abilities. Abilities that I could put to far better use than playing childish games with the IRS."

"Really?" Kohl questioned skeptically to see what the General might reveal.

"Properly directed, I could fit you all into my organization and personally make you the beneficiary of extreme wealth and power," the General continued, throwing out his chest with pride as he spoke. "I have reached a point in my own endeavors where I could use someone with your level of intelligence and trustworthiness. There is no limit to what we could accomplish jointly. And since you are already a part of the family, so to speak, you would be the natural heir to such an empire. That is my one sadness, you know. I never had a son of my own. You could be that person. Go back to Arizona, take some time to think about it, if you like."

"Sorry General. No deal. Not under any circumstances."

"Didn't you hear what I said? I can..."

Kohl waved him off. "Didn't you hear what I said?"

The General grumbled loudly and leaned back in his chair, his empty stomach beginning to bother him. "Don't be such a fool. How could you refuse? Perhaps when you become aware of the true extent of my operation and my resources."

"I don't care about your money or your empire."

"What then? What do you care about?"

"Nothing you can offer. Besides, it wouldn't work anyway."

"What wouldn't?"

"None of it."

"None of what? Explain yourself!"

"This isn't some episode of Star Trek. We can't just turn the transporter on and rematerialize the van."

"What are you saying?"

"It's really gone. Disappeared! Forever!"

"But where? Where did it go?"

"Have you read any good physics books lately?"

"We used to have such briefings when I was at the Pentagon. What are you referring to?"

"As a consequence of some of the theoretical dilemmas they get themselves into, physicists have recently postulated the existence of an infinity of parallel universes. Not that any self respecting scientist really believes it, of course. It's simply a concept that alleviates a problem in mathematics, like string theory, true randomnicity and chaos, Stossahlansatz or a time symmetrical universe."

Obviously not comprehending, the General just looked at Kohl. Kohl reached over and knocked on the desk top.

"The illusion, General. Is the desk solid or is it not?

130

On this level it would appear so. On the subatomic level, however, it is composed of far, far more space than it is of matter. The nucleus of an atom is analogous to something the size of a pea in the middle of a football field with the electrons circling it out at the periphery of the field some one hundred and fifty yards away. An impossible ratio. All the rest is space. Room enough for a vast number of other particles to be zooming around in there without interference, wouldn't you say? And then, are protons and electrons themselves really solid? Maybe they are electromagnetic energy fields instead, blinking on and off, all a small phase difference away, sharing in several universes at once. Not that it really matters, I guess. Just suffice it to say that whatever the real truth is, that is where the van and the laser are now. Somehow they have been relegated into some other dimension. One from which they cannot be recovered."

The General sat morosely pondering words he would have difficulty arguing with. Somehow, it seemed plausible. A noumenon. The van had disappeared from right under his nose, no doubt about that. What a waste, what a damned waste.

"Well, okay," he said at last, resigning himself to it. "But what about that IRS stuff? Let's talk about that."

"There's nothing to talk about, General."

"But," the General persisted. "I still don't understand. How are you and your friends able to do things like that? Where does all that awesome power come from?"

"Out of the fire mist."

"What does that mean?"

"Out of the fires of creation! Hell, General, I don't know. What difference does it make? Let it go and just consider the fact that if you don't release Daphne, we just might have another little ceremony. I can't decide, however, whether we should make you disappear personally or whether we should just take away all your toys and make all your bank accounts evaporate," Kohl said with extremely hostile emphasis, even though it was a bluff. "Or, on the other hand we might effect something

131

more on the personal level, something to do with your manhood, perhaps."

Fortunately, or unfortunately as the case might be, the spirit world could not be manipulated for such things as material gain, personal power, revenge, control or other non altruistic ventures. It didn't work that way. Not the part which Kohl understood, anyway. On the other hand, it might be used to provide unselfish, beneficial acts such as helping someone who is ill or in danger so if this mad dog didn't come to his senses pretty soon Kohl would be on his way to Colorado to see just how Grey Hawk might help him rescue Daphne.

The General weighed Kohl's implications thoroughly. Could they really do such a thing? he seriously wondered. It sure as hell looked like they might be able to. Now what? Maybe he should render Kohl immobile with the tranquilizer gun and cart him off to Costa Rica, then shoot him full of Amytole or something. They could learn all the secrets and then dispose of the body. It might be a start. But then, would it work? Would knowledge alone be enough. Maybe not. What if it took more than one person to accomplish these mysterious feats. It certainly looked to be a shared thing, somehow. What if it was in the coming together that somehow amplified the thing and made it work...Then, unfortunately, he would have to find all those Indians and do the same thing to them, too.

The General reconsidered. Maybe he had best find out a little more about it before he did anything quite so irrevocable as tracking them all down, draining them dry and then killing them all. So where was he? At an impasse. But not stupid, never stupid. He smiled. For the moment there was nothing left to do but to concede. He would wait and learn. Other opportunities would present themselves. "All right, you win," he said at last and reached for the phone.

TWENTY

Daphne was standing on the edge of the bathtub doing her best to ram the end of the chair leg she had broken off through the ceiling of the bathroom. She was not about to sit idly by and let that scum bag soldier of the General's, the one she had named Arnold because he was even uglier than the movie actor and thought he was tougher than Robo Cop, make any more passes at her. She had already told him that the General would cut his balls off if he touched her but he had only laughed and it was only after she had screamed and Rapier had ordered him out of her room that he had left. She needed to escape. She would escape, she decided, or die trying. Her clothes and her hair were covered with white powder and chips of plaster as was the inside of the tub, but, something was wrong. She reached up, stuck her fingers through the hole and pulled on the edge of the opening to make it bigger. A chunk of the fragile material broke loose and came down, almost causing her to loose her balance. She put her hand into the opening. Damn! What was up there?

She stood on her tip toes and squinted into the darkness above. Then she sat down on the edge of the tub. The bastards had nailed a strong wire mesh over the top of the ceiling joists up in the attic. She wanted to cry. The place was a veritable stronghold. The ceiling had been her last hope. Fighting her depression, she stood up and began brushing the powder from her clothes and shook out her long hair. Then she became angry again. There had to be a way. What was it?

Subconsciously, she reached for the broken chair leg and hefted it. It was fairly substantial. Given the right opportunity, it might make a good club. Thinking of that possibility, she left the bathroom and closed the door behind her. No sooner had she done so than there was a knock on the door and she heard the key in the lock. Silencer equipped weapon in hand, Rapier came into the room and looked at her as she stood waiting with the chair leg lowered to her side out of sight.

Could she maneuver him into a more vulnerable position, Daphne wondered. And what if she failed to subdue him with the first blow? Would he shoot her? More than likely. Warily, she studied him. He raised the pistol and spoke. "Come here," he ordered. "And turn around."

She stood still. He cocked the weapon, pulling a round into the chamber. Slowly, she complied, still holding the club. Rapier shouted to the guard. "Take that stick away and handcuff her," he directed as Arnold came in the room.

"What for?" Arnold asked suspiciously.

"The General wants to see her."

"He didn't tell me."

"Just put the cuffs on her. I'll explain later."

Arnold looked at Rapier. He did not like the man and trusted him even less, no matter what degree of confidence the General had granted him. Was he telling the truth? It wasn't like the General not to keep him informed. Especially if the prisoner was to be moved. He stalled and quickly found himself looking down the barrel of Rapier's pistol. Complying roughly, Arnold grabbed Daphne's right arm and twisted it upward behind her back as the club fell to the floor. He snapped on one cuff and reached for the other arm.

"Back away," Rapier ordered sharply when he was done. Arnold stepped back. It was the last thing he would ever do. There was a loud pop as the silenced weapon erupted and a soft nosed slug entered his forehead and ripped away the back of his skull. Daphne screamed and fainted.

There was no response to the loud knock on the door. Angrily, the General tried again, pounding even harder than before. Nothing. He tried the knob. The door swung inward. Kohl followed the red faced man inside. There was a half empty can of beer on the table and a burned out cigarette in the ashtray but the front of the converted old house was empty. They made their way to the open door in the rear. The General stepped through and cursed in a shocked voice. Kohl rapidly assessed the grisly scene and moved quickly through the quarters which had been Daphne's prison, finding her attempt to escape through the bathroom ceiling. His heart sank.

"What the hell does that son-of-a-bitch think he's doing?" the General bellowed as he looked at the dead man's frozen stare with a touch of remorse over the waste. A lot of time and money had gone into training him. He would be hard to replace. "And what the hell good does he think that girl is going to do him?" he shouted in frustration.

After all this time he still referred to her as, that girl. It was about as personal as he would allow himself to get. Women had their place in the world and filled a compelling physical need, no doubt about that. But as for this one, she might have all her super endowments but she was far too damned independent, that's for sure, and he had little sympathy for her. None, actually. The little bitch didn't know her place at all. Such undisciplined women were an insidious threat to the future. Unchecked, they could bring about serious imbalance in the bigger scheme of things. Besides, she had been his pawn, his to bargain with, not Rapier's. How dare that audacious little bastard turn on him like this. Especially after he had taken the trouble to rescue him from the dismal depths of professional failure. And why, after all that, why had he done it, that was the unanswerable question. How ungrateful could one get? Had he gone totally mad? How could he ever hope to better his situation by doing such an irrational thing?

"You had just better hope that whatever his reasons", Kohl warned. "He values them enough not to harm her."

"Yes, I suppose you are right," the General conceded.

"So, where do you think he took her?"

Quite bewildered, the General looked at Kohl. "I don't have any idea," he said quietly.

TWENTY ONE

"Follow him," the General ordered the special team he had quickly assembled, telling them about Kohl. "Follow him night and day, around the clock, wherever it takes you. I don't care if you have to walk in elk shit up to your eyebrows at that Indian's place, sleep in a tree or drink bus station coffee. Stick with him. Sooner or later Rapier will contact him and he will lead us to Rapier. When we find that little piss ant we'll have a new French delicacy on the table and it won't be escargot, Goddammit."

"Yeah," said Lieutenant Kouslip, the man in charge, as he brushed back the bristles of his blond, crew cut hair savoring the thought of Rapier's capture, a man he had come to thoroughly despise and hate. Not only did he not like having had to put up with his haughty attitude all the time but the popsicle sucker had shot and killed his twin brother Barnold. "Diced testicles sautéed with butter, onions and vintage wine," he said with a malicious laugh. "I can't wait."

Even the General was forced to laugh. "Get moving," he said after they had their fun.

There was a lightness in Grey Hawk's step and a glow in his eye that Kohl had never seen before. It was more than just Claudia, the new woman in his life. It had something to do with the community he had created. Ten people were living on the property when Kohl arrived from Washington. Grey Hawk, Claudia and two young women resided in the main house where all the meals were served and the rest slept in the older house Kohl had spent so much time trying to repair. Grey Hawk promptly relegated two women together into one bedroom and Kohl was privileged to have the other. Then, by the time those arrangements were made, dinner was on the table. Thus far there had been no time for Kohl to explain his reasons for being there.

Claudia was a definite contrast, both to Renee, Grey Hawk's former lady, and to the other two women. Somehow Kohl had expected someone a little younger, a little flashier, a little more self centered, but, she was none of these. Instead, she was a good woman whom Kohl decided he liked. The other two, however, an affected redhead and a hair tossing blond, left him feeling skeptical.

Running Deer, Spotted Owl, One Hand, Rainmaker

136

and James were all there too and joined them around the table along with another woman named Benji whom Spotted Owl had obviously claimed for his own. Five Indians, four white women, a black man and Kohl. The outward disparity was complete. Inwardly, however, there was a common bond. Grey Hawk's teachings and philosophy. The prayer of thanks over, everyone began eating with gusto, except for Kohl. He ate meagerly and talked less, his concern for Daphne's situation growing steadily. Finally someone asked, "How's Daphne? Why didn't you bring her along?"

Kohl was silent.

"What happened?" Grey Hawk wanted to know, sensing the emotion Kohl was trying to suppress.

"Let's wait until later," Kohl said as all eyes turned to him.

Grey Hawk nodded and the others turned back to their food. When the dishes had been collected and coffee served, Kohl and Grey Hawk went outside and sat on the long porch that extended two thirds of the way around the south. half of the house. It would be another ninety minutes or so before the sun went down but there was a stream of clouds on the horizon and the suggestion of a brilliant sunset already in progress.

"She's been kidnapped," Kohl told the Indian and filled in the details.

"Not good," Grey Hawk said, contorting the muscles of his mouth and chin. "Not good at all." They sat together in silence as Grey Hawk reviewed the story in his mind and Kohl went over things for the hundredth time, still grasping for a plan. Finally the Indian spoke. "Go tell Spotted Owl to come here," he said.

"Get the sweat lodge ready," he instructed Spotted Owl when he appeared and the younger man headed off without a word. Half an hour later all the men had been smudged by Grey Hawk and crawled into the misshapen, blanket covered lodge after him. The redhead was tending the fire, the blond had been designated stone carrier. Grey Hawk gave the order to begin. The blond grappled with the

137

fork, finally got the first glowing rock out of the flames and promptly dropped it half way from the fire pit to the lodge. She then giggled, maneuvered it back onto the fork and brought it to the door whereupon Grey Hawk instructed her to put it back on the fire and bring another one.

She dropped the second one. Only this time she didn't giggle, but swore. Sitting next to Kohl along the western wall, Running Deer snickered and Kohl could see the half scowl of reaction on Grey Hawk's face in the dim light. The third stone made the full distance and found it's rightful way into the shallow grandmother pit inside the lodge, as did the following six. The flap of a door was lowered. Round one was underway and was completed without further incident.

Other than for the exceptionally hot stones the women added to the growing pile in the lodge and the oppressive clouds of steam that were generated, round two went relatively smoothly also, as did the beginning of round three. But then, when the prayer circle had moved around to Running Deer he began to ramble on at great length in a very disorganized manner about the meaning of spirituality until finally Spotted Owl, who shouldn't have had seconds and thirds at the dinner table, got to feeling sick and had to leave before the round was completed. Although he did his best, Grey Hawk had difficulty in re-infusing any vitality into the disjointed ceremony after that. It was dusk when they came out. The dying western sky was a streaked paintboard of black, gray and blood red.

Grey Hawk and Claudia retired to the master bedroom as Kohl waited his turn for the shower, then dressed and came back out to sit by the fading embers of the fire. He was soon joined by the blond whose major concern was to talk about her father. In her own words she said that her father had been visited by the "Grays."

"Who are the Grays?"

"You know. Those short, gray looking extraterrestrials with the large almond shaped eyes."

"Oh them," Kohl said as if it were an everyday

occurrence. Where was this conversation headed, he wondered. They had taken control of her father's mind, she confided, and told him that it was his duty to kill Grey Hawk. Great, thought Kohl, wishing he had brought a good book along. He sighed and looked at her. She was cute, almost pretty, but from the neck down there were more bumps on a bean pod than there were curves on her body. Not the kind of woman Kohl thought the Indian would be attracted to but for some reason Grey Hawk was quite enamored with her and excused her for things that any of the men would have received serious reprimands for. Inept, superficial and air between the ears.

So if it wasn't her body and it wasn't her brain, what was it, he wondered. What it was about her that caused Grey Hawk to allow her into the ceremonial circle, even if just to carry stones from the fire pit to the lodge. By every criteria that Grey Hawk had ever previously uttered, she didn't fit. But yet, here she was. Did this sudden confessional about her father have something to do with it? And what the hell kind of a loony tunes story was that? Whatever the source of her father's wild imaginings, the Grays or God himself, Kohl hoped Grey Hawk was at least taking the killing part of it seriously.

But then there was also the redhead. She was equally unqualified to be there. Did her father belong in a straight jacket, too, Kohl asked himself as he and Running Deer drove into town a little later to have a beer. Obviously angry and troubled, Running Deer was having a hard time. Was it one issue, or several? For one thing there was a bitterness about the two women.

"What about them?" Kohl asked.

"They're Woman Wives," he was told.

"Woman wives? What's a woman wife?"

"Grey Hawk claims they were signed to become his other wives."

"You're kidding? Grey Hawk wants more than one wife? And Signed? What does that mean."

Running Deer laughed derisively. "Ha!"

"Well, explain it."

"The redhead was out in the woods and squatted down behind a bush to go pee and claims to have seen a Sasquatch footprint in the dirt. That other hollow head found a stone on her father's farm that had a bunch of scratch marks on it."

"Okay. So?"

"This is supposed to mean that they were destined to come here and bear children."

Kohl shook his head in bewildered amazement.

"Exactly," Running Deer said.

"So what do you think it's really all about?" Kohl asked.

"Who knows? Lots of stupid things, none of which make any sense. The redhead is, or was, a part time hooker. The other one helps her old man grow marijuana on his farm back in Ohio. Two screwed up, nothing going for them, young females looking for easy passage into nirvana. Along comes a Medicine Man, also screwed up, but for another set of reasons, still unclear. Whatever, why ever, what for, he's willing to take them in and teach them about spirit. They think they can enhance the process by spreading their legs and the next thing we know he's reaching for their pussy. What's happened is that he's changed, man. He's changed a lot."

"It does look that way," Kohl said, if it were really true. Or had something happened between Grey Hawk and Running Deer? Although Running Deer certainly didn't impress him as being the kind to resort to such gross character assassination it wouldn't be the first time a woman or two clouded men's minds and it wouldn't be the first friendship to hit the rocks over such an issue. "That's not the man I thought I knew, either," Kohl said, however, waiting to hear the rest of it.

"What I don't understand is why did he think he had to come up with such a wild tale to justify his behavior. What the hell. If he likes a little extra pussy and Claudia is willing to let him get away with it, let him have it."

"What wild tale?"

"I thought you knew, maybe even had a hand in it."

"Running Deer, now what are you talking about?"

"The Star People. Those Pleidians. One calls himself Ptaah and the girl, Semjase. He says they are still making visits."

"Really," Kohl said. Somehow he had hoped that entire issue had gone away. Especially since he still wasn't sure that he had ever believed it in the first place. But, not wanting to hurt Running Deer's feelings, he stayed with the story line. "I thought he considered them to be the enemy?"

"They have converted him. It's like he suddenly got religion. Now he not only talks about the coming earth changes but also about the universal brotherhood. What the hell. I believe in the prophecies. Look at all the weather changes, hurricanes, floods, fires, earthquakes, heavy snow, severe cold. And look at the human race. There's war and disruption everywhere and crime and craziness. Something big is going to happen, I tell you," Running Deer said with certainty and drained his beer bottle dry. Kohl nodded to the bartender as the Indian continued.

"And soon, too. Maybe by the turn of the century as they say. Anyway, the Christians think there will be a second coming of Christ. But, as I seriously doubt, Christ was not the immaculate son of Mary and here I think the Talmud might even be right, which I have also read by the way. It says Christ was the artificially inseminated bastard son of a star person. And, according to Grey Hawk, it is he who is returning, not to punish the sinners and save the Christians, however, but to help lead the survivors of all the coming catastrophes back to a new and more sensible way of life. Repayment of some sort of karmic debt because he screwed up so badly last time around and wants another chance at doing it right."

Yes, Kohl was familiar with that story, too. "But, what does that have to do with Grey Hawk directly?" he asked.

"He claims his visitors have told him he is supposed to acquire seven women wives and that one of them will

141

be the mother of the new Jmannuel, or in this case, an Jmannuella."

"Goddamn. Seems like I heard something like that once before."

"That's his excuse for jumping all these young broads, anyway."

"What about Claudia?"

"She seems to be adjusting, almost as if she believes it herself."

It was too much for Kohl. The inner workings of the human mind can be a little odd at times.

"There's more," Running Deer said, however.

"How could there be?"

"He claims the Grays are coming around and that they are trying to abduct the blond because she keeps coming up with these stories about how someone is trying to lift her out of her bed in the middle of the night."

"I thought they were only interested in her father?"

"That, too. So, guess what? We have been ordered to take shifts around the fire all night standing watch."

Holy mother Mary. Who was playing who? One group of ET's was telling Grey Hawk that he will be the father of the next great prophet and that one of his women will be the mother. Such a privilege might be hard to resist, even for Grey Hawk. Not only that but there were probably thousands of bored, borderline little girls out there who would willingly jump out of their panties for a crack at that one. Stir that all up with another group of ET's who are trying to get the father killed and steal back one of the potential mothers and what have we got? How could anyone believe such a story. On the other hand why would anyone want to make up something that bizarre?

Again Kohl cautioned himself. Here was the man who had made the van disappear. No doubt about that, he had done it. And here was the man who had come to his house that first time, shook out of his mind with anxiety and fear when he had claimed to have had that first visit from the people in the shiny craft. A fear that had looked as real as any fear could ever get and nearly impossible to fake. Here, too, was a man who could have all the women he wanted without generating all this wild, unnecessary, convoluted story telling. So what the hell was really going on? Kohl's mind was spinning with questions. He was in the middle of something he didn't understand. If he jumped to conclusions either way it could seriously jeopardize his friendship and relationship, not only with Grey Hawk but also with Running Deer. The only choice was to wait until morning.

After a long, semi-sleepless night, sunrise came with a burst of promise. The sun was warm, the sky cloudless and the birds were singing. Grey Hawk's voice was also strong and reassuring, his prayers fluent and well structured with a special addendum pleading for Daphne's safety and well being. Perhaps Running Deer had exaggerated, Kohl thought. Maybe he had even lied. Maybe there really was some behind the scenes hidden conflict between the two men festering away in Running Deer's mind which had provoked him into acting in such a confused, usurping manner. Jealousy, perhaps, of Grey Hawk's success, envy of his power? If so, Grey Hawk needed to be aware of it and needed to deal with it. There was no room for underhandedness here, his newly established community would never survive. But did Kohl have to be the bearer of bad tidings? It wasn't what he wanted, at all.

Fortunately, or unfortunately, as the case might be, it didn't come to that because Running Deer wasn't lying. Without betraying confidences, Grey Hawk freely confirmed everything he had said, right down to being under siege by the Grays. Kohl didn't say anything, he just listened apprehensively as Grey Hawk reiterated the whole story. Whether or not the Indian really believed everything he was saying was another thing. However, there was a fire in his eye when he said it and if he didn't believe it, he was the most effective liar Kohl had ever met in his life.

"Just remember, Coyote is out and about," was all Kohl could say when it was over. "And as you well know, he wears many different skins." Coyote was an integral part of Indian lore, the trickster who loved to meddle and confuse. Coyote was akin to the raven in some societies and sometimes the rabbit. A role played out there on the edge of things, keeping them stirred up, thwarting man's good intentions, making a game of mocking him, laughing at him, keeping his ego in check. Beware, Grey Hawk, coyote is out and about. Grey Hawk nodded. Yes, he hadn't forgotten about coyote.

After breakfast they all gathered under a great, spreading old oak tree, sat in a circle in the grass and did another ceremony, one designed to see if they could gain insight into Daphne's whereabouts. Nothing came of it. They repeated it that afternoon with the same results and did another sweat lodge in the evening, all to no avail. That night after all the lights were out and Kohl lay in his bed worn out from thinking of Daphne and ready to drift off to sleep he was disturbed by sounds coming from the living room. Grey Hawk's low voice was mixed with giggles from the blond and noises made by the couch. No wonder the medicine man's magic wasn't working very well.

TWENTY TWO

Rapier had his own second thoughts about the impetuous act he had committed. He had acted blindly, he knew that now and it bothered him. But, when the General had been ready to give up the girl with nothing in return, it was too totally overwhelming. Just like General Bart, he had also been sure Kohl would concede and that after having been offered some rather large sums of money, he would even cooperate. But no, Kohl was a stubborn, idealistic fool of the worst sort, in love with an equally difficult and impossible to deal with woman. If only he had joined the General's team.

If he had, Rapier would even have been willing to leave him alone for awhile. Until that other bastard, Mike, had shown up, anyway. That was the opportunity he was waiting for. Then, zip, he could obliterate the two of them together, once and for all. Deep in the back of his mind that had been the plan all along, he could see that now. More than a plan, actually, an obsession that was still alive inside, gnawing away at him. And like the hungry rat that he was, he had been quite willing to bite off the toes and the ears of the man who had let him live in his house.

Most certainly there would be an attempt at retaliation on the General's part, but not for a while. He was confident that he knew too much about the inner workings of the General's operation to be in any immediate danger, especially with an insurance policy composed of old Bart's computer printouts stashed safely away. But someday, someday when old Bart had grown more powerful and had covered his tracks a little better, then...well, he had best stay alert and keep out of the alleys, Rapier warned himself. In the meantime, however, there was still a lot to be done.

Daphne's body was bruised and sore. Blindfolded again and still handcuffed, she had been forced to kneel down on the floor in the back seat of the car while Rapier had driven across town and out into the countryside somewhere. At least that's where she thought they had gone because all the traffic sounds had eventually disappeared and all she could hear was an occasional vehicle going the other way. Finally she worked her way up into the seat. "Get down, Dammit. Unless you want to feel the butt of my pistol on your head."

"I have to go to the bathroom," she said, thinking he might stop, and if he took the blindfold off temporarily she might get a chance to figure out where she was at. He refused to stop, however, and told her it would only be another half hour, wet her pants if she had to.

The road got bumpy after that and she was tossed about a lot before they finally stopped. The rear door was opened at last and she was dragged out and allowed to find her feet. The path was rough and hilly, there were trees around, she could smell them. Some pine, maybe some dogwood, other smells too. She stumbled and skinned her

145

knee. He helped her up and pulled her along, banging her toe on a rock. Inside at last he took the blindfold off, temporarily removed the handcuffs, pushed her into the bathroom and pulled the door shut. "Don't take too long," he warned her.

God, what a foul place, she thought. The tiny room smelled, the floor creaked, cobwebs hung down, the toilet bowl was full of rust and scale, the sink was falling off the wall and worst of all there was no soap. Reluctantly, she finished and came back out into what had once been a living room, equally decrepit and offensive, only to be forced back into her constraints again. Then he pushed her down into a sturdy old wooden chair, tied her legs to the chair legs and handcuffed her arms behind her and down so she couldn't lift them. Then he disappeared out in the back somewhere and returned with a hammer and nails and nailed the legs of the big chair to the floor.

When he was done he smirked at her. "Scream," he said. "Scream all you want. The nearest neighbor is five miles away."

Then, without another word, he turned and left the ramshackle building. When she heard the car start in the distance, she began to do just that. She screamed and screamed until her throat was dry and worn herself out. Her head began to droop. At last she heard the sound of the car again. She jerked awake. The day was nearly over, the house was growing dark inside. Rapier came in carrying two paper sacks full of groceries which he sat down on the pealing linoleum of the counter top and flipped on the bare bulb of the light hanging from a frayed cord over the table.

The first thing he removed from the sacks was a bottle of scotch. The second was a six pack of beer and the third a red and white box of take-out chicken. "Jesus," she said, but then her stomach growled and she decided that by now she could probably eat most anything. She sized him up carefully as he freed her from the chair. Not too tall, maybe one hundred and sixty pounds but on the wiry side. If she could find the right weapon and catch him unawares, maybe she stood a chance. Rapier, however, was extremely cautious. She was allowed to put her arms out in front of her but the handcuffs were still on and when they went to the table to eat, he sat well out of reach opposite her. The pistol, with silencer removed, lay there next to his own can of beer, pointing at her.

They ate in silence as Daphne forced herself to consume more than she really wanted. Who knew when the next meal would come. After they were done he gathered up the bones, put them in the box and tossed the whole thing out into the front yard. Then he ordered her across the room to the old couch and forced her to help him drag it nearer to the bathroom door. "Sit," he said then, pointing to the big chair and handcuffed her to it.

Then he went to the counter and brought back the other sack from which he extracted a long length of chain and two padlocks. One end of the chain was tossed over an exposed ceiling beam and locked to it. The other end he tried to wrap around her right ankle.

"You rotten bastard," she said and kicked him in the chest. His eyes went hard and cold as he righted himself and slapped her strongly across the face, making her lip bleed.

"There," he said when it was done. "You can get from the couch to the bathroom and back and you'd better not make too much noise doing it tonight or I might just shoot you anyway." With that he found a blanket, tossed it at her and went into what must have been the only bedroom in the house.

"You'll be sorry for this, you wimp," she shouted after him. "If the General doesn't kill you for it, Kohl will." The only answer she received was the creaking boards of the floor in the adjacent room. Still handcuffed, she picked up the blanket, shook it as best she could, smelled it, decided it wasn't too bad and did her best to arrange it over the frayed material of the sagging couch. Then she laid down and let the tears flow.

TWENTY THREE
The light was flashing on the answering machine

147

when Kohl arrived home from Grey Hawk's in Colorado. A man's voice stated an area code, a phone number and an extension, nothing more. There was no other message. The phone number was an answering service company in Richmond, Virginia. Kohl asked who had rented that particular extension, even though he already knew. "What is your name sir, may I have your name please?" the impatient operator asked him for the second time.

"Just tell that party that I'm home," Kohl said. "I'll be waiting for his call."

"What is your name, sir?" she asked again. Kohl answered by hanging up.

His phone rang at five the next morning while he was still in bed. He reached for the light, turned it on, got up and went down into the kitchen, picked it up and waited. "Do I have the right number," a voice said.

"Yes," Kohl said. Although it had been nearly two years since he had heard that voice, he recognized it immediately. His hands suddenly felt cold and a wave of hatred passed over him.

"You and Mike for the girl," he was told.

"Impossible. I haven't seen nor heard from Mike for more than a year. You ought to know that by now. You've been following me long enough."

There was a period of silence on the line. "You then," Kohl was told. "Be on the eleven fifteen flight out of Phoenix tonight. Someone will meet you at National in the morning."

"What Airline?" Kohl asked, but the line was already dead. Slowly, he put down the receiver. The house was chilly. He shivered, found some clothes and dressed, put the kettle on the stove, began calling airlines, found the one that had an eastbound flight at eleven fifteen but there was no reservation in his name. "Any space left," he asked.

"It's fully booked," he was told after a few moments.

"It's a serious emergency," he said, speaking the truth but ready to lie about it if he had to. His father had a heart attack, his mother was dying of cancer, his sister had been

148

hit by a train. Worse, Daphne was being held captive by a cold blooded scorpion of a man and there was nothing make believe about Daphne. She was a real person, the most important person in his life. If he didn't get off that plane when it landed tomorrow morning, what would happen to her?

"Just a moment," the voice said as he began to worry. Then, "We do have a cancellation. Would an aisle seat be all right?"

"Perfect," he replied, relieved that it was so simple, and made the arrangements. Then he told himself he should go back to bed, get some rest, be prepared for tomorrow. He went outside instead, coffee cup steaming in the pre dawn air. A dim, reddish hint of the new day was becoming visible over the horizon.

He built a fire in the fire pit, piled on wood until it crackled and danced, sat down on the old sycamore log they used for a bench nearby and stared back into the flames. What else could he be doing? he wondered. Surely there must be something. If Grey Hawk wasn't all messed up and were in this situation, what would he be doing? And without Grey Hawk, what was it that he might do himself to help shield Daphne and make sure that everything turned out all right? He sat almost motionless until the fire began to die, then he rose and threw on more wood, went back to the house and returned with the ceremonial pipe Grey Hawk had given him and the elk hide drum he had made for himself. Carefully, he placed them on the ground a safe distance from the heat and sat down before them, his mind full of turmoil and tangled thoughts, feeling very alone, reaching, reaching. The sun was near its zenith before he began to make some sense of it.

Yes, it was true. No matter how hard he tried, he would never be an Indian. Not in this lifetime, anyway. He could play at it, do all the things, maybe even learn to speak Grey Hawk's native tongue, but it wouldn't change anything. He would still be just a white man. Hopefully,

149

however, that was not the point. It couldn't be. They had conducted ceremony together when Grey Hawk had made the van disappear, the same when they tampered with the government's computers. But where had the power itself come from, the power that made it happen. From the rituals, Grey Hawk's prayers, the beat of the drums, the words that were spoken? That was a part of it, to be sure, but which part? In the end they no doubt helped focus and intensify but the deciding factor had to be in the power of mind of the individuals involved. Their combined will. What else could it be? That, and the belief and the knowing that it was possible to begin with.

The important point was that if there was Spirit, if Spirit was the basis of all, then he was as much a part of that spirit as any other man, no matter what his heritage. True enough, but there was still a difference. The redman had been gifted with a tremendous advantage. He had been raised from birth in the ways and traditions of such higher knowledge and he had thousands of years of ritual and close association with nature stored up in his genes while both Kohl's ancestry and his whole life prior to the last few years had been an expression of everything that was totally contrary to such thinking. He could see now that it had been wrong. God, what he had been lied to about by his family, his teachers and society in general. What self limiting things he had convinced himself of, what greater wisdom he had missed. But also, now, looking back, what great change had been wrought upon him. He had tested and proved himself in many ways. But if things became desperate and he had to stand alone without Grey Hawk, would it be enough?

He picked up the ceremonial pipe and filled it with tobacco, then faced the sun. Somehow, although he honored it and respected it, he could not raise it nor find the words to speak. He stood there desperately wanting to pray, ready to plead. Begin, he told himself. Do the pipe ceremony. There is both a humble, appealing beauty about it and a powerful symbolism embedded in it. If nothing else it will help bring you to center. "Grandfather," he said at last, raising the pipe. But he knew it was wrong. Not for Grey Hawk, but for him. If he had learned what he had learned and believed what he believed, it was not the way. Grey Hawk was Grey Hawk, he was Kohl. One could not come to power by emulating the other. The answers were there, at the root of his own identity, not in imitating Grey Hawk, nor anyone else. Where else could they be?

Nowhere else, his inner voice told him. You are yourself. Be yourself. Your power lies within the moment point of that knowledge. Seek that.

Kohl didn't know who he had expected but it wasn't Rapier and he was a bit surprised to see him standing there at the end of the concourse. It told him one thing. Rapier was apparently acting alone. If so, it certainly improved the odds.

Kohl worked his way through the crowd towards his adversary but when he was still some twenty feet away Rapier merely nodded and started towards the parking facility. Rapier had left his rental car on the top deck at the end where there were few others. It was now seven thirty in the morning, Washington time. A cold breeze was blowing in off the Potomac and there was a hint of fall in the air. Kohl zipped up the light jacket he was wearing. When they reached the rental car Rapier was using he indicated to Kohl. "If you don't mind," he said.

Obligingly, Kohl bent over the car with his hands on the roof and his legs spread as Rapier patted him down. Then, thinking he would be taken somewhere, Kohl started towards the passenger side door. "Stop there," he was told when he reached the rear of the car. Rapier's hand went inside his jacket. He removed his weapon, now with silencer reinstalled, and pointed it at Kohl. Then with his free hand he fumbled in his pants pocket and found the car keys. "Open the trunk," he ordered as he tossed them to Kohl.

"You want me to get in there?" he asked. "No way Rapier. Not until I see Daphne and know that's she's safe."

"You're wasting time. Open the damned trunk."

Jesus, Kohl thought. Would he have put her in there? He put the key in the lock, turned it and lifted the lid. "You son-of-a-bitch," he said when he saw what was inside. He reached to help her. Both her hands and feet were tied and there was a gag in her mouth. She moved her head and blinked at the sudden light that rushed into the dark world where she had been all but immobilized for the last three hours. Then she was able to focus on Kohl. She looked into his eyes and began to relax.

Kohl removed the twisted scarf from her mouth. "Are you okay," he asked before he noticed the bruises on her face. She nodded, unable to speak because her mouth was so dry. Finally she managed a weak response. He began untying her hands. She was almost free when another car appeared on the deck. Rapier moved closer, the gun now hidden by the flap of his jacket. "Shut the trunk," he barked at Kohl. Kohl hesitated, eying the approaching vehicle. "Do it!" Rapier said with a hiss.

Kohl hoped it might have been a man but unfortunately it was an older woman in the car. "Hang on," he told Daphne. "It shouldn't be long." Then he shut the trunk and leaned on it, watching Rapier, his anger swarming over him, taking possession. He contemplated rushing him. If only the little bastard were a few feet closer. Dammit!

Although he was tired and off center from lack of sleep, the bruises on Daphne's face had sent a rush of adrenaline into his veins leaving him ready to spring at the slightest opportunity. If only Rapier would just turn his head momentarily and look at the approaching car. The timing would have to be nearly perfect but he might be able to manage it. He was ready to try. But the opportunity never came, the man was much too cautious. He would just have to wait. Once Daphne was safe, however, his chance would come. He was sure of it.

The woman turned into a slot half a dozen spaces away, shut off the engine, reached in the seat beside her, picked up a small briefcase and got out, not once even glancing at them. When she turned the corner of the elevator tower, Rapier indicated his approval and Kohl reopened the trunk. Daphne had untied herself the rest of the way by now and was ready to be helped out but when her feet touched the concrete she nearly fell. The ropes had been too tight. Kohl held her and hugged her to him, turning her slightly so that Rapier couldn't see that he was whispering in her ear. "Go stay with your mother. I called her last night. She doesn't know the whole story but she's expecting you. It's the safest place for now."

"But what are you going to do?"

"Go with him."

"No, Kohl. You can't," she said, backing away slightly so she could see his face.

Looking at the bruise on her cheek he kissed her carefully. "I have to," he said.

"God, no. You can't. He's a maniac. He'll kill you."

"No he won't," Kohl said, trying to reassure her, realizing full well that he might be wrong. Somehow the odds didn't look as good as he had thought they might be earlier. But if she was to be saved, he no longer had a choice. Daphne began to cry. "I love you," Kohl told her and she pulled him tighter again.

"That's enough." Rapier said quickly. "Move apart." Reluctantly they separated. Kohl reached into his pocket and withdrew an airlines envelope but there was no ticket in it, only some cash and a long note. He handed it to her.

"You. Woman!" Rapier said to Daphne. "Walk over to the elevators and wait where I can see you. As soon as I get in the car, you can leave. If you don't wait, I'll shoot him. Is that clear?" Daphne glared at him with hate in her eyes, then looked at Kohl for approval. He nodded and she started to walk away. "Satisfied?" Rapier asked.

Kohl waited until she had reached the tower and said, "Yes."

Daphne stopped and turned around. Kohl was still watching her. What was she supposed to do? Where was Grey Hawk anyway? Or her step father, the bastard? Somebody, anybody? My God! It might be the last time she ever saw Kohl alive. Then she saw Rapier toss a pair of handcuffs to Kohl, saw him put them on, saw Rapier motioning to him with the gun to get into the trunk of the car, saw Kohl comply, saw Rapier slam the trunk shut and get into the car. She turned and began to run, made it around the corner and slammed into Lieutenant Kouslip.

Daphne recovered and stepped back quickly, ready to keep on running but then she looked up and saw his face. She cried out in horror. This man was supposed to be dead. She backed up two more steps and stared at him. Kouslip was as surprised as she was. He had never seen her before but he had been given a detailed description and recognized who she must be almost instantly, in spite of the disheveled way she was dressed and the discoloration of her face. It came as a relief. Part of his assignment had been to find her and see that she was safe. "Miss Layton?" he said eagerly as Daphne jumped back even further.

She eyed him cautiously, looking nervously over her shoulder towards the elevator doors and the staircase, ready to bolt. "You're dead," she said after she caught her breath.

"Hardly. That was my twin brother he killed," he said, looking at her with the hard eyes of a killer bent on vengeance. "I'm Lieutenant Kouslip. I also work for your father."

"My father!" she said with indignation. Dead brother or no dead brother, there was no compassion in her voice. "You mean the General?"

"Yes ma'am."

"The rotten bastard," she said, starting to edge away. "He's not my father. Don't you ever call him that!" But then something made her stop. "What do you want?" she asked.

"I was following your boyfriend. My job was to use him to lead me to Rapier and to you, free you, save your boyfriend and then cut off...a, bring Rapier in so the General can deal with him," Kouslip said as the sound of a car interrupted. He peered around the corner. "Is that him in the blue car?"

Confused, Daphne refused to answer. She didn't trust

him either but the look in her eye was all the answer he needed. He reached for the two way radio on his belt and spoke urgently. "He's on his way down. Blue Oldsmobile, new. Only one person in the car. Don't lose him. I'll follow." Then he looked back at Daphne. "I have to go. The General will have my head if he gets away. Are you all right? Do you need some help?" he asked, already turning away.

"I'm okay," she said, unwilling to admit anything to him.

"Good," Kouslip said and headed toward the elevator. Then he stopped in afterthought. "What happened to your friend? I didn't see him in the car."

Suddenly uncertain, worried about Kohl, Daphne hesitated. "He's locked in the trunk," she finally said, hoping to God it was the right thing to do.

At last the long, bumpy ride was over. The car had finally stopped and Kohl was ready. It was now or never. He had to take Rapier when he was getting out of the trunk. He heard the car door open, felt the slight movement of the vehicle with the change in weight, again heard the door being slammed shut. He tensed and waited but there was nothing.

Finally, after some long minutes there was another sound, a very large sound of someone pounding on the trunk lid of the car with a hammer. Then, with a last blow, something punctured the metal and he could make out a long thin rod protruding inward. It was the shaft of a screwdriver. Rapier had knocked a hole in the trunk. What for? A breathing hole? Was he just going to leave him in there? He had already explored the latch mechanism with his hands in the dark but it was covered in such a way that he couldn't release it. The trunk compartment was also too shallow to allow him full use of his legs in trying to force it open. Christ, maybe this was to be his coffin, Kohl thought with fading hope. He grabbed for the screwdriver and hung on but it was pulled from his grasp and the hole went dark. Next he heard a hissing sound and a strange smell. A funny, hospital kind of smell.

When he regained consciousness, Kohl found himself outdoors, sitting on the grass and leaves, propped up against a gnarled old tree. He blinked, groaned and tried to move. His feet were handcuffed together, his hands were handcuffed behind him and there was a long chain around him under his armpits holding him to the tree. Rapier was kneeling, resting on his haunches some four or five feet away smoking a cigarette. Oh shit, Kohl said silently.

Rapier apparently had been staring at him for some time. When he saw Kohl try to move, he smirked evilly, dropped the cigarette to the ground and stood up. Then he laughed insanely and came closer.

"Now perhaps you can tell me where your friend Mike is," he said somewhat gleefully. "If you want to get out of here alive, that is."

"That's a joke, you little smuck ass. You'll never let me out of here alive and you know it."

"Goddamn you. You'll tell me one way or the other," Rapier said. Removing the heavy pistol from his belt he hit Kohl across the face with the barrel. "All right, I can shoot you or beat you to death. What's it going to be?"

"You decide," Kohl said, sneering back. It was all Rapier needed. Something snapped inside. He reacted by shooting Kohl in the foot, right through the ankle, tearing half of it away.

"Where is he?" Rapier screamed. "Where is he, damn you. I hate you, you bastards," he went on, raving away at Kohl, pouring out his guts and the foul smell of his misguided soul into the surrounding air, blaming Kohl and Mike for all the misfortune he had ever suffered in the whole of his sick and tainted life, talking in circles, repeating himself, waving his arms, contorting his face, blubbering, almost slobbering on himself as Kohl lay helplessly before him, his eyes closed in excruciating pain, bleeding to death.

Finally, Rapier stopped. Then he bent down and stared at Kohl with glazed eyes, not comprehending. It looked as though the man had gone to sleep. How dare he do that? He was supposed to be listening to him, damn him to hell, anyway. How could he do that? It wasn't fair. It wasn't fair at all. Then, with that last thought, he raised the pistol to Kohl's forehead and pulled the trigger.

TWENTY FOUR

"It's Lieutenant Kouslip," the receptionist said. "Line one."

The General leaned forward in his chair, pushed the lighted button and asked, "Have you found him yet?"

"We have him but I don't think you want him."

"I want him."

"Sorry to be so obtuse, sir, but I don't really think I should bring him in."

"Why not? What's wrong?"

"He went in his pants."

"What?"

"He went in his pants, General. Honest to god."

"What the hell are you talking about, Kouslip? Don't play games with me. That's an order!"

"I'm not, sir. It's Rapier. He gone stark raving bonkers. We found him sitting on the ground in front of this tree with a chain wrapped around it. He had his gun up to his head trying to kill himself but it was out of ammunition and he just sat there crying, pulling the trigger over and over. Now he's totally incoherent and he stinks like all hell, General. Nobody wants to get near to him and we certainly don't want him riding in one of the cars."

"What the devil happened? Where's Kohl? Wasn't he supposed to be locked in the trunk of Rapier's car? Isn't that what you said when you called in last?"

"Yes Sir, that's what the girl said but we looked. He probably was in there but it's empty now. We checked the house, the old shack out behind and scoured the woods, looked up in the trees, in the bushes, everywhere. There isn't a trace. Nothing except that deranged idiot, two pairs of handcuffs on the ground, the chain around the tree and a large bloodstain on the ground near it."

"And Rapier's vehicle is still there?"

"Yes sir."

"Did you see any other cars on the road?"

"Nothing. Not a soul for miles. This place is really no-wheres-ville."

"How could it have happened?"

"I don't know, General. We came on in the moment we heard the first shot."

"Hmmm."

"What do you want us to do?"

"I'm thinking."

"Yes sir."

"Kouslip."

"Yes sir."

"Find a rope or use that chain. Whatever. Drag that treasonous son-of-a-bitch out into the woods a mile or so and leave him there. I understand there are bears in that part of the mountains. If they can get past the smell, maybe they can have him for lunch."

"An excellent idea, sir."

TWENTY FIVE

Half hidden by a pile of bubbles, Daphne laid back in the oversized tub in her mother's bathroom and closed her eyes. Her mother brought in a cup of hot tea and placed it on the tile ledge next to her then pulled up the velvet covered vanity stool. She took the thick, soft washcloth and gently bathed her daughter's face. Daphne sighed, opened her eyes and found the teacup. Then she leaned back again and began to talk.

Daphne talked for more than an hour, pouring out her life and her soul and every last detail of what had happened to them in the last couple of months as her mother listened to each and every word, fighting back her own burgeoning emotion and tears. Daphne's words filled her with anger, remorse and pain. Her own pain and the pain that came from witnessing her daughter's pain, reaching her in a way that nothing had ever reached her before. Finally, when Daphne was drained and could not go on, her mother helped her out of the tub, dried her carefully with the heavy towel and tucked her into her oversized bed. Within seconds, Daphne was fast asleep.

Her mother quietly pulled the bedroom door shut behind her, went down the hall and into the study. She picked up the phone and dialed a number, one that she had rarely ever used. "Let me speak to the General" she said in a stern voice when it was answered. "His wife," she stated when asked who it was. "Put me through," she added. "It's important."

"Ann?" the General questioned with a note of consternation in his voice. "What's the meaning of this? Why are you calling me here, don't you know how busy I am?"

"No Bart, I don't. How would I? And don't hang up on me either you arrogant, self centered, power hungry SOB. Don't lie to me either, not now and never again."

"Ann, Ann. What is going on? What in hell's name are you so upset about?"

"Where is Kohl, Daphne's young man? What have you and your little army of Nazis done with him?"

There was a very long silence on the line. "Listen to me Bart," she continued. "I may have shut my eyes and turned my head all these years to things I didn't want to know or to hear or to believe but now I know that I saw them and heard them and I have taken care to put together a little insurance policy. Do we understand each other?"

As yet she hadn't really done anything to protect herself, however. That part of it was a bluff but it soon wouldn't be. It would be real before the General would have time to move on her, she would see to that.

"Well," said the General. "What brought this on?"

"How would you like me to file a complaint for kidnapping?"

"I didn't kidnap her. This man Rapier did. All I tried to do was to help. It's not my fault he went crazy."

"Maybe we should let the authorities decide."

"I see. Yes. Well, we don't know where he is. Somehow, he has disappeared."

"What do you mean, disappeared? I thought your men

159

were following him?"

"They were, and they were right behind him. They heard shots and moved in immediately. It took ten or fifteen seconds at the most and they were there, but he wasn't. Just this bast...man, Rapier."

"Well where did he go? Did you look around? Maybe he crawled out a window and caught a cab or something."

"You don't understand. It's an isolated place out in the Virginia mountains. Probably the same place he took Daphne."

"What are you going to do about it? Did you call the authorities?"

"Ahh...yes," he lied. "But I don't think it will do any good. I think those drum pounding damned Indians were smoking loco weed in their pipes again and sent him off into one of those other realities they seem to have a key to. I'd bet my knickers on it."

Daphne's mother hadn't considered that possibility, mostly because she didn't think it was one. When Daphne had told her about Costa Rica and Kohl's van she attributed it to her daughter's somewhat vivid imagination. Of course the part about the IRS had bothered her. By now everyone recognized that something very mysterious and unexplainable had happened there, all right. Was it possible that Daphne really was involved? How fascinating. With that thought she summed up her conversation with the man who was, technically, still her husband. But not for long. "And by the way," she said before hanging up. "I'm getting a divorce."

TWENTY SIX

That was curious. The shadows of sunlight through the trees told him that it had to be late afternoon. How did it get to be late afternoon, Kohl wondered. It should still be morning. Or maybe not. He had certainly worked up an appetite over something. What had happened? He turned his head back and forth, lifted his arms, moved his legs. Everything felt like it was functioning normally. Then he looked at his right foot. What was wrong with his shoe? It had a big hole blown through it.

Suddenly, the morning's events came rushing back. He had been sitting under this very same old giant of a tree, chained to it in fact, with both his hands and his feet cuffed. But where were those restraints now? Even the chain was gone. He made a special effort to move his foot. There was no pain. He took off his tattered shoe and blood stained sock and looked closely. There wasn't the slightest break in the skin, it looked and felt just as intact as it had been that morning when he had walked off the airplane. There was something else, too. If his recollection of the morning's event were correct, his brains ought to be spattered all over the tree, but, obviously they weren't or he wouldn't be sitting there. Still, he felt the need to check. Amazing! That part of his anatomy was just as sound as the rest of him. It was far too good to be true.

Well, maybe that was it. Maybe he was really dead, still imagining himself to be in his body as it was before. That had to be it, didn't it? But then, if he were dead, how come he felt so hungry? It didn't make any sense. He got to his feet and felt the tree. It was solid enough, as was the ground he had been sitting on. Think, Kohl think! Go back to the moment that should have killed you. Rapier flipped out. First he shot you in the foot, the pain was almost unbearable. But then what happened? he asked himself, trying to penetrate the viscous, spidery, opaque veil that had been drawn over the event. He continued to work at it, trying to part the screen. Finally, there was a slight dawning.

You know, don't you? he said to himself. It was something you started to become aware of sitting up on that rocky, canyon ledge in the burning sun all those many days without food over a year ago. The contents of the vision. The white snake that fell from the sky. *"I am the belated messenger from other realms,"* that's what it said. *"It is on yon side of self where promise and fulfillment both begin and where true and abiding destiny awaits. THE KEY RESIDES IN YOUR OWN MIND, seek and prepare, it will show itself."*

161

That was it, wasn't it? That and the voice that had spoken to him by the fire before he came to get Daphne. It was shutting out the world that had made it happen, turning inward, far inward, all those many extra steps beyond the mystical mood of ordinary meditation. Pierce the veil, find yon side of self, like in the vision. Grey Hawk had alluded to it on occasion, too. Thus then, in his darkest hour, his moment of deepest need, there it was. He had simply slipped sideways through an invisible doorway and disappeared out of harms way, only to reappear again when it was safe to do so, all intact. Spirit, the all pervading, unifying force, the underlying common denominator of the physical universe, the oneness of mind and matter had saved him. He had saved himself.

However, regardless of what had happened to him in that one crucial instant, and for whatever reason, it was obviously not something that could be turned on and off at will and with ease. The everyday world of the body still had its own set of rules. He needed food and drink. Some sleep would be nice, too.

The rotting porch of the house felt like it would collapse at any moment but Kohl made his way across it and pulled open the sagging front door. There was no food inside that he could find but a half empty plastic bottle of mineral water sat on the table. It looked safe enough to drink. Then, in the last light of the day, he explored the remainder of the abandoned dwelling, deciding that this must have been the same place where Daphne had been held. Had she been there she would have laughed at him for, just like her, he picked up the blanket lying on the old couch and smelled it, concluding that it might be sanitary enough to spend the night on. But then his thoughts turned back to Rapier.

If Kohl had believed in the devil then surely he would have had to say that Rapier was a man who had become possessed. If there was a force of evil loose in the world, then Rapier was the real life manifestation of it. Where was he now, where had he gone? And what if the madman came back? Kohl had been lucky this time but if he stayed here and fell asleep, it might really be all over. Besides, since Kohl had disappeared from right before his eyes, crazed as Rapier was and as frustrated as he must feel now, he might just go after Daphne again. Kohl needed to find his way back to civilization, wherever that was.

Two and a half hours by car was a hell of a ways on foot. If he was lucky he might find a ride once he got back on the highway. However, the bumpy last leg of the journey had been at least half an hour long and Rapier hadn't slowed down very much in driving it. Kohl's body had attested to that. So how far was the highway? Fifteen to twenty miles, perhaps. It was going to be a long, weary night. He had best get started.

TWENTY SEVEN

"Look at this little item," Inspector Spinnet said to his boss one morning as he was passing his superior's office on the way to the coffee machine.

"What is it?" Branch Head Digand Pry asked as he took the computer print out that had been handed to him. "Well, well, well," he said with satisfaction as he read the report. "At last. Justice prevails."

A body had been found in the hills of Virginia. Identity-John Paul Rapier. Cause of death-unknown, autopsy pending.

Digand smiled. The over bearing, arrogant, little smart ass was no more. Digand was so pleased that he got up from behind his desk and accompanied Spinnet down the hall where he paid for his assistant's coffee. Then the bigger picture occurred to him. What about that case they had been assigned some months back? The one regarding the IRS that he had delegated to Spinnet. Not that he had seriously expected any progress. The whole idea that Kohl and a bunch of Indians could have been responsible for totally disrupting the IRS computer system was so farcical that he had completely dismissed it long ago. Still, the bulletin had raised the question and he was forced to ask. "Nothing conclusive," Spinnet replied. "Just what's been in my weekly status reports."

"Yes, of course," Pry said, even though he didn't. Darn that dratted sixteenth Masonic degree he had been working on for so long, anyway. He had been spending far too many of his spare moments trying to memorize those reams and reams of ritualistic mumbo jumbo that were necessary to elevate himself in the grand order of his societal brotherhood. So many, in fact, that he hadn't had time to even keep abreast of his employee's status reports, let alone remember what they might have said. Darn that degree, anyway. He might just get himself demoted before he achieved his goal if he wasn't careful. Regardless of how hard he tried, however, it all ended in confusion because he kept getting grand wizards, grand wizers, grand litany and grand aggrandizement all mixed up with grand juries, grand larcenies, grand aggravation, graduated aggrievement and other legalese terminology. It had to be some kind of legerdemain his mind was playing on him.

Not only was it detracting from his professional performance at the office but his wife was also beginning to make innuendos about his performance in the boudoir. At the dinner table, no less, right in front of the boys. It was bad enough that the oldest one was already hiding Playboy magazines under his mattress even though he had yet to make it into the seventh grade. Good grief! What was the modern world coming to? Darn, darn, darn. Now he would have to go back and reread three months worth of Spinnet's status reports all over again because he couldn't remember even half of an iota of what, if anything, they had said. Or if in fact, he had really read them at all.

"Darn," he said, out loud this time and put two more quarters in the coffee machine. This cup was for himself. If he had to read that stuff, he would need it.

Spinnet didn't ask what the, "darn," was all about because his boss was always saying, darn, and it got a little tiring after while. Dammit, if only he would say, damn, once in a while. Or maybe even, goddamn. Now that would really be refreshing. But, true to form, predictable Pry didn't. Instead he took a sip of his coffee, made a face and headed back to his office wondering where he had last seen the pile of reports that Spinnet used to justify his paycheck with.

Well, that was it, wasn't it? Just as he had expected, Pry said an hour later. Nothing significant, more time and taxpayer's money down the tube. Darn! But then he took the additional time to run it through his mind once more, just in case. Like a good trooper, Spinnet had not only made the effort to drive the two hours and eighteen minutes up the Interstate to Sedona to spy on Kohl, he had also followed him clear on up into the Colorado mountains. He would have also gotten on the plane with Kohl and his girl friend when they went to Costa Rica under some alias. But, at the time, however, he had been reluctant to pull rank and bump someone off the, full to capacity, airplane without his boss's approval, and his boss hadn't been available that day.

Pry checked the date against his appointment calendar. Hmmm. So much for that. Better not bring that one up, but, what the heck was in Costa Rica? He confirmed the date that the IRS computers had gone blitzen. It didn't correlate. Then he looked at the date Spinnet had put down as having been the time when he had listened to all that weird drum pounding and pipe smoking going on in Sedona. Curiously, that date did match. Hmmm, again.

Then his left armpit began to itch. Now that was a powerful sign. When his left armpit began to itch that was a strong indication he was onto something important. Now if his right eyebrow would only begin to twitch, then he would know he was on the right track. It did. By golly, that darned Kohl was involved after all, wasn't he? But how had the fowl deed actually been accomplished? That was the big puzzler.

No doubt the ceremony had been a diversion of some sort while the real goings on had been instituted. Quite possibly by remote control from some super high powered energy beam or something like that infrared laser Kohl

165

was supposed to have invented, only one that emitted anti-gigabyte wavelengths in the computer frequency domain or something of that sort. Maybe they had even re-invented the Philadelphia experiment which had made a battleship almost disappear way back in the time of the second world war and had made some time, phase-sync refinements on it, or whatever.

Pry wasn't exactly sure of all the terminology but it didn't matter for now. He could visualize it and that was what was important. Maybe they had beamed it up to a synchronous satellite or maybe even bounced it off of one of those large abandoned Russian missile boosters still floating around up there. The actual ground base was probably down in Mexico or Belize or maybe on Santa Catalina island.

Pry reached for the intercom. "Get Spinnet a ticket on the first flight to Costa Rica," he instructed his secretary. "And send Parsons in here."

"Parsons is in Pasadena, sir."

"What's he doing there, for heaven's sake?"

"You said he could take his annual leave, sir. He's on vacation."

"Ah, yes. Well, cancel it. And then get the Washington office. See if the Chief might have time to run over to the White House and ask the President a couple of questions about a meeting he had a few months back with a Mr. Rapier."

"Is it important, sir? You know how the Chief is about such requests. He thinks they are bothersome."

"Darn it, Lois. This is a priority matter. I'm the boss around here now, remember?"

TWENTY EIGHT

It had once been a drafty old blimp hanger at Wright Patterson Air Force Base in Ohio. Now it was the location of a most unusual laboratory, one where Albeit Keener the third, Project Manager on the "Fog Bank" program sat and looked at the wall. Fog Bank was the code name for a hastily put together, Top Secret endeavor into the dark and

166

mysterious world of psychic phenomenon which had been quite appropriately placed in his dedicated hands.

Yesterday Keener had spent five hours staring at the west wall, three hours completing his notes, two hours reviewing the input of his staff and one hour attending to his administrative duties. And, if today was normal, it would, with one minor exception, be a repeat of yesterday. The exception was that today he was staring at the south wall.

Dimensionally, the room was in the form of a precise cube. The ceiling had been painted to represent the night sky with a full bevy of stars beaming down, all back lit with tiny bulbs that glimmered when the rest of the lights were turned out. The floor of the room, in perfect harmony, had become a green meadow with grasses and flowers and even had little ants and bugs painted on it. Unexpectedly, however, the walls were juxtaposed in a state of jarring, total disparity. Instead of being nature scenes that one could mentally look out upon or even scenes of man made structures such as views of a city, they were brightly painted, extremely complex, geometrically contrived mandalas that Keener, himself, had personally designed. With the help of a mildly depraved old girlfriend, that was, one who had provided him with many constructive comments during the layout phases. Comments that were based upon some of the more illuminating things she had gained from her several brave trips into LSD land, a place where she claimed to have personally reached out and touched the universe itself, in all its grandeur, with her very own fingertips.

Regardless, had the mandalas had their origins in the chewing of peyote buttons instead, or from pages torn from comic books, it wouldn't have made half a tantra of difference to Albeit. Albeit loved mandalas right from the very first time he had ever seen one way back in his college days. It didn't matter that it had been hastily hand painted on the back of a dirty T shirt worn by a flaked out hippie pill popper laying face down in the gutter on Powell Street back in San Francisco some twenty years ago. It had still sent his mind soaring. And, in the end, mandalas had become the subject matter for his Master's Thesis. Ultimately he even credited it with leading him into his present pioneering career where he was trying to prove that the human brain is more than just a protoplasmic blob of interconnected electrochemical impulse transceivers. That instead of that, it transcends that, and by a whopping great big bit. In other words, a whole lot, and mandalas were the key, he was sure of it.

When people asked Keener about mandalas he tried to remind them that mandalas had been passed down through centuries and ancient centuries inside the old occultist, secret societies. They were devices reported to have been portals into the back door of the mind. Portals that had allowed the high priests and holders of the arcane wisdom to utilize it and pass it on to new initiates. Not verbally, of course, with spoken or written words all forced to find their place into the tedious, linear fashion of modern man's sentences, but conceptually, where whole worlds of ideas and ideations are caused to permeate into the mind where they burst complete into the greater consciousness and give one the "knowing." And when that happened it opened up the flood gates to even greater possibilities and grander powers.

It was true. Keener really believed it was true. And now, lucky man that he was, he might have just been handed the funding, the staff and the facilities to prove it, to show scientifically that with proper technique, and, through the exclusive use of mental force alone, one can make a material object disappear. His first task was to determine, categorize and define that technique in a manner sufficiently adequate to allow the training and deployment of suitable personnel for its use in adverse field situations. Then, once that has been accomplished and fully documented, he was to find out how to make those things reappear again elsewhere, at some pre selected site. Do that, Albeit Keener the third, he told himself, and your place in history would be forever assured.

Appropriately enough, the south wall had been dubbed the purple wall for although it had spots of white and tiny bursts of yellow in it, it was predominately purple in color. Now five hours was a long time to have to sit and stare at a wall with purple designs on it but Keener didn't mind, for he had the mind for it. He had also done it before and he would, no doubt, be doing it again. The trick wasn't in doing that, however. The trick was while doing that to be concentrating with all the intensity and power that the mind could bring to bear on the empty noodle soup can that sat out of sight behind him on a small, cleverly designed pedestal and attempt to make it disappear.

The pedestal had been made from a converted digital electronic postal scale rigged so that, if the object should indeed disappear, the circuitry would notice the weight change automatically and set off a beeper inside the room. This way the operator, or the conjurer as the case might be, could let his eyes loose themselves in the mandala while he focused his higher consciousness on making the can disappear without ever having to turn around to see if he had achieved success, thus breaking concentration and spoiling the experiment.

Although Albeit had a civilian staff of five, as well as a genuine private to drive the military jeep that had been issued to him, not a one of them had ever been allowed to set foot inside the lab once the mandalas had been put in place. It wouldn't have worked. PhD's or not, they were all pristine products of occidentalism and therefore not to be trusted with such delicate departures from the mundane. He had wanted to hire two fakirs, an aboriginal medicine man, a voodoo witch doctor and an old Zuni named Morice instead but the secret Senate committee that provided the funding for the project threatened to fire him if he did so, so he was forced to concede and accept the more conventional graduates of American universities.

Therefore, instead of letting them waste his time by having them participate directly in the experiment, he made research assistants out of them and sent them off.

They were to explore libraries and laboratories, back alleys and bailiwicks, elsewhere and everywhere to seek out and bring back supporting evidence of his theories. In the process they were to eventually make their way to Russia, Zurich, Tibet, the Australian outback, the Brazilian jungle and the back streets of Bombay to see what atavistic wonders they could come up with and funnel into their lap top computers.

In all he estimated they would be gone for at least a year, which should give him more than adequate time to accomplish his mission. After all, in many respects he had a good head start. As a young boy he had accompanied his Uncle Exide, who sold car batteries, to India and had seen a toothless, shriveled up, bare chested old man with his ribs sticking out put a seed in a pot full of dirt and make the plant shoot up to a full grown, flowering shrub right there in front of his eyes.

Some years later he had also witnessed the arrival of a Tibetan monk who had walked barefoot twenty miles through foot deep snow in bitter cold with nothing on but a thin, moth eaten robe. There had been other happenings, too, but the one thing that had always stuck in his mind was the story told by an old Navajo elder wearing a sheepskin. A historical event which was, for the most, later confirmed by modern archeologists.

The inhabitants of such places as Chaco Canyon, Mesa Verde, Canyon de Chelly and many other sites in the American southwest had all vanished around twelve hundred AD. For the record, many theorists had postulated periods of long drought or other natural changes as being responsible for their disappearance and it was this notion that had made its way into the predominate literature of the day. The over riding fact of the matter, however, remains that the population didn't gradually dwindle out over some long period of years and slowly fade away. Instead, it was as though everyone literally got up from the dinner table one day and disappeared off the face of the earth. A supposition which had indeed been verified by later unbiased looks at the evidence.

When asked what stories had been passed down and how the Indians accounted for this, the Navajo elder said that the ancient ones had all decided to move into a different realm because they were under threat from the star people. Well, star people or no star people, the Anasazi had certainly disappeared as if in a flash. It was another fascinating story that added credibility to Albeit's belief. If old men could make plants grow and walk barefooted through the snow and if whole tribes of Indians could take themselves off into another world somewhere, well then Albeit Keener damned well ought to be able to make a simple little second hand soup can disappear, even if he was the son of a Wall Street stock broker.

On the other hand, if things didn't work out here in the Mandala Room, maybe they could find the culprits in the IRS scandal, lock them in a screen room, lift off the tops of their skulls, wire up their brains and find out what was going on first hand. Once they had recorded the basics on magnetic tape maybe they could develop a brain wave synthesizer, interface it with a computer and do all kinds of things. Wouldn't that be something?

TWENTY NINE

"Either you flush those damned things or leave the premises," Judge Julius J. Hapgood said to the two men sitting across the heavy wooden conference table from him. "Now," he warned in his deep voice.

Judge Hapgood was a big man with a rough face and gave the impression he might have just stepped inside from splitting rails for a log fence he was putting up around the Supreme Court Building all by himself.

Senators Blubluster and Filcher almost dropped the stogies they had lit up when Hapgood had gone down the hall to get something from his office. Blubluster put down his ball-point pen and removed the foul smelling cylinder of rolled up plant leaves from his mouth. He brushed the cigar ashes off his yellow legal pad and stammered, "But Judge, this tobacco was grown and harvested in the hallowed land of my very own constituents. The least I can do is to smoke it."

"Not here, you won't," the Judge said and swore. Why in the name of justice had he agreed to a meeting with these two half wits in the first place, he wondered. It certainly wasn't out of loyalty to the administration because he had been appointed to the highest and most august court in the land three presidents back. Nor was it done as something of a personal favor to the present chief executive. Not at all. He believed that the country was headed for real trouble with this smug ass, visionless twerp, as he called him. Better pray to god a real crisis never came along or this slick, grinning, womanizing fool would lead everyone off the edge of the world. No, Judge Hapgood had done it with great reluctance and when he finally conceded it was more out of a genuine sense of duty than anything else. Not so much for his country but for the human race in general, for that and that alone had been the criterion he had weighed every judicial decision against that he had ever made.

So here he was, sharing his private conference room with these gross misrepresentatives of the people who personified everything that was ever wrong with the system, forced to listen to the most ludicrous concept he had ever heard in his life being bandied about. A special Senate subcommittee had been appointed at the President's insistence to prepare a legislative package that would make the practice of conjuring a federal offense, and, if government property was involved, one punishable by life imprisonment. Judge Hapgood had already spoken his mind about it on several occasions but the glorious leader of the people had insisted anyway. Now he wanted the judge to give the committee a hearing and an opinion as to how such farfetched gobbledygook might be constructed so as to pass some test of constitutionality, should it ever come to that.

As insane as it was, it had still been a barely tolerable situation up until then. For three and a half days he had listened to them as they wrote and rewrote indecipherable requiems of intertwining circumlocution that would ultimately be offered up as self evident truths instead of the sandiverous scum it really was. Bah! Enough! the Judge finally decided. Chewing tobacco was one thing. Smoking it was another. Now they were stinking up the precious air of his room with something that smelled more like horse dung than anything else, the stench that had blown the Judge's cool. Wisely enough, the senators looked around for an ashtray. There were none to be found.

"Out the window," the judge said and they got up to oblige him. "Leave it open," he instructed. When they regained their seats, he scowled heavily.

"Sorry, your honor," they said, avoiding the flinty look in his eyes. "We won't do it again."

"Damned right you won't," the judge said. "Because the party is over."

They looked at him wide eyed. "What do you mean, the party is over?" Senator Filcher asked.

"What's the point?" the judge stated.

"The point of what?"

"This meeting. It's pointless."

"How can you say such a thing?"

"Well," the judge said. "Let's just suppose that you do write this bill and that by some weird quirk of fate you somehow get it through both the Senate and the House and the President is stupid enough to sign it. What then? The police will love it, of course. They will be able to use it as an excuse to lock up everyone who has even as much as looked cross eyed at them. Okay...but what does the prosecution do? How do you tie the alleged criminal to the crime, where is the smoking gun and the bullet with rifling marks on it, so to speak? Where is the hard evidence, the physical cause and effect? How do you prove such a thing beyond a reasonable doubt? Don't you see what you're trying to do? Witches and witch hunts. Such a piece of legislation will take us back to the middle ages."

"Jesus, Judge. You're so naive sometimes. Where the hell do you think we are now what with ten year old kids shooting each other dead on almost every damned street corner of the whole damned country?" Senator Blubluster put forth.

"And how do you suppose we got there?" the judge answered.

"Well..." came the start of an answer but, for lack of inspiration, the senator was unable to finish. He could only sit and stare back at the judge.

"How did we get there, Judge?" Filcher finally asked, not wanting to miss anything.

The judge studied the two of them. Would it be worth the trouble to try and explain, he wondered. Probably not, but there was always a small chance that someday, someone would hear him. "Take a good look at yourselves, gentlemen," he said.

"Now wait a minute, Judge. What the hell is that supposed to mean?" Blubluster wanted to know. He had come in good faith and certainly didn't want to be talked to in that kind of a tone.

"Nothing," the judge said, having decided he was going to pass after all. Maybe what Thomas Jefferson had said more than two hundred years ago was still true. People weren't ready for self government, then or now and one look across the table at what the present government was all about sort of proved that. Maybe that was the real bottom line. It didn't matter how many laws men wrote or how well crafted they were. There could be a stack of them from the earth to the moon, but as long as men continued to embrace their purely materialist views of the world and looked to the law books for their answers, the laws weren't worth the paper they were written on. Materialism had taken the place of god and man's laws had taken the place of god's laws. Not only did honor and common decency no longer play a part in the everyday scheme of things, they made it almost impossible to survive if they were taken too seriously.

When human actions ceased to be based in human kindness and decency, then laws became necessary. And if man's intent is not honorable then he is always seeking out the inherent deficiencies in the law and looking for ways to circumvent them. As a consequence, the body of man-

174

made law must forever be amended and added to in a never ending attempt to close loophole after loophole because, without recognition of higher law, almost anything is permissible. Criminals always find the guns the honest man is forced to give up. Laws don't make for more freedom, but less, and ultimately serve to pull the good down to the level of the bad. The criminal doesn't care about the law. If he wants something badly enough, he finds a way to take it anyway. And, as crime rates rise the system gets so clogged that the chances of getting caught become less and less. Without a higher authority man answers only to his own lust and greed to the point where there is everything to gain and little to lose, and that was the way it was as far as the judge was concerned, and he lived accordingly.

In many such respects the judge thought that the business of formulating man made law was analogous to the pre-Copernican concept which placed the earth at the center of the solar system instead of the sun. Attempts to describe the movements of the sun and the other companion planets with respect to the earth became equally as ludicrous as modern law because the mathematics had to encompass perturbation upon successive perturbation to even approximate the orbital reality of all the respective planetary movements. Eventually, the calculations became totally unmanageable, just as modern society had.

Finally, when man acknowledged that perhaps he wasn't so supreme and that he wasn't at the center of all existence, then, in the scientific sense, things suddenly became deceptively simple and far more beautiful. Unfortunately, while man was at last able to assimilate a concept of celestial mechanics which placed him far out on the edge of things rather than in the privileged center, he still lagged tragically behind in the realm of morality and social justice, and that is what made the judge's job particularly difficult. So long as modern man still thinks he is at the center of the universe and therefore only answerable to himself, life will become progressively more complex, complicated and precarious as things proceed to change for the worse. On the other hand, if man would but allow himself to see beyond himself to the bigger truth of things, then life would suddenly become intelligible and beautiful again.

So what the hell, the judge thought. He had no way of controlling such people as these. About all he could do anymore was to sit on his judicial bench and do his best to try and filter out the worst of the small portion of questionable legislation that ever made its way up to the higher court. He summed it all up with a final comment. "I think that's about it. My docket is full. I can't help you anymore."

"All right," Filcher said in a perturbed way for he was more than a little put out about the whole thing. "But we are going to do this bill with or without your help and between us and the President we have enough strings we can pull to get it passed."

"And, quite frankly, we don't care if it stands up in court or not," added Blubluster.

"So, now we have it don't we?" the judge said. "You don't care. You just need a good excuse to lock someone up and keep them out circulation for a while. Maybe just long enough to have some unexpected tragedy happen to them. Is that the picture?"

The two senators simply shrugged.

"Well," the judge said. "Just remember. It's not a done deal yet so just be careful. If this is all being done for the reason I think it is, you might just find that a lot more will have disappeared than just those IRS files before you get your way."

"You mean to tell us you approve of what's happened?"

"Damned right," the judge said. "I never thought the income tax was constitutional to begin with but the issue has never been presented to the court in my time on the bench or I'd do my best to throw it out. In the meantime I think what's happened is hilarious and long over due and if I knew who these people were and how to do such things I

176

think I would be out there helping them myself."

THIRTY

The General had decided that he didn't dare kidnap anyone else. If he did Kohl had promised him that no, he wouldn't make his balls disappear, he would give him Alzheimer's disease instead. How degrading. In his opinion, that would be worse than being dead. If he kept forgetting who he was and had to wear diapers to stay dry, what good would everything be that he had worked so hard for? There would be nothing he could recall to brag about. And, much, much more serious, he wouldn't be able to remember who his enemies were. But what were the alternatives? He had seen the laser, he had touched it, and if he couldn't have that one he wanted one just like it. And as for someone having the power to make it disappear, the thought of that was even more delicious than his recollection of the night he had lured that long legged Las Vegas stripper with the bouncing melons up to his hotel room.

In an effort to see if he could at least make part of his dream come true he had solicited nine different high tech companies to work up quotes to build him his own laser. Unfortunately, so far four had flatly said it was impossible. One said it would take them at least four years and cost more than three million dollars without any guarantees that it would work and the remaining ones had asked for more time to study the feasibility of his request. As for the rest of it, he set upon it with equal determination. First, he hired a television camera crew and sent them off to survival school so they could hopefully hide in the woods long enough to film an entire ceremony without getting caught. Second, he sent one of his people out to penetrate the laboratory of one Albeit Keener who was supposed to be doing government research in that area and last, he had headed west.

So far he had talked to a Cherokee, a Chippewa, a Winnebago, three different Sioux, a Zuni, an Apache and a

177

Pagoda but thus far all he had been told was, hah, hah-hah and hah-hah-hah. Such a response should not have been considered unusual, however. What else could a pushy gringo expect? All he had offered them was money. Anyone who didn't have any more savvy than that didn't deserve to be told much of anything except which direction was the quickest way off the reservation. But to hell with that, Bart stated. He hadn't been kicked out of the US Army for nothing. There were at least four dozen other tribes still out there, scattered around the country. Sooner or later he would find the man he was looking for and when he did he would settle things with all concerned. Kohl, his step daughter and his, soon to be, ex-wife. There was retribution due and by Henry and by George, he would have it, damn them.

Screw it, Spinnet told himself. Tomorrow he was going back to the states and try to catch up with Parsons. He had been down here in Costa Rica for nearly a week now and all he had learned was the name of the bartender in this thatched roof shack of a place where he came to eat and have a little snort before going to bed. Or at least he thought he knew the bartender's name. It was hard to tell. The bartender was from Norway and spoke Spanish with a Norwegian accent, but no English. He stopped in front of Spinnet and motioned to his glass. Spinnet nodded. While he was waiting for his refill, two men came in dressed in camouflage fatigues. Jesus, Spinnet said to himself. Look at that one. He thinks he's Arnold what's his name? God, what a big mouth, what a jerk.

His drink came. He took a sip. What's wrong with that fool, anyway, he began to wonder after a while. He keeps staring at me. The bartender sat four bottles of beer in front of the two men. Arnold picked one of his up, looked at Spinnet and raised his glass in a toast. Spinnet grumbled to himself and nodded in recognition. Twenty minutes went by. Spinnet had finished his drink and was about to head back to his hotel. He was just getting up from his bar stool when Arnold put his hand on his shoulder.

178

"You sure look awfully familiar," he said.

Good grief, Spinnet thought. Is this weirdo trying to pick me up, or what? He shook his head in vehement denial.

"No, seriously," Arnold said. "I know I know you."

"Couldn't be," Spinnet assured him and tried to leave.

"My name is Arnold Kouslip," the man said.

Jesus, Spinnet thought. His name really is Arnold. And he sounded straight enough. He took another look. A picture of an overgrown mongrel dog flashed through his mind along with the face of two young boys but it made no sense. He again tried to leave.

"No, wait," Arnold said and Spinnet waited. "Where did you grow up?" Arnold asked.

Reluctantly, Spinnet answered. "Boonsville, Iowa. Why?"

"Ja," Arnold said. "Ever been in Doudy?"

Spinnet was a bit taken aback. He looked at Arnold carefully.

"My grandmother used to live there," he said.

"So did mine," Arnold said. "My twin brother and I used to stay with her every summer."

"No shit," Spinnet said. Then it occurred to him. "Arnold! You son-of-a-bitch. That was your damned cur dog that bit me on the leg in the summer of sixty two. I still have the scar. Here, look at this," he said pulling up his pants leg. They both laughed and shook hands. Kouslip bought Spinnet another drink. Spinnet bought Kouslip a drink. Kouslip bought Spinnet a drink, and so forth. At last they got around to talking about what each of them was doing in Costa Rica. Well, well. Wasn't that interesting?

Unfortunately, even though he had apologized for it five times already, Kouslip was still feeling guilty about letting his dog bite Spinnet as a boy so when he learned of Spinnet's reasons for being there he began to share information with him. Before the night was over Spinnet knew practically everything Kouslip knew. Then, when he found out Kouslip was on the way to Colorado, they had another drink and Spinnet agreed to meet him there.

179

THIRTY ONE

Taking Daphne's mother's car, Kohl and Daphne had left Washington in the middle of the night and drove as far as Illinois before stopping to rest at a little bed and breakfast that was off the highway. Feeling quite certain that they hadn't been followed, they were back on the road again at nightfall. Two days later they were in Utah. Daphne had changed the color and cut of her hair, Kohl had let his beard grow and began wearing a western hat when they were out in public. As an added precaution he also had a second drivers license in his wallet with a different name on it, just in case.

There were many parts of Utah that held an appeal for them, perhaps because they reminded them of what Sedona might have been like before the developers and the merchants had came along and nature had been forced to give way to greed. After some searching they found an isolated old ranch far to the south of a small town along the road that was about half way between Zzyzx, which was in California, and Paradox, which was in Colorado. A secret place which even the author of this book is not supposed to know exactly where it's at. Once moved in, they sent for Daphne's mother who had decided that it was time for new adventure in her own life. Then, when they had become somewhat settled, Kohl left for Colorado. He felt he owed his old friend Grey Hawk one more try.

With the exception of an impending mutiny amongst the men, little had changed since Kohl's last visit. The girl, Benji had left and had been replaced with another. The new face belonged to an unsettled female named Betsy. In her late thirties, she had passed that way on a previous occasion and had donated her old personal computer to the cause so that Grey Hawk would have something to begin publishing a newsletter on. Intentionally or not, the computer came with a unique bonus. She had forgotten to erase some files off the hard drive memory. They inadvertently contained personal accounts of her love life and a number of one night stands she had indulged in over

180

the last few years in her misguided search for self.

As soon as the young men learned of it they whisked the computer away to their abode in the lower house. While on the one hand it served to brighten some of the long nights, the very detailed and livid descriptions also served to add to their frustration, loneliness and lack of warm skin to rub against. Especially since Grey Hawk had declared all the women off-limits to everyone but himself and had suggested that a state of celibacy might be good for all the male apprentices who were living there. Then Claudia got wind of things and ordered the computer back up the hill. Shortly thereafter Betsy showed up again in person and moved into the main house along with Grey Hawk and the rest of the women.

In all truth, Betsy wasn't all that bad looking. Her blouse had a tendency to bounce when she walked and there was a, come hither, gleam in her eye when she smiled at the men. By the time Kohl had arrived, Spotted Owl was buying her presents and One Hand was threatening to take her by force. To resolve the issue fully Grey Hawk declared her to be one his women-wives, claiming she had also been "signed." How? After having dropped off the computer the last time through she claimed she had been compelled by some higher force to stop at a tattoo parlor on the way home and have a bluebird permanently imprinted on her left buttock. Grey Hawk had seen a blue bird land in the yard the same day she had told him about it and that was enough. It was enough for Claudia, too. She had threatened to strangle them both.

Running Deer was standing by the road with his thumb out looking for a ride to almost anywhere when Kohl pulled up. So, before going up to the main house to say hello, Kohl suggested the two of them do the usual thing and go have another beer or two together and talk things over.

"What do think happened?" Kohl asked after they had their arms on the bar rail.

"He's completely lost it," Running Deer said,

descriptively.

"That's what you said the last time."

"It's gotten worse."

"How so?"

"As you know, he began to get a little strange right after that visit he claims to have had with the star people."

Kohl nodded. It was strange, all right, and as he listened it got stranger. Not only was Grey Hawk still making everyone stay up all night to keep the fire going so the Grays didn't abduct the blond, he was conducting special ceremonies to improve the fertility of his women-wives and shooting his rifle at weather balloons. Additionally, he was doing exorcisms on the blonde's father to get the Grays to leave him alone so he won't kill anyone, especially Grey Hawk, the man who was keeping the couch springs limbered up with his daughter as filler in the sandwich.

"He's becoming pretty damned bitter about Vietnam, too. Mostly the part about being dropped behind enemy lines on jungle hilltops that had been drenched with Agent Orange, then getting overrun and damned near killed. But you can't blame him for that. Then he gets into the purity of race, thing. He says that in every reincarnation he has ever had he has always been a red man. He even claims to be related to Crazy Horse and Sitting Bull. They were cousins, as you know. But this time around he turns out to have some mixed blood. That's got him going, too."

It sounded like a lot to deal with, all right. Fighting a meaningless, thankless war that had begun to make your body fall apart. Seeing, or thinking you saw people from outer space, feeling compelled to have seven wives when you claimed you only loved one of them, winding up at war with yourself over the two sides of your heritage. Yes, Grey Hawk, by some slight slip of the old loin cloth on his grandfather's side, had a touch of French swimming around inside him. So, it wasn't all that easy, was it? But did it excuse any of the erratic behavior Grey Hawk was exhibiting? That was doubtful.

"Doubtful," Running Deer said, confirming part of

Kohl's thoughts. "But maybe since he likes to think he is more red than white it kinda explains the women. Except for that skinny assed little blond, he doesn't seem to like them all that much. Perhaps the notches on his belt are another way of getting revenge on the white man, I suppose. Screw all his women for a change."

"What's with the blond?"

"I told you about the scratched up rock she found. Well, he swears he loves Claudia but that he is bound by spirit to sleep with these others to produce offspring. But, guess what? This one has a birth control patch sewn into her arm and can't even get pregnant."

"Does gets to be a little bizarre, doesn't it?" Kohl said, thinking of Claudia and what she must be going through.

Running Deer could only shake his head in dismay. Silently, he drank his beer, leaving Kohl to face the quandary he found himself in. They had a third bottle and a fourth. Finally Kohl told Running Deer about the place he and Daphne had found in Utah and told him he was welcome to come and stay for awhile, if that was what he really wanted to do.

"How about the others?" Running Deer asked. "They're ready to bail out too."

"Damn," Kohl said. "If I show up and everyone comes with me, Grey Hawk will really be pissed."

"Might do him good for a change."

An hour later Kohl was headed down the road with a fully loaded vehicle. Except for Spotted Owl, they were all there. Running Deer, James, Rainmaker and One hand.

"I'll be along in a bit," Spotted Owl told Kohl. "After I get myself a taste of that stuff first," he said, referring to Betsy. It had nothing to do with the color of her skin, either. Spotted Owl just liked women and he had convinced himself that this particular one needed him. She was in heat, he had stated, and he felt he had a duty when it came to that sort of thing.

People will do what they will do. All Kohl could do

was to laugh and wish him well. His main concern was for Grey Hawk at the moment. He had left him standing on the front porch with arms crossed and an evil glare in his eye. Where was the truth, Kohl wondered. What was really at the bottom of it all? What had turned this once wise and generous man into this disreputable, misled individual? That was the real mystery. And what could be done to help? That was the real question, the one that left a heavy feeling in his heart.

Betsy dropped Spotted Owl off in Monticello five days later and Kohl drove down to pick him up. They had actually left Grey Hawk's place the day after Kohl had been there but had stopped at a lot of motels along the way. Although he looked a little pale for an Indian, the smile on Spotted Owl's face lasted for nearly a week. However, whatever he was replaying in his head to keep the smile going didn't interfere with his participation in the group's activities and that was fortunate because the agenda was full. Kohl hadn't planned it that way but it looked like they were building a community of their own.

The area behind the little house was ringed with tents. The sweat lodge and medicine wheel were in place and they were clearing land for a garden as well as laying foundations for guest cabins. Who knew, someday they might serve as retreats for others who needed to get away from the madness of the city. Like Daphne's mother, perhaps. Daphne's mother had gone into town the day she arrived, bought the first jeans she had worn since high school and soon discovered how refreshing and renewing it was to work outdoors.

Sometimes, in the midst of a task, she would just stop, sit down in the dirt and stare up at the sky, catching a bird in flight or studying the clouds. She loved to watch her busy daughter also, and to see her working and being together with Kohl. Then too, she enjoyed her long walks alone out into the vastness of the surrounding terrain, climbing over the swirlings of the slickrock, counting the colors, marveling at the sand, wind, water and time produced carvings and discovering for herself all the creatures that somehow managed to live out there in an area that she would have once dismissed as being totally barren.

She was equally awed by all the ceremony and underwent her first sweat lodge. Then she began to sit in on the evening discussions that often lasted until well past midnight. They raised many issues varying from, how to help Grey Hawk, to making preparations for the coming earth changes and what to do when the electricity went off and you ran out of batteries and bullets. From old native Americans to new native Americans to perhaps even a new America itself. She saw the contrasts between the individual members of the group to be enormous but was constantly surprised at how such diversity of opinion, background, taste, habit, manners and mores could result in such ultimate harmony and common purpose. It was all so foreign to her. What was it that made it possible? Looking back at the life she had left behind in the city, she puzzled over it. At the time she had convinced herself that her former existence had been quite exciting but now it all seemed so boringly pretentious, presumptuous, preposterous and practically meaningless. Ugh. But why? What was the reason, she asked Kohl one day.

"When you go somewhere in the city and are introduced to new people, what is the first thing they try to do?"

"I'm not sure. Probably ask a bunch of personal questions."

"Why?"

"So they can do some kind of instantaneous rating thing, I guess. The trouble is, I never had anything very impressive to say in that regard. I wasn't a doctor or a lawyer or a writer or a senator, or anything much."

"But why should that be so important?"

"It shouldn't be, but it was to them. All they want is to find out if you might be in a position to do them some good, otherwise they dismiss you."

"People preying on people."

"Exactly."

"Maybe that's the only way they know how to deal with each other, anymore. I think it's a sign of insecurity."

"Insecurity?"

"Why else do people feel the need to compete so heavily, both socially and economically. Emotionally secure people do not need status to make themselves feel good. That doesn't mean that everyone who has status is insecure, of course. The question is, if you took all their money and power away from them, what would you have left? If you would still like to know that person, then you have the basis for a real relationship."

"That might be refreshing."

"So why is everyone so afraid to approach others with that in mind, instead? Why does it become a kind of invisible boundary which they are reluctant to cross, not only with others but with themselves, too?"

"I'm not sure, Kohl."

"Neither am I, exactly. But it takes more than clothes, cars and bank accounts to make a real person. And there you have it."

"Have what?"

"The predicament. Science has somehow convinced the world that man had his origins in the chemical equations of pond scum and survival of the fittest mechanics and that through successive mutation he has finally risen to the point where he now has dominion over the entirety of creation.

Whether or not scientists are able to admit it, however, man does have another side. Just because physics and astronomy have intellectually banished the supernatural doesn't mean it no longer exists. In those few cultures which are left that haven't been ruined by western thinking, we find people we choose to describe as primitive, living quite happily together without written law and modern conveniences but also without crime, mayhem and madness. Why? Because all of these cultures recognize the spiritual side of man. They believe there is a ubiquitous spiritual world and that the physical world is simply a manifestation of it. And that, I think, is the reason things work so well here. Our common bond is that we believe in the spiritual side of our nature."

"So do I, I think. Except I'm not completely sure what that means exactly."

"It means that all things have their basis in Spirit, they come from Spirit and are sustained by Spirit. Everything is alive and deserves to be considered in that context. Animals, plants, bugs, birds, rivers, the sky, the entire universe. In our little group we practice a way of life that attempts to honor that. It is not a religion. We do not have, a God. We don't have idols. There is no dogma, no concept of guilt or penance. There is an occasional, life honoring, spontaneous ceremony but no one is compelled to attend and anyone can make changes to what we consider an on going process. And as far as those other ceremonies which were conducted to make the van disappear and do the IRS thing; as I'm finding out, the magic was never in the ritual, it was in the minds of the people involved."

"Yes. I guess I can see that, but it's so hard to change one's thinking and let it all in."

"I know. It would be a lot easier if spirits just showed up in broad daylight where everyone could see them. Then we would be forced to accept that side of things. On the other hand, why should it be so hard? We all admit that there are such things as love and hate, compassion, ambition, desire, loneliness and fear. These are the driving forces of the world. We don't have a problem admitting that they exist. But where? We can't see them, weigh them or measure their circumference. We can't see the wind either, only the effects of it, yet we don't deny it. So why do we do such a good job of denying the also invisible, spiritual side of creation and the deeper reality which surrounds us? Why do we go on hiding behind the little we think we know because we fear that which we don't? Logic and intelligence should lead one beyond the materialistic, not keep them trapped in it. Does that make sense?" Kohl

187

asked, feeling he tried to say too much.

Instead of giving him a direct answer, however, Ann thanked him and told him she was going for a walk. It was a lot to digest. She returned just in time for dinner and found that when she sat down they had come up with yet another new plan. Spotted Owl explained the why and what for of it.

"America wasn't discovered," he pointed out. "It was taken by force and collusion, divided up amongst the victors and self righteously treated as private property. The few poor survivors were deprived of their humanity and forced to fend for themselves on a few scattered and nearly useless parcels of land that no one else wanted at the time. In one respect, done is done. In another, however, wouldn't it be nice to admit a bit of the truth and leave a monument to some of the heroes of the original American people? The ones who had called it home for many thousands of years before the latecomers stumbled onto it?"

So, he explained, they would go to Mount Rushmore. They would go and test some of the new ceremonies they had developed. They would go and take Grey Hawk with them because, when all was said and done, he had been the messenger that had brought them all together in the first place. If nothing else, they at least owed him for that. And, if it worked, it might just help him get his act together again. Additionally, to make it really complete, they would see if that wise old man who had been responsible for getting both Running Deer's and Spotted Owl's lives back on the Red Road would lead the ceremony. Thunder Cloud, an Oglala Sioux, a still living, bonafide relative of Crazy Horse himself.

Grey Hawk, however, after Spotted Owl had driven down to see him, wanted no part of it or of any of the people involved. He was particularly angry at Kohl, claiming he was a traitor who had lured all his people away.

THIRTY TWO

At first, a shock wave of total silence passed through

188

the crowd as they stood dumb struck and watched the solid rock mountain walls change shape right before their eyes. Finally someone screamed. It was an eerie, out of this world scream that sent another chill through the ranks of the people. Seven different women fainted as a number of old men searched through their pockets looking for their nitroglycerin tablets. Soon there was yelling and shouting and shoving. By the time the rangers had left the visitor's center to see what was going on, a mad stampede was well underway as everyone began running for their cars. Except for an old man being pushed back to the parking area in his wheelchair, it took all of seventy three seconds for the entire crowd to disband and disappear.

When the melee was all over the only visitors still left was a family of five local Indians who had stopped by to repeat the weekly prayer they had been making for the last ten years. If the white man had wanted to honor his leaders, why hadn't he put their carved faces back in Washington, DC. where they belonged. Putting them out here in the Blackhills of South Dakota was like rubbing salt in the many wounds the red man had suffered here in the stolen land that the Indian had loved so dearly and had fought so hard to keep. Here where the land was made red, not only with the blood of warriors but also with that of his defenseless women and children. The faces in the stone were, in reality, a monument to genocide and slavery, the ultimate high in hypocrisy, the ultimate blasphemy against the Indian and against all humanity in situations where, might had become right. To disfigure the sacredness of the earth for such a purpose was both fraudulent and evil.

It was six minutes after one o'clock in the afternoon. The tall Indian man with the pony tail in his long hair began to smile. His wife began to smile. All the children began to smile. They hugged each other for a long time and thanked Waken-Tonka for the gift he had brought them on this most appropriate of days. After some time the man released himself from his family and went back to their old, rusted out Chevy to find his camera. He hoped it still worked and had some film in it because he wanted to have a picture to show to his ninety six year old grandfather. When he returned, a very pretty, middle aged white woman in blue jeans and an old shirt stepped out from behind a tree.

"Here," she said, indicating his camera. "Go stand by your family and let me take the picture with all of you together."

At first the man stared at her reluctantly. Then he nodded. How more appropriate could it be than to have a white person take the photo. "Thank you," he said when she handed him back the camera.

"My pleasure," Daphne's mother said, for she had come to see the results of the ceremony, not to participate in it. "It's a day to be remembered, isn't it." she stated with a pleased look as she headed back to her car, leaving them to enjoy the scene alone.

And so that is what happened on that same July 4th that Parsons had been sent back to Phoenix and Spinnet and his childhood acquaintance, Arnold, were up in the Colorado woods together sharing sardine sandwiches and watching Grey Hawk's house through binoculars. Fortunately, Spinnet had thought to bring along a deck of cards and his cribbage board because this day had been especially boring. Even more boring than all the other days they had been up there hiding, hoping that before long Grey Hawk would be up to something and they would finally catch him in the act. Then, one hundred and fifty three yawns apiece later, at exactly four o'clock in the afternoon Grey Hawk emerged from his double wide, factory made home with his entire entourage of women. That perked Spinnet's and Arnold's interest. They had never before all came out of the house at once.

"Not bad," Arnold said as he checked out all the females with his binoculars. Then he noticed that Grey Hawk was carrying his ceremonial pipe. "Ah ha!" he stated, jubilantly. "Get your video cameras ready," he said to his camera crew as he shook them awake in their hiding places behind the trees.

Now I'll show them, Grey Hawk said to himself. Won't they be surprised to see my handsome face looking down at them from the cliff when they arrive. Convinced that Kohl and his former apprentices wouldn't begin their ceremony until after all the crowd had gone home in the evening, he was determined to beat them to the punch. That would teach them that there was nothing wrong with his powers. He didn't have to drive all the way up to South Dakota to do what he wanted to do, either. No sir. He could make it happen from clear down here six hundred and twenty three and a half miles away.

The camera men adjusted their five hundred millimeter telephoto lenses and followed the procession out into the large circular area in the middle of the driveway and began shooting. Spinnet began to sweat. God, he was excited. What would disappear today, he wondered with anticipation. He took out his ball point pen and noted the time on the inside of his left wrist. Four-o-six. If only he had known. It was exactly three hours after all the faces at Mount Rushmore had begun swimming around and changed into something else. It was already, all over.

THIRTY THREE

The Attorney General of the United States tried to keep a straight face when he said it, but it was difficult. "Defacing," he said to the hastily assembled group before him. "Defacing a national monument is already a federal crime. We don't need any new legislation. What we need is to get out there and make some arrests. Bring those sons-a-bitches in here. Hang them from the top of the Washington Monument and cut their hearts out. Wiping out the IRS files was one thing, but this... This disfigurement of famous faces, by damn...What they have done is far worse than burning the flag, I tell you."

Assembled together with the Attorney General were the Vice President, Senators Filcher and Blubluster, the

191

head of the Department of the Interior, the head of the National Parks Administration, the heads of the FBI, the CIA and the BIA (Bureau of Indian Affairs) and old Judge Hapgood. The President would have been there had he been able but he had caught a severe case of the flu when he had been out trying to stir up support for the health care package he was trying to force through congress.

"I agree," said the head of the BIA. "But not wholeheartedly. We specifically waited until clear up to nineteen seventy six to make it legal for the damned Indians to practice their native religions and rituals and do they appreciate it? Hell no! It's just like that heathenistic Ghost Dance they began practicing back in the late eighteen hundreds. We do need new legislation, yes. But we need to take away all their rights this time. We need to take away their feathers, rattles and drums, tattoo numbers on their foreheads and string up cyclone fencing and barbed wire around every damned reservation in the whole blessed country because we've got a bunch of damned Geronimos on our hands again."

"I also agree," said the Vice President, "but we have to come up with a far less burdensome plan financially. Can you imagine how much all that fencing would cost to put up. And we just couldn't stop there. There would have to be guards along it, too, or someone would always be trying to climb over. Look what happened in Berlin where they had a twenty foot high wall instead of just a fence. And then we'd have to feed them and clothe them and house them and build laundromats and find a place to park all their pickup trucks and, anyway, there are more important things that need funding. Just because the Soviet Union is no longer in the picture doesn't mean that we still don't need every last one of those thirty five hundred nuclear bombs we have and all those new Trident missile launching submarines we are building. We need fifty times overkill, not ten. We can't afford to cut into something as important as that."

"I second that," said Senator Filcher. "And think of all the other ramifications. We'd be losing all those bingo parlors and gambling casinos out west in the process. Where would I take my wife on vacation, for heavens sake? The Indians would stop making jewelry, baskets and Kachina dolls. What would the tourists think? They wouldn't have anything to shop for and there wouldn't be any public ceremonial dances or pow-wows to take their video cameras to. They'd come totally unglued. And think of all that lost sales tax. Arizona, New Mexico and Utah would go broke. Not only that but who's going to climb up on that high steel and put all the new skyscrapers together that are in the planning stages across the country?

And what would I tell my wife's brother in-law? He's a half breed and he's our accountant and financial manager. How can he advise me if he's locked up somewhere, like back in Oklahoma where his mother came from?"

"Well," said the head man of the Department of Interior. "I suppose we should try and remember that the Indians gave us tobacco and potatoes and corn and canoes and snowshoes and beans, squash, tomatoes, peppers, maple syrup and peanuts so we have to try and be a little fair about this."

"Bilge water," said Blubluster. "Those things were here when we got here and we wouldn't have had them if we hadn't taken them away from the natives. I say, lock them up. A good Indian is a locked up Indian."

"I thought it was, a good Indian is a dead Indian?" someone quipped.

"Yes, but we don't dare do that anymore. We would be invaded by the United Nations."

"We are the United Nations for all practical purposes, you dummy. We can't invade ourselves."

"Lincoln did it."

"Right, but the Indians haven't tried to succeed."

"They would if they had any sense. Now you take the Hopi. They are the only tribe in the country that has never signed a treaty with the government. In essence they are really a sovereign nation, if you want to get right down to it," the Head of the National Parks Administration pointed out.

"For Christ's sake, Joe. Will you shut up with that kind of talk. And don't let that kind of thinking leave this room, either. We have enough trouble on our hands already," said the Attorney General as he glared at the man. "I though your department was a part of the Department of Interior. Isn't it?"

"Yes sir. It is."

The Attorney General then turned to the Head of the Department of the Interior. "Tell him to shut up, will you. If he wants to keep his job."

Finally Judge Hapgood got to his feet and held up his hands. "Gentlemen. Gentlemen, please. If this is the best you can do then perhaps it is you and not the Indians who ought to be behind the barbed wire. From what I can see, they are far more civilized than we are."

"Goddammit Judge," Blubluster said. "Why are you always insulting everybody all the time? Who the hell do you think you are?"

"Actually," the Judge said. "My mother was part Choctaw and part Comanche so I guess that makes me part Native American. Now if you want to try and shut me up or lock me up, just go ahead."

Blubluster coughed at that and started to apologize but he was interrupted by the head of the FBI. "All right, all right," he said. "But no one can argue with the fact that we must have an orderly society, no matter what the ancestry. We must have compliance. Maybe we are wrong to generalize and to bad mouth all these, ah, Native Americans. Obviously it is only a very small group of them that's creating all the problems, so let's concentrate on that.

Now the FBI has had a lot of experience in these matters in recent years. We have to say that we learned a lot at Wounded Knee trying to put them people in their place as well as up there in Oregon shooting at that man and his son locked up in their cabin and also down in Texas ganging up on them Divinity folks as well as jumping the gun in the Olympics bombing. Yes sir. This

194

time we would use different tactics. We'll find them, but, we won't make the mistake of telling anyone about it or taking any prisoners. No public and no media to screw things up for us, either. As near as we know, there may be only about a dozen of these radicals creating all these problems. We have five hundred specialists in our ranks now. We can drop them in by helicopter, seal off the area and blow them off the map before anyone even knows what happened. Then we'll bury the bodies and tell the press that it was just a training exercise."

"It might be better than apprehending them and bringing them to trial. That would just make heroes of them. Then we would have a real uprising on our hands," the head of the CIA pointed out.

"Just a damned bejiggered minute here now," Judge Hapgood said in his loud voice, interrupting again. "Unless you are already thinking of injecting me with something to make it look like I had a heart attack, there will be no cover ups. Besides, not only do I know about it, but, so do other people."

"Name one that anybody really gives a damn about," the head of the CIA said. "Besides yourself, of course."

"Ex General Bart Winsome," the Vice President pointed out. "And we sure as hell can't afford to hand him something like that. He'd love to embarrass this administration with something like that and since your job comes through appointment and since you are not as fortunate as the Judge here to have a lifetime lock on it, perhaps ..."

"And don't forget," Blubluster said. "We have it on good authority that at least one of them is a white man and another possibly black. What about that aspect of it? Picking on one minority is bad enough but two is out of question, especially since I come from Virginia. And whether I like it or not, there is an election coming up and black people are a sizable part of my constituency these days."

"And just how do you happen to know that?" the Vice President said. "How do you know there's a white man and a black man involved? And who are they, anyway?"

Blubluster groaned. How did he always manage to get in the middle of such things? Why was the President always withholding information from the Vice President? Did he enjoy having him look like an un-informed fool all the time? Doing a political sidestep, Blubluster looked at the head of the FBI as if he were the man that was somehow responsible. "Well?" the Vice President said, looking at the new culprit.

The FBI head rubbed his eyes with both hands then started drawing little circles all over his note paper as he tried to explain how they thought that the man who was at least partly responsible was the same man who had been involved in the disruption of Hoover Dam and all the other anarchistic acts a couple of years back. The Vice President's face took on a really confused appearance at this time, then slowly turned an angry, burnt red.

"Why wasn't I told this earlier?" he asked.

Since no one knew the answer or wanted to risk an opinion, the meeting came to an impasse. Except for Judge Hapgood they had all come there to set policy on the matter and establish a course of action on how to deal with it. As for Hapgood, he had merely been out for a stroll and had seen Filcher and Blubluster scurrying through the back gate into the White House so he had followed them in. Then, since no one seemed to question his presence there, he hung around to see what was happening.

After five minutes of uninterrupted silence the Vice President finally decided that the meeting had stalled out because it was now eleven ten. Low blood sugar. He promptly sent word for coffee and donuts as the CIA head left to go to the men's room. Blubluster took out a cigar, looked at Hapgood and put it back in his pocket. The donuts arrived, the CIA head returned. The head of the National Park Service noticed that he had only stuffed in half of his shirt tail and it reminded him of something. "When can we begin work to restore the monument?" he asked the Vice President.

"Gee, ah...,hmmm, let me see. Now what was that I heard. It was yesterday afternoon just before I left to go to the dentist," he said and scratched the back of his neck. Then he picked up the phone sitting on the conference table and dialed two digits. "Get the senior senator from South Dakota on the line," he said, keeping the phone to his ear. "Let's see, this is Saturday, right? He's usually over at that pool hall in Georgetown I think." He put down the phone. "Shouldn't be long," he said.

Everyone got up and helped themselves to the coffee. "What a bunch of cheap skates," Senator Filcher said as he pawed through the donuts. "The last administration used to spring for eclairs and jellied. There isn't even a powdered sugar one in here," he complained and finally tore a glazed in two and stuffed half in his mouth. Well, at least they had finally stopped using styrofoam cups.

The phone rang. The Vice President picked it up. "Yes, Senator. Thank you for calling. I wonder if you could go over those statistics again that you started telling me about yesterday. Go slow so I can repeat them to the people here... What people?... Senator, that's confidential, but I assure you they are important or I wouldn't be calling... Thank you... Really? You say the polls are showing that of those Americans surveyed, seventy six and a half percent think that what happened to Rushmore is a great idea and they all say that they're heading out to see the new wonder of the world just as soon as they can get some time off from work... What?... You're petitioning the President to keep the park open twenty four hours a day for the rest of the summer... There isn't a vacant motel room within two hundred miles of Rapid City, South Dakota, Greyhound has shut down all routes except those going to Rapid City and diverted all its buses to service that area. There are thirteen, 747s in the air full of Japanese tourists right this minute. Mac Donald's has ten new hamburger palaces under construction and ten more on the drawing board... My God, Senator, that's wonderful. Yes, I know I should have canceled my dentists appointment... Yes... Thanks Senator," the Vice President said and hung up.

"Does that answer your question," he asked the Parks Administrator. "And as for the rest of you, I suggest we go very slowly on this one. It just might turn out to be the biggest windfall we've had in years. Of course I can't say that officially, what with the President camped out in the bathroom as he is, but I'm sure he would agree. Instead of locking up Indians we need to think of some way we can take credit for what's happened, that's what. So let's get out of here and go do that. Let the good times roll, I say."

With that, everyone rose. All except for one man. "What bullshit," the FBI head said in a loud voice and hammered on the table with his fist. "What about the IRS? What about all the income taxes we have been unable to collect? What about that, dammit. I say a very serious crime has been committed and by God, someone needs to be incarcerated for it," he said in an angry tirade and rose to his feet just as everyone else sat back down. Then he picked up his briefcase and headed for the exit.

"Where do you think you're going?" the Vice President asked, ready to reopen the discussion now that he had been reminded that the federal treasury was without its main source of revenue.

"Out to kick some ass," the FBI head stated.

With that the CIA Director also got up and followed him through the door. "If you need backup, let me know," he said. "Our wives made enough money from their bake sale to buy us some of those of those surplus, wire guided rocket launchers."

THIRTY FOUR

"Darn it!" Digand Pry said. Who could be calling him at home at this hour of the evening. And right in the middle of his favorite sitcom. "Yes," he said somewhat indignantly but was quick to change the tone. "Yes, sir," he said. Holy shit, the Chief himself was on the line. All the way from Washington. "I'm not sure, sir," he said after a moment of listening. "But I've got my best man on it. How about if I call you back first thing in the morning?"...

"What? Tonight?... Yes, sir."

"You've got twenty minutes," he was told.

Pry considered asking for more time so he could watch the rest of his program but decided against it. The Chief sounded pretty grumpy. He hung up, dialed a number and counted the rings. Darn it, where was he? On the nineteenth ring a sleepy voice answered. "Spinnet? Are you awake?"

"Oh, is that you boss? What's up? Did you run out of Knockquill again?"

"No, nothing like that. The Bureau Chief is on the phone. I need you to give me a run down on the Havoc case again.... Yes, I know it's on my desk but one of my boys got expelled from school yesterday for shooting his sling shot at the principal and that took all day to straighten out."

"Gee, I'm sorry to hear that boss," Spinnet said, knowing full well that his report had been on Pry's desk since Monday. But like a good trooper, he pushed aside his feelings and proceeded to bring Pry up to speed.

"Very good Spinnet. Now go back to bed so you are fresh in the morning," Pry said to him after he had listened to the lengthy review. Then he called Washington.

"At last", they all shouted in jubilation. The long dry spell was over. They didn't have to over play this one, trying to make something out of nothing. No, sir! It was exactly the kind of thing that careers were made of - and lost over. It was news. Real, honest to god, genuine news. News to be exploited to its fullest. And, at a time when the media had again become desperately, desperate. The IRS computer mishap was many months ago in the past and, unfortunately, old news is no news. Besides, it had never made the big time to begin with. It hadn't been allowed to. Totally forbidden. No doubt something serious had happened to the computer network and the IRS's ability to enforce the tax code but to this very late date there was still an official denial and complete blackout in place on the subject.

Of course the grapevine knew and as a result the public knew and were taking happy advantage of it, but officially there was no real news. The one and only IRS employee who had dared to confirm what little anyone knew of the truth had been promptly arrested and incarcerated in some unknown maximum security facility in up-state New York. Or was it Nevada? Wherever it was, it was a bad place because that part of it had been publicized widely. As a result there had been nothing of sufficiently tangible nature to risk putting in print or on the networks. Only rumor. And in that regard, the FCC had promised not only to withdraw broadcasting licenses but to also lock the doors of any establishment foolish enough to cross that line.

Worst of all, the blackout on everything related to the IRS mishap couldn't have come at a worse moment in broadcasting history. There were no serial killers or insane snipers on the loose at the time, no unusually mad warlords in a murdering streak, no racial genocide being committed, no buildings being bombed and no political assassinations. No life destroying earthquakes had happened either, no tornadoes, hurricanes, or airlines crashes. No public figures had been bashed, no private citizens' penises had been whacked off. There were no serious cases of wife beating or child molestation, no public figures coming forth to condemn their parents or their spouses. There hadn't even been an old movie star who had passed on in all those long, long months. It was instead, a time of tranquility in nature and relative peace on earth. People were doing little to harm each other.

Of course, as always, lots of good things were happening. Most people were going quietly about their own business, occasionally even helping their neighbors and taking care of the animals and the planet. But by every known definition of the word, that was not news. Nor was it the slightest bit newsworthy in the opinion of the executives and the commentators. That was boring. That was disallowed.

"We have spent more than forty years and almost as many billions of dollars turning the viewing public into pathetic, paranoid couch potatoes and we aren't going to let them down now," the CEO of BCA said at the annual stockholders meeting just the day before it had happened. "Stalin once said that religion was the opiate of the people. Well, he was wrong. Television is the opiate of the people. They are starved for sensationalism and addicted to violence, therefore, in the best interest of the future of the human race, it is our solemn duty to keep them saturated with that kind of material and that is exactly what I have sworn to do," he stated to the sound of clapping hands.

The CEO kept on with his barrage because he had recently gained the impression that he was about to loose his grossly overpaid position if the network didn't come up with something newsworthy in the very near future. Finally, he launched into a summary of what they were trying to do to keep their ratings up. He explained how they had been fortunate enough to outbid the competition for the life story of last year's mass murderer. All theirs for only half a million. They had also commissioned a major screen play writer to come up with another version of the chain saw murders for a new Movie of the Week, only this time using a pair of twelve year olds as the grisly executioners. "It will be a major sensation," he assured everyone.

But when the meeting was opened up to questions he had to admit that, other than that, well... that was it. Even though they had established the healthiest fund of any network to acquire the rights to any story in such major categories as, most heinous crime committer, most bizarre act of the century and, most despicable thing done to another human being, they were back to reruns of reruns in the areas of violence, suffering and tragedy. There was no way out of the dilemma. The pressures on over paid executives were tremendous. One company president had spent more than a hundred thousand dollars on psychotherapy alone in the last year. Another, even more grossly over paid, prime time female news commentator, driven by guilt at being paid so much for doing so little, had attempted to jump off the Brooklyn Bridge. And then, just when things had sunk to their lowest, when the pond of news everyone siphoned from was about to turn into a dry lake, just in time to save every newscaster's pampered butt, there it was. Rushmore! An undeniable fact of life. Onward to South Dakota, everyone. All the government pressure in the world couldn't cover that one up.

There were so many television crews, reporters and interviewers there during the first week afterward that the park rangers were forced to close the monument to the public. The major question of the day, however, wasn't what had happened, but, what was behind it all? Surely there had to be some deep, dark and very sinister machinations involved. Bribery, murder, drug money, something. After the fifth day, however, the only sinister thing that had happened was that two competing network helicopters had a mid air collision and had fallen on the satellite up-link van of a third network and cut them off the air. Conspiracy, the third network had shouted and threatened to sue. After that it was time to begin the person to person interviews. They started with the Indians. One hundred and sixty three different ones were confronted. "What do you think of it?" was the first question asked.

"About time," was the standard answer.

"Who do you think did it?" was the second question.

"Spirit," they all said happily and walked away, leaving no room for any further discussion.

"Okay, start the panel shows," the troops were all told, so out they came. The world's experts were promptly escorted off their first class seats at La Guardia and Los Angeles International, hustled into waiting network limos and driven to the studios where they were paid five times the going rate to show up on prime time live.

First came the Sheriff of Blackhawk County and all his deputies, then the National Stone Cutters Association. Next is was the geologists followed by the nuclear physicists. After that it was the psychologists and the parapsychologists, fifteen witches from New Salem, the steering committee of United UFO Watchers of the World, The Soothsayers of America and, The Brotherhood to Save the World From the Anti-Christ.

The Sheriff claimed to have felt deep, earth rumblings the night before but his boys claimed that it was only his dyspepsia acting up again. The stone cutters disavowed the whole thing saying that no earthly crew could have done such a deed. There wasn't a single scrap of fresh cut rubble anywhere around the base of the monument. The geologists stated flatly that it couldn't have happened and therefore it hadn't happened. They postulated a strong energy field surrounding the area which, once you walked through it, caused a hypnotic illusion to appear. The physicists were inclined to agree because when they had set up their magnetometers, isonometers, biometers, diometers and triometers, they found not the slightest wiggle in any of their chart recordings. It must indeed be some kind of mass illusion that was so strong even camera film recorded it.

While the psychologists agreed wholeheartedly with the physicists, the parapsychologists attributed the happening to the paranormal and tried to take credit for it by saying they had talked about such things at their last convention. The witches said, yes that was true but claimed that one of their own membership had caused it to happen one moonlit night when she had fallen over a grave in the local cemetery on the way home from a beer party. Which grave? They couldn't remember for sure because they had split a half pony of dark draft amongst the six of them prior to having set out into the night but surely it was the grave of an Indian.

The UFO'ers said it was the next logical step after the giant face that had been carved on Mars and crop circles put into being in fields all around the world. These were phenomenon that their new age buddies claimed was an indication that the Pleidians were on the way and they would all soon be "stepping into the light". The

Soothsayers all stated that if the public didn't like what had happened that they should all get together at exactly eleven o'clock on the eleventh day of the eleventh month and shout "SOOTH" as loudly as they could. The monument would then return to normal. What the Brotherhood to Save the World From the Anti-Christ said, however, was both unmentionable and unprintable and was censored before it could get out. With that, the story began to fade. In a last ditch, desperate attempt to keep the issue alive, the networks put up a standing offer of five million dollars to anyone who had verifiable evidence as to what had really caused the national monument to take on its, "change of faces." But no one stepped forward.

Back to fear, they decided. Use the incident to promote fear. Fear will keep them home and keep them tuned in. "It could happen to you," commentators came on the big screen and said with pointed finger. "Anywhere. Right in your own home. Something evil is out there, lurking in the shadows. Your own neighbors might be involved."

About that same time a fledgling reporter asked his superior why they insisted on using such tactics. "Because," he was told. "If you want to manipulate the public, fear is the first law. Guilt is second, greed third. It works in advertising, religion and politics. Never tell people that only a small percentage of the population is doing the bad things, convince them that it is far worse. Promote the image that man is inherently bad, not decent and good. Let him think that lurking around every corner is a fatal virus waiting to jump out and infect him, a lunatic to shoot him down, a disabling accident ready to cripple him for life. It is natural to be diseased and threatened at every turn by fate and misfortune. Start early. Smother the children in TV violence, justify it by saying that the programming is merely a reflection of life in the modern world, get them addicted to it, too. It helps guarantee that we will have all that much more gory news to report in the years to come. Keep it up long enough and pretty soon you get what we have got. A paranoid society, afraid of living, afraid of dying. But man, does it sell prime time advertising."

"Yes, but it seems rather deceitful to me."

"Grow up boy. Grow up. Don't you see that the media, out of its own necessity, is forced to drag every one down to the same brain dead level. Sports, sitcoms, talk shows, movies. They aren't supposed to stimulate. Good shows just don't make it. The public has been exposed to shit for so long it no longer recognizes or wants quality time. The few who do are in such a minority that the sponsors don't care and aren't willing to spend money on advertising because people who think are also less likely to be swayed by advertisers exaggerated claims and less likely to impulsively buy worthless, sloppily made goods they don't really need or want in the first place. Christ! The whole economy would fall apart. Is that what you want? Don't you like your job?"

"Well, don't get me wrong. Of course I like my job. Somebody has to make the payments on that big screen, home entertainment center we just bought."

THIRTY FIVE

"What the hell is this, Pry?" the head of the FBI demanded of Digand as he looked at the hand painted little sign nailed to a tree on the hill above Grey Hawk's house.

"I don't know, Chief," Digand said and turned to Spinnet. "What the hell is this, Spinnet?" he questioned in turn.

"Hmm," Spinnet said. "That wasn't there the last time. How did he find out we were here?"

"What we have here is a real wise-ass," the Chief said. "We should have burned his butt a long time ago." And with that he did his best to rip the sign off the tree. A sign that said, "Please pick up your gum wrappers when you leave. Signed, Grey Hawk."

"Not exactly a very covert operation, huh, Chief," a voice said from behind them as they all jumped and turned around to see ex-General Bart Winsome standing there in green fatigues with an AK-17 assault rifle slung over his shoulder.

"The place is surrounded. How the hell did you get up here?" the Chief demanded as soon as regained his composure. "And who the hell gave you permission?"

"I don't need permission," the General said. "I believe we are standing on National Forest land. That's public property the last I knew."

"Well, I suggest you stay out of the way or I'll have you taken into custody."

The General laughed raucously.

"Shut up, you fool. This is supposed to be a surprise encounter," the Chief told him as the General laughed even louder.

"Christ. How many men have you got here, anyway? Looks like the whole damned US Army." he asked.

"A hundred and twenty seven, if you really have to know."

The General almost passed out with hysteria. "Do you think you can handle it?" he asked when at last he caught his breath. "There are two men and four women in that house."

"And just how do you happen to know that?"

"I had breakfast down there."

"Excuse me? You had breakfast down there? What for?"

"I don't think that's any of your business."

"Don't you realize you're associating with a known criminal."

"Maybe he was, but he's not anymore. If he were I'd have hired him."

"What's that supposed to mean?"

"He didn't do the Rushmore job."

"What! How do you know that?"

"Rushmore happened at one o'clock. Grey Hawk didn't conduct his ceremony until four."

"Impossible."

"No it's not, sir," Spinnet said, interrupting after he had put one and four together.

The Chief was flabbergasted. Spinnet explained how

he had written the time of Grey Hawk's ceremony on his wrist and how it hadn't totally washed off for more than a week. Colorado was in the same time zone as South Dakota. There could be no mistake.

"All right," the Chief said to the General. "Since you know so damned much, where is this man Kohl and all those other Indians? Tell me that and I promise not to have you arrested."

"Arrested? What for?"

"Conspiracy, treason, anarchy, plotting to overthrow the government, illegal weapons possession, to name a few."

"Yes. Well, its been nice talking to you," the General said and started to walk away which caused the Chief to draw his own weapon. It was only a thirty eight and no match for the General's big rifle but Pry was reaching for his, too, and the General still had his back turned.

"Stop or we'll drop you in your tracks," the Chief ordered.

Slowly, Bart turned around, his hands out from his sides but still holding the rifle. "Okay, okay," he said. "I don't have the slightest idea where all those people are. If I did, I think I'd shoot that Kohl son-of-a-bitch myself. Not only did he threaten to give me Alzheimer's, now he's run off with my wife."

"Just stand still and drop your weapon," the Chief ordered.

"Are you out of your mind?" the General said as he took a step backwards, tripped on a rock and fell down. "Ouch. Goddammit," he said from his position on the ground. "Jesus H. balls. What the hell was that? Something bit me."

He sat up and looked at his leg. The scorpion that was clinging to his pants stung him again. He became panic stricken and started slapping at it wildly, swearing the whole time, only to wind up also being bitten on the hand and the arm. Of all the things in the whole world that he dreaded most, scorpions and spiders were at the top of the list. He'd rather look down the barrel of a five inch howitzer any day. Rolling around in the dirt, swatting crazily away, he began to run out of breath and his chest began to hurt. A thought flashed through his mind. Holy shit! He was going to die.

Equally in a state of panic, the poor scorpion was now on the ground doing its best to keep from getting crushed. Seeing it trying to get away, the Chief pointed his revolver at it and fired three shots, ultimately connecting on the third.

At the sound of gunfire a number of things all began to happen at once. All one hundred and twenty seven of the Federal Bureau of Investigation's best, raised and cocked their high powered rifles and pointed them down towards Grey Hawk's house as the General began having a genuine heart attack. Hearing the gunfire, Grey Hawk turned off the afternoon soap opera he was studiously watching, grabbed his own rifle and stepped out on the front porch of the house. Suddenly seeing him standing there with weapon in hand the feds opened fire. A hail of bullets kicked up the dirt by the front steps of the house. Another salvo of lead slammed into the fake log siding of the structure and tore up the redwood planks of the porch all around Grey Hawk's feet whereupon Grey Hawk, who was still in one piece, threw his rifle up in the air and ran back inside.

"Cease fire, Goddammit. Cease fire," the Chief ordered as soon as he was able to find his bullhorn and turn it on. "Cease fire," he yelled again. Suddenly a blanket of silence settled over the wooded hills as the echoes of the indignant gunfire faded away. Off in the distance a pair of Ravens began squawking and the General let out a low moan. Pry bent closer and saw that the General's face had turned from red to an ashen gray.

"Better get an ambulance," he said. "I think he's about had it."

"Too bad," said the Chief, having finally realized that here he was, about to have a serious shoot out with a wild Indian and he had forgotten to include a team of medics in

208

his planning. "The nearest hospital is seventy miles away."

"But, sir. He'll die."

"Well, start giving him mouth to mouth. It'll be over an hour before anyone can get here."

Pry looked first at the General, made a face and looked at Spinnet. "Give him mouth to mouth," he told Spinnet.

Spinnet wiped his shirt sleeve across his mouth then just stood there nodding his head. "Sorry, sir. Not me," he said.

The Chief then summoned his nearest troops but, for one reason or another, all refused to become that intimate with the bull faced man on the ground. Then, before the next squad had been able to make their way up the hill through the trees the General looked at the one lonely cloud in the sky, thought he heard someone calling his name, took one last, mighty gasp and succumbed.

"What a bunch of dumb fucks," a husky voice said as a rugged faced red man stepped out from behind a tree.

The Chief stared at him. "And who the hell are you?"

"Grey Hawk, you dumb shit. Who else were you expecting."

The Chief quickly suppressed his surprise. "Ah, ha," he said and began to smile valiantly. "Put the cuffs on him boys," he ordered.

"Wait just a damned minute now," Grey Hawk said and held up his hand.

"Read him his rights," the Chief barked.

"I said, wait a damned minute, you numskull."

"Read him his rights."

"Okay. Good idea. Nobody here seems to be able to hear but maybe someone can read. Wouldn't that be interesting," Grey Hawk taunted him. "Because the sheriff and all his deputies are on the way as well as the State Police and the local contingent of the National Guard."

"Hold it," the Chief said to Spinnet, seeing that he had finally found the little printed card that had come about because of someone named Miranda. Then he

209

looked closely at Grey Hawk.

"Honest Indian?" he queried.

"Better an honest Indian than a forked tongue white eyes, asshole. You bastards shot up my house, scared the pants off all my women and I'll bet my damned chickens won't lay any eggs for more than a month. And, for the record, my attorney is also on his way here. Now what about that? Are you ready to bury the hatchet?"

Now that was a whole different matter, wasn't it, the Chief decided. How was he going to save face and get himself out of this one? Visualizing Grey Hawk's house burned to the ground with all traces of occupancy gone, he had felt so confident of his mission that he hadn't even bothered to obtain any of the necessary warrants.

"All right," he conceded at last to Grey Hawk. "Go back to your house. I'll be down in a minute. I'm sure we can work out some kind of compensation."

Then, as soon as the Indian was out hearing range he ordered Pry and Spinnet to quickly pass the word for the men to evacuate the area. "Promptly, Dammit! Promptly! Get a move on now," he growled, wanting only himself, Pry and Spinnet to be there when the locals arrived. It was too much. He was angry now, and for good reason, he told himself. Damn these people anyway. They were making a complete mockery of the justice system and, by God, they weren't going to get away with it. This pot bellied scalp stealer might have the upper hand at the moment but, sooner or later...

In the meantime he would bring all his resources to bear in a different quarter. Kohl and the rest of those renegades were still out there somewhere and somehow, fair or foul, they would find them. And when they did, well, guess what? He could almost taste the pleasure of it. But then Spinnet interrupted the chain of his sweet thoughts.

"The men are loaded and moving out, Chief, but what about all the bullet holes in the house?" Spinnet had the audacity to ask.

The Chief gave him a disconcerting look. "One thing

at a time, Dammit," he said abruptly, as if he really had things under control. Then he took out his wallet and looked in it. Two fives and three ones was all it held. Pry in turn had thirty seven dollars and Spinnet forty three. It would take more than that to keep the Indian quiet.

"Stop those men," he ordered. "Get them back up here. We need to take up a collection."

THIRTY SIX

Two weeks later Grey Hawk was sitting in his favorite rocking chair out on the brand new front porch of what was really Claudia's house soaking up the beauty of the day and wondering what he might spend the rest of cash on that he had come into. Back and forth, back and forth. Although the sun was a little warm on his face, a light wisp of a breeze comforted and lulled him. Everyone else had taken the pickup truck and gone into town for the rest of the day. All seven dogs were asleep back in the shade, the chickens were quiet, having not cackled once since the big ruckus took place, and the ravens were all circling high over the next hill more than a mile away.

Grey Hawk's eyelids began to flutter and to droop. Soon, the mighty rumble of snoring flowed out over the surrounding terrain. One of the dogs woke up, realized who was responsible and went back to sleep. At last, one of the roosters started to crow and off in the distance a coyote howled out in a pathetic note but Grey Hawk noticed it not at all. He was out of it. A dream began to form in his head, or, wherever it is that dreams form. Somewhere.

Face painted, feathers in his hair, eagle bone necklace and breastplate on, lance in hand, he was on the bare back of a great white stallion racing along over the rolling breast of Mother Earth, chasing the wind, for the wind had summoned him. Upward to the hilltop the mighty beast carried him and there he commanded the animal to stop so he could see what it was on the far horizon that had caught his eye. The great horse stopped but flared it nostrils, snorted, pawed the earth, tore up the grass and reared,

211

anxious to go on but he kept it there for a moment longer to get a good look. Then he spoke and the beast was off again, running with great, long strides that ate up the distance.

As he drew nearer he saw something shining in the sun. A strange, round object that glistened like polished silver. What was it? Now, even the horse who had run so strongly became cautious and held back, circling warily around the thing that was taller than two men and bigger around than the largest of teepees. Grey Hawk raised his lance and shouted at it in challenge. He heard a slight noise and rode to the other side to see what it was. There was an opening in the object. Standing in the opening was Claudia and the red head along with his other woman. Each was carrying a child. Beside them stood a tall white man and a fair skinned woman with long hair the color of honey. Two other men appeared and pulled Claudia's baby away from her, then pushed her out of the opening. And then, somehow, he was on foot. The horse was gone, the shiny thing was gone, Claudia was gone and he was standing there naked, all alone. Then his knees buckled and he fell to the ground, unable to get up.

He woke with a start, almost tipping over in the chair. He looked around, listened, looked again. What was it? What had woken him? He rubbed the base of his neck and massaged his forehead. Slowly, the dream came back. Son-of-a-bitch, he didn't like it one bit. The meaning was all too obvious.

Then he remembered the conversation he had with Kohl on Kohl's second to last visit. What had he said? "Although on the surface it might look to be of little consequence because our planet is just a little speck way out on one of the spiral arms of our galaxy, I could still believe that if we blew it up, such an act might have repercussions which we don't understand. Repercussions which could extend outward into the universe with adverse effects. In such a case, intervention would be justified. But, for anything less than that, it is not. What right does

212

anyone who does not call earth home have to interfere with man's right to self determination? No matter what wayward course mankind might appear to be on or what the good intentions, they certainly don't have the right to impregnate earth woman or even to have one of their dead reincarnate in an earth human no matter who the father is supposed to be."

There was more to the discussion, too, but that had been the crux of it. Being all too enamored with what he thought had to be a hand in a greater destiny for himself, Grey Hawk had dismissed it at the time. Now, perhaps, it was time to reconsider.

Presently having some difficulty with his bout of bone cancer, he was also thirty five pounds overweight, hardly able to walk five steps without puffing and pushing the age of fifty with nary a thing to show for his life but a small disability pension that barely covered the cost of his cigarettes. What now? His apprentices had all left, his power had failed him and to top it all off, both Claudia and the redhead were pregnant. Where had he gone wrong? Had Spirit not spoken clearly? Had he misinterpreted, distorted or overlooked something? Or was it really Coyote? Had that sneaky, long haired little rascal nipped at his heels and tripped him up by whispering lies into his ears when he thought he had been talking to someone else? Maybe Kohl had been right all along.

Annoyed by the sudden confusion taking place in his head, he got to his feet, stepped down off the porch and began walking towards the woods. Fifty yards in he rested, then walked some more, rested again and at last came to a small, almost chapel like clearing amongst the trees. He lowered himself onto the carpet of leaves and grass, leaned back against a rust colored, lichen covered rock, put his chin in his hands and looked down at a trail of little black ants hurrying back and forth between his legs. Fighting desperately to save his soul, he started to pray.

Kohl had his own dream that night. He dreamed that he had been out walking somewhere. A blanket of fog

213

covered the ground, softening and blurring the outlines of things for the most part indistinguishable, yet the path beneath his feet looked clear and straight. Following it he passed through what might have been an archway and beyond the archway stood Grey Hawk. At first the Indian did not act as though he was aware of him but then he turned and his bluish black eyes looked quietly into Kohl's and his hand went out in a gesture of greeting and goodwill.

Kohl spoke of it at the table in the morning. "What do you think it means?" Daphne asked before she was cut off by the phone ringing. She went to it, picked it up, said hello and listened. "I don't know," She said into it. "I'll have to ask. Can we call you back?"

"It was Claudia," she said after returning to the table. "She wanted to know if you could meet somewhere with Grey Hawk. He would like to talk to you."

Daphne's mother didn't think it was such a good idea, however. Seven wives and a sky full of UFO's were one thing but she had also learned about his attempt to subvert them at Rushmore. Strangely enough, it had come to her through her attorney whom she had sworn to secrecy about where she was living. The attorney had called to tell her that the General had expired, leaving no will, but that the divorce hadn't been completed so she stood to inherit the house and all the personal bank accounts because they had been held in joint custody. The rest of it, however, was in probate which meant that the General's greatest enemy, the government, would probably end up with the bulk of it.

Somehow during the attorney's discussion with the FBI about the details of the General's death, the attorney had discovered that Grey Hawk had also conducted a ceremony on the fourth of July with the specific intent of changing the structure of Mount Rushmore. A ceremony which the FBI had initially contended was the prime cause of the event.

But as everyone at Kohl's knew, Grey Hawk had prior knowledge of their own plan since he had been invited to participate in their attempt to alter the monument. What

214

Grey Hawk hadn't known was that they had changed their minds about the time of day. At first they thought it might be wisest to wait until evening when the park was empty but, on the way to South Dakota, Daphne suggested that it might have more impact if they could pull it off right in front of a live audience. She had been right, of course, but that was not the point. Grey Hawk had behaved very badly.

"So why would you want to talk to him?" Daphne's mother asked. She didn't understand.

Daphne herself, was somewhat inclined to agree but waited to hear Kohl's answer. "Well," Kohl said. "Remember when Spotted Owl first talked about Rushmore and we decided to invite Grey Hawk because we felt we at least owed him something for being the one that brought us all together in the first place?" He looked at Daphne. "You and I might not have met again if it hadn't been for him. None of us probably would have and none of this would ever have happened. The van would never have safely disappeared and the IRS would still be in business. Neither would we have done the Rushmore thing. Good or bad, in his own way, he made it all possible," Kohl stated, then he grinned. "Besides, I kind of like the scoundrel."

"Well, I don't," One Hand said rather cryptically. "And as far as I'm concerned, let him go hang." It was a typical statement for One Hand lately. Not only had he become depressed and sarcastic, he had also begun to behave rather strangely and erratically. Although he wouldn't discuss the matter it must have something to do with the detour he had made over into Montana on the way back from Rushmore. Life was becoming difficult for everyone around him.

Running Deer was convinced that he was doing drugs, the two women thought he needed psychiatric help and the rest just felt it was time for him to leave. They were tired of it. To Kohl, however, there was something about One Hand's behavior that was fundamentally wrong. Something which, by itself, might be good enough reason to talk to Grey Hawk. Since Grey Hawk had known One

Hand's family and much of his background, perhaps he would be able to offer some advice. It might also serve as an opening for a renewal of their friendship.

Daphne had become even more addicted to the natural beauty of the southwest than her mother and if she had her way they would have spent the next ten years exploring all the back roads and by ways of everything from the Rockies westward. Crossed and criss-crossed with cement, asphalt and gravel though it was, it was still a vast land that never ceased to make her wonder. She was forever like a child, staring out the window at the passing panorama, pointing at something, everything, chattering happily away, making Kohl stop the car so they could get out and look, take a picture, or walk back off the road. Sometimes just to make love outdoors. And today was another special day for her. Today they were headed east to Black Canyon of the Gunnison. It was where they had decided to met Grey Hawk, mostly at her suggestion, because she was sure she could persuade Kohl to detour down through Mesa Verde and Canyon de Chelly on the way home. Two more places that held special intrigue for her.

Grey Hawk was sitting alone on the masonry wall of North Point Overlook when they arrived, stoically staring down into the depths at the dark ribbon of river far below. He looked up when he heard the car and waited as Kohl got out alone. Without words they shook hands like two old soldiers who had been together in battle. Kohl sat on the wall next to Grey Hawk.

"Well, it's a nice day," he said at last, looking up at the sky.

"Yes it is," Grey Hawk stated in return.

Daphne left them alone for more than half an hour. Then it was her turn to say hello and she noticed a subtle change in demeanor on Grey Hawk's part. He was treating them differently. But how? She couldn't quite clarify the feeling. Only later, after they had talked, then she knew.

They were no longer apprentices to him, but blood brother and sister. At the moment, though, there was little to be said about the ill feelings which had transpired between them. The fact that Grey Hawk was even there were words enough, so instead they talked of other things.

Kohl told him about One Hand. Grey Hawk shook his head in the way he was prone to do when he already knew what the answer was. "Possession," he said with authority.

"Possession?" Daphne said.

Grey Hawk grunted in the affirmative. "Does he appear a little somnambulistic at times, then swings over and gets hostile, depressed and just generally coaybtete-leranous?"

"Yes, to the first three, but you got me on the last one."

"Churlish," Grey Hawk smiled, for he still loved to throw in the use of an occasional big word or two.

"He is that, all right," Daphne agreed wholeheartedly.

"Well, there you have it," Grey Hawk said. "It happened to his little brother a couple of years back. I heard he committed suicide not too long ago."

"Oh, my," Daphne said, saddened by the prospect of such a thing. Once One Hand and the rest of the men had stopped looking at her as a sex object and started treating her as a complete person, they had all become good friends. She would hate to loose any of them, for whatever reason. "But how?" she questioned with regard to One Hand. "What can we do?"

"So far, you've been lucky," he said. "Just like Kohl, I don't believe there is such a thing as a, *force of evil,* loose in the world that somehow permeates space and lays there lurking in the shadows waiting to jump out and grab someone. What there is instead, now that you have become aware of the spiritual world, is that not all entities who are on the other side have good intentions. It's not the spirits of the plant, animal or mineral worlds. It's those who were once human who somehow can't separate themselves from the particulars of the life they left behind. They're the ones who create problems. They look for people like One Hand.

217

People who themselves are not totally focused and present in this earthly life. And when their defenses are down they step in and take over. After while, as is often the case, the person looses the ability to regain control."

"How do you help them?"

"Exorcism!"

"But that's what Catholic priests do." Daphne said.

"Don't get upset. There is an underlying common denominator."

"Which is?" Daphne asked.

"First of all, faith and trust in the healer. Secondly, some understanding of what has really happened to the victim and lastly, some knowledge of what it takes to drive the entity out. Not so complicated, really. Except..."

"Except what?"

"Well..." Grey Hawk said.

Kohl waited.

"Now that you have come into your own power you will find that some of these entities don't like mere mortals messing around in their back yard. So, they do things to interfere. I think you referred to it as, Coyote being out and about," Grey Hawk said as he glanced at Kohl. "So what I'm saying is that, we especially, have to be careful."

Daphne and Kohl studied his face.

"How well I know," Grey Hawk added with a sheepish grin.

"So when can you come up?" Kohl asked.

"You don't need me," Grey Hawk stated. "You can do it with a little instruction."

"But we want you to come. It would be good for everybody," Kohl told him.

"Yes, please do," Daphne added and took him by the hand.

"Okay," he agreed. "Just me and Claudia," for as they were to learn later the blond had been sent back home to her father and the redhead had decided to marry an old boyfriend from Australia willing to accept her in her present condition.

With that they shook hands once again and said good-bye. Grey Hawk remained sitting on the wall where he had been the whole time. When they drove off he rose painfully and hobbled slowly to his car. The remission he had enjoyed for so long had ended. The bones in his once good leg were in trouble also.

There was an interlude there, in the midst of all the chanting and the smell of sweet sage and tobacco smoke that filled the air, when it took all Kohl, Running Deer, Spotted Owl and James could do to hold him down. But, when it was all over, One Hand came to his feet with an overwhelming grin, grabbed Grey Hawk and hugged him dearly. Then he took hold of Daphne's mother and danced around the room with her. "Yahoo," he yelled the whole time.

"Ah-ho, brother," Grey Hawk said to him when he had settled down. "Walk in peace."

About four in the afternoon Betsy arrived, shook hands with Grey Hawk, smiled politely at Claudia and put her arms around Spotted Owl. Then the real party began, except for Grey Hawk. He said he was tired from the long drive and went off to take a nap, hiding the agony of walking as best he could.

Much later they built a fire to fend off the darkness. Then the moon came up crisp and bright and before it was time to sleep the Big Dipper had rotated more than a quarter turn in the night sky. Somewhere in there Grey Hawk arose and came outside to warm his knees by the fire and talk to Kohl.

"There are two things I'd like to do before I die," Grey Hawk said. "Maybe three. Somehow, I'd like to do something about the Pentagon. Not just blow it up or make it disappear. I'd like to fill it up, solid full, with concrete or something like that so they can't even tear it down. So it has to stand there like some special monument. Like those concrete dinosaurs you see along the road here and there. An archaic monument to everything that is uncivilized in the world. A monument especially to the Vietnam war and

219

the middle east war, the ultimate in stupidity. And if he wasn't already dead, I'd fill old Lyndon Johnson and Tricky Dick Nixon up with concrete also and make them stand up on top of it for half an eternity," Grey Hawk said with a certain finality.

"Maybe you could just do away with the Oval Office," Kohl suggested. "That might make the people who sit there think a little before they commit to war for all the wrong reasons."

"Yeah, well...That was kinda second on my list."

"And the third?"

Grey Hawk paused, rubbed his knees and looked up at the moon. All he really wanted was to be able to have about six months of feeling half way decent so that he might put his affairs in order. But that is not what he said. Instead of a direct answer he asked Kohl if he had any brandy. Half a glass of that might help him make it through the night.

When Grey Hawk left around noon the following day, One Hand got in the car with him. James and Spotted Owl looked at Kohl to see his reaction.

"Well," Kohl said. "I believe you guys were committed to an apprenticeship."

They looked at him more carefully. He nodded and with that they went and got their things. James and One Hand climbed in the back seat of Grey Hawk's car and Spotted Owl slid in next to Betsy in her's. "See you in about a week," Running Deer said, indicating that he would be coming too.

Kohl and Grey Hawk shook hands and hugged each other, Daphne kissed him on the cheek and her mother handed over a large sack of her home baked pastry to take along.

"Let me know if you want to help," Grey Hawk said to Kohl, referring to the conversation they had the night before.

Two days later Kohl, Daphne and her mother took Running Deer into Moab to catch the bus. Then, when they arrived back home, her mother told them that it was time for her to leave also, time to go back to Washington and wrap up the legal affairs associated with the General's death. She also wanted to put the house on the market and tidy up a few things in her own life. Maybe a month or two and then she would be back. Promise.

THIRTY SEVEN

Weeks went by, swallowed up by the moments of the days. Kohl had finished the second of the cabins and was rebuilding the fireplace in the main house where a pile of firewood had already been stacked up on the back porch. Daphne had diligently learned to hoe weeds, pound nails and mix mortar, push a wheelbarrow, drive the truck, run the chainsaw. Her clothes were worn and torn, her nails ragged, her hands rough, but happiness has many faces, sings many songs, wears many strange garbs and speaks many languages.

That was now, but she knew that tomorrow might well be different. Living with Kohl, there was a good chance that it would be. It was almost guaranteed. Still, there were no regrets. They made a good couple, each finding reprieve in the other for the inherent, questing restlessness that bubbled in their veins. But she clearly understood that one of these days a new challenge would surface and then they would be off. All the work they were doing, however, was still for a reason. It would always be their place to come home to. In the meantime, "Trust in Spirit," as Grey Hawk would have said. And what she was learning was that trusting in Spirit meant to learn to trust in oneself and ones own abilities to cope and to mold life into something both significant and beautiful.

She knew all too clearly now that life was not an accident and that there was no room for fear or worry. So, perhaps out of all this a way to help others was also beginning to emerge. That was the ultimate challenge. It was one thing to shock them and frighten them and make things disappear and try to make them think a little. But somehow it didn't always address the point directly. There is dignity and significance to human life. It can have purpose and meaning. But how do you help people learn to recognize and re-embrace themselves in the bigger sense of the word? If they could just figure out how to do that, then they would really have done something.

One day Daphne woke feeling that they were going to have a visitor. "Is someone coming?" she asked Kohl.

"Yes, I think so," he said. "Maybe today."

That evening when she went for a walk to pick flowers for the table, she thought she heard a car. But it wasn't a car. It was a new, four wheel drive truck that made its way up the long drive through the trees and stopped in front of the house. Daphne came around to the driver's side to see who it was and was greeted by a grinning, good looking, mustached face with a discolored tooth in the front. She looked from the man to the woman. The woman appeared to be tall and slender and had long, dark hair and deep blue eyes that contrasted heavily with the olive tones of her skin and Daphne was sure they had never met before.

But as for the man, she looked back at him, closer this time. What was it about that crazy grin. Her head spun. Oh, no. Could it be?

"Mike?" she asked. "Mike? Are you Mike?" she asked him once more with a joyful laugh and then, when she knew it was true, she had to blink away the tears because she knew how happy Kohl would be to see his old friend again.

The following dawn broke cool and clear. The sun was no more than thirty minutes above the horizon when another vehicle made its way down the drive. A very long, low, nineteen year old Cadillac limousine that someone had recently given to Grey Hawk. It stopped in the yard near the front door of the house. Grey Hawk and all of his apprentices emerged from the interior as Daphne, Kohl, Mike and his woman friend, Jana, came out to greet them. Although they had never met, Grey Hawk already seemed to know who Mike was. After shaking hands all around he announced that they were on the way to Washington, DC.

Kohl looked at him skeptically. If he was right about what Grey Hawk had on his mind, were they ready for such an undertaking? He didn't think so. It wouldn't be like hiding in the brush in the jungle, either. There were more security minded people around Washington than fleas on a stray dog.

"I've learned a new trick," Grey Hawk stated, however, after they had discussed it further. "Come," he said and led them in the direction of Mike's new truck.

They stopped about twenty feet away. Grey Hawk looked at the women. "Now, young ladies. If you would do me the honor. Go stand by the front fender of that shiny new toy over there."

Daphne and Jana complied, quizzical looks on their faces. Grey Hawk walked slowly to a place about four feet in front of the truck. There was pain in his legs but he had a sneaky smile on his face and he hoped it would work as well here as it did back home. He reached in his coat pocket and removed the leather pouch he carried. From it he extracted a handful of finely shredded tobacco and carefully laid down a fine line along the ground that completely encircled the truck and the two women. He then returned to where the men waited, had them face away from the truck, became silent and shut his eyes for a short moment as everyone watched him. Then he opened them again and gazed back at the women. From the men's point of view, they were not to be seen. Both they and the truck were surrounded by a ring of thick, high shrubbery formed out of plants indigenous to the area. Creosote mostly, with a few manzanita, rabbits foot and low mesquite thrown in for effect.

From where they stood by the side of the truck, however, the women were able to look back at the men as if nothing had changed and they wondered at the strange expressions on Kohl's and Mike's faces. They were even more puzzled when Grey Hawk instructed Kohl to walk through the bushes. What bushes? They didn't see any

223

bushes.

Kohl, however, proceeded towards the ring of green which appeared all too real to him, raised his arms to part the dense foliage and worked his way through it. Once on the other side, he stopped, completely baffled. There was nothing inside the ring of bushes. Both the truck and the women were gone. Puzzled, he reached out and walked further ahead. Nothing! Just the gravel underfoot.

Daphne and Jana cried out when he reached the truck because the heavy metal side of the vehicle began to part and enfold Kohl. In vain, Daphne moved to stop him but her hand passed on through his shoulder when she tried.

Unable to either see or hear them, Kohl continued to walk on through the machine as if it weren't there, came out on the other side, made his way through the far side greenery and stopped, a strange expression on his face. Then he began to smile. At this point Grey Hawk snapped his fingers and everything returned to normal. Kohl turned around and started walking back, this time forced to walk around the front of the truck. He caressed the polished hood with his hand as he went by.

"Well?" Grey Hawk asked. "What do you think?"

"Fantastic. A one way mirror that really works!"

Good, Grey Hawk said to himself. Now if the feat could be repeated just one more time, that was all he needed. It wasn't that he was actually creating something from nothing. He didn't have the power to do that and he hoped no one else on this plane did either. All he was did was move things around a little, talking to the plant spirits, asking them to project themselves into a different location for a while. However it happened, it worked, so why bother to question it.

Across the Potomic from Washington, DC, however, things would probably be much more difficult. He was on good terms with the plant life here in the west and knew all the individual characteristics and feelings of all the separate varieties and had joined in consciousness with them on many occasions. Back east, though, it would be different. They would need something quite a bit taller and denser back there. Something like a thick row of Italian Cypress about thirty feet high. But damn, he had only melded with wild things in the past, never to a domesticated, decorative plant or tree. He hoped they had something in common. Maybe the part of his blood supply that was French would help. He understood his Grandfather on his white side had come from southern France and southern France touches a part of northern Italy, doesn't it? Maybe it would work. Otherwise he would have to do some scouting out in the Blue Ridge mountains for something a little more humble and native but that would take a lot more time and effort, and time was the one thing he felt he didn't have much left of.

Then there was the matter of all that concrete and why in the hell did they have to go and make the Pentagon so ostentatiously damned big for? If his arithmetic was correct, he would need at least three million tons of it to do the job properly. So far he was at a loss as to the specifics and the logistics of that part of the plan. Maybe they could locate some abandoned highrise buildings first, drive all the rats, insects, drug pushers and homeless outside into the streets, teleport it closer to the site, change it into rubble and use it as a partial filler. Then they could block off five miles of the closest interstate highway and finish the job with recycled concrete. Whatever the approach, he would need all the help he could get. It was paramount that everyone come with him, including that new guy, Mike, and his girlfriend.

But would Kohl come? He hoped so because he needed him most of all. If he lived through it, this caper would demand every ounce of his strength and will. It would also sorely deplete all his reserves, suck up his blood, dissolve what was left of his bones. When it was over he still wanted enough strength left to be able to turn the ignoble structure a bright orange least they forget the Vietnam veterans and to put some unremovable symbol on top of it that commemorated those who had acquired Gulf War Syndrome. And then, last and forever, he wanted to make it home to Colorado.

225

There was already enough hard cash buried under the house in plastic pails to provide for Claudia and the baby for the rest of their lives but he needed to get to the top of the mountain behind the house. It was a tall mountain, rugged and wild, born out of cataclysm and fiery upheaval, thrusting to the sky. There were elk up there, and bear and wolves and coyotes. It was a place where the clouds came to rest sometimes, before dropping their rain and moving on. It was a place of silence and mystery, scraggly trees and lightening strikes, winter snows and summer sun - a forever place, infinitely old, eternally new. He would meet with coyote there, have that last dance with him.

But he would need someone to carry him that far and someone brave enough and wise enough to leave him there alone. Claudia could not be trusted. She would put him in the ground and let the worms have him. The apprentices might do it but they would make too big a deal out of it, say a lot of prayers, dance around the fire, feel sorry for him, pile up a mound of rocks somewhere to memorialize him.

No, that was not the way. It had to be done silently and peacefully. Kohl would understand. And afterward Kohl would be able to stop and look up and listen to the wind in the trees and know that he had not really gone but had only returned to the place of all new beginnings.

> May the Gods bless, and the Spirits be kind.
> May you find your way out of the Fire Mist
> And into the safety of your own power and
> Greater comprehension
> Where the real beginning, begins.